THE JALOPY CHRONICLES

BOOK II

LOST IN THE TIME BELT

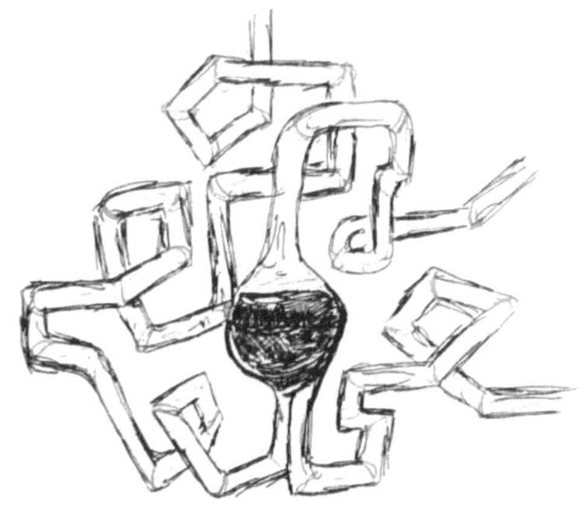

BY CAELI ENNIS

Illustrations by Claire McDonald,

Elyzabeth McDonald, and Brigid McDonald

Printed in the United States of America

Hardcover ISBN: 978-1-959096-55-9
Paperback ISBN: 978-1-959096-56-6
Ebook ISBN: 978-1-959096-57-3

Canoe Tree
Press

4697 Main Street
Manchester Center, VT 05255
Canoe Tree Press is a division of DartFrog Books

To my little fuzz, my sweet Ennis Bowser. I hope the rainbow bridge is full of milk bones and cheese, and that you can howl to as many piano tunes as your heart desires. I would give anything to have more time with you.

"Mysterious thing, Time. Powerful, and when meddled with, dangerous."
—*Albus Dumbledore*, Harry Potter and the Prisoner of Azkaban, *by J.K. Rowling*

The Jalopy Chronicles

Book 1: Across the Universe
Book 2: Lost in the Time Belt

Contents

CHAPTER 1

ENTERING THE TIME BELT

una McHubbard sat helplessly on the sandy beach of Dikson, Russia, listening to the chaotic and warlike sounds streaming into her ears from every direction. The darkness around her was nothing new—she had been blind for most of her life. What terrified her was that no one around her could see, hear, or touch her. It was her worst nightmare.

After several attempts of trying to get anyone's attention around her by shouting, waving her arms, and even going out of her way to trip over the nearest Olfinderian, she gave up. She could only hear the sounds of the GeoLapse, the terrorist group that had originated on Earth whose predominant goal was to take over the universe. And, well, they did . . . in the future. But thanks to her mother, Henrietta, the final battle to eradicate the GeoLapse was underway. The resistance force Henrietta had so cleverly planned had grown into a universal army that now had a chance to defeat the GeoLapse once and for all. The army had travelled to Earth—and nearly eight years into the past—by crossing the Time Belt, a mysterious area of the universe where time runs in reverse. Upon reaching Earth, the army split into battalions and fought the GeoLapse at their various headquarters on each continent, aiming to weaken them before they could grow to a point where they could take over the universe again. Luna was still in shock that her mother had been behind the whole plan. Henrietta had led the Earth Rehabilitation Association in this great scheme, all the while managing to keep it a secret for all these years.

Luna could hear the huffing and puffing of the Epitonians as they hurled some GeoLapse over the side of the cruise liner that served as the terrorist group's headquarters in Asia. She heard the entrancing sounds of the Olfinderians, little furry creatures who noised mesmerising, hypnotic songs out of their cone-like foghorn mouths. Their springy coiled feet bounced with a series of *boings* as they galloped along the sand. Luna also was able to decipher the flapping of the Antympanicans' parachute-like wings as they deployed into downward arcs, as well as the faint squashing of the Ciptons as they bounced and hurled themselves bravely against the terrorising GeoLapse forces. Just moments before, Luna herself had been on the cruise liner fighting off a few GeoLapse. They had bashed up her face and bloodied her up quite a bit before tossing her over the side to what they thought was her death. And now she was here, alive . . . or was she dead? She wasn't sure. She remembered the stinging blows and the wetness of blood in her eyes. And yet now, when she gingerly felt her face, there was no pain, no blood, seemingly no wounds to prove what she had just been through.

She was, however, having a hard time breathing. She felt constricted in the safety suit the ERA had given her so that she could navigate the

Earth's uninhabitable environment. Maybe the cramped body suit was impeding her breathing, although it could have been just anxiety at her dire situation. To calm herself, she unfastened the top half of the suit.

Luna inhaled deeply. She could taste salty particles in the night air. She wasn't entirely sure what she was breathing in, since the Earth's atmosphere was still entirely destroyed and therefore fully fatal to any human who was exposed to it . . . except for her. Why her? She ran her fingers through the smooth sand. What a strange feeling it was to touch something in the outside environment of Earth! Luna had never been able to experience the outside world of Earth in her twenty-five years of life. The sand felt soft, and she almost wondered how something so soothing to touch could be part of such a deadly environment. Holding handfuls of sand firmly in her fists, she wiggled her toes as she dug her still suited-up legs underneath the sandy surface. Her dark red hair, long and wavy, blew lightly backward in the hot wind. However horrifying the Earth had become, however uncertain her existence was at this point, she felt temporarily calmed at the thought of basking in the outdoors.

A member of the GeoLapse was approaching, or so Luna thought. She could hear human footsteps creeping along the sand, but it didn't matter anymore. She figured that since no one seemed to be able to detect her, she was safe in her spot in the sand. Unfortunately, that also meant that she couldn't warn anyone of an impending attack. But she trusted her mother's plan. She chuckled to herself, thinking back to the times when she teased her mother, saying that she must have gotten her brains from her father. She was wrong. Hopefully, wherever her mother was, she was proud of her.

As Luna continued sifting the sand through her fingers, she started to think about her siblings. Were they doing the same as she was at this moment? She shook her head, thinking of Riff all the way in Prague, Ann Lou in Mt. Cameroon, and Elbina in Washington, D.C. They must be frightened. Or perhaps, if they were lucky, they didn't notice anything had happened yet.

Coming back into her current space, Luna wasn't entirely sure what to do at this point. Was she stuck in this spot forever, or could she leave? Curiosity bubbled up in her, and she hopped up and walked away from the beach. Luna recognised the feeling of the ground as it turned from sand to rubble and then stone.

The battle sounds grew fainter as she strolled away from the chaos until she heard nothing at all except her own footsteps. She had no other intention than to walk. Luna usually could figure out the answer to anything, or at least provide an educated guess. But since no one could see, hear, or touch her, there were no imminent threats, no problems to solve. She finally had a moment to take in her surroundings in peace: no siblings to argue with, no GeoLapse to fend off, not even one of her books to read. There was nothing to do except walk within her darkness.

"Argh!" Suddenly something propelled Luna backward onto the ground. It felt as if she had walked into something—but not anything hard. It was more spongy.

She picked herself up and walked to the left instead. Again, she was pushed down.

Luna growled under her breath, infuriated by the opposition. She extended her arms out in front of her and felt the springy obstacle not just resisting her but closing in around her. She twirled around, hoping to find a gap in this mysterious shield, but there was none. It was a forcefield, and it was slowly caving in on her.

Luna suppressed her claustrophobic terror and held still. The forcefield wrapped around her, moulding around her tall, thin body. She could not even move her arms. Then she felt a warming sensation envelop her. A blinding white light struck her immediately, causing her to gasp from the sudden and extremely unexpected visual stimulus. She had seen and felt these sensations before, while entering and exiting the Time Belt on her way to and from Harvinth.

The air around Luna began to swirl. Within moments, it lifted and spun her. A widening spiral swirled her and all of Dikson into the blinding white light. Luna felt slightly nauseated but managed to quell the discomfort by pinching her eyes shut. She felt her hair wrapping itself around her face. Her arms and legs flailed for some sort of ground to grasp. Finally she face-planted onto a soft, plushy surface, bouncing a few times before rolling to a stop. Luna opened her eyes, and to her astonishment she was still seeing the bright white light around her.

But there was more. As she sat up, the light morphed into blobbish shapes. These blobs then turned into sharper images . . . things she recognised from many years ago. Luna caught a glimpse of her body—two bony hands, long, lanky stick legs, unusually long and thin feet, her silvery ERA safety suit, and long threads of red hair poking into her visual field. She gasped, grasping her hair with her long, ghostly fingers. She could see again—but how? She looked around, but the visual input was overwhelming. It seemed as if her mind had to link up the sights with her existing knowledge of the world to re-learn what everything was. She lowered her gaze toward the ground and focused on her feet, wiggling them back and forth.

"Weird," she whispered.

She then worked her way up her body, touching everything she saw. Her trousers were made of a highly reflective, aluminised material that hurt her eyes to look at. Moving up, she saw the red-and-black checkered pattern of her fuzzy flannel shirt. She noticed how almost translucent the skin of her hands was, with blue veins just below the surface. She reached back up to her hair and pulled a few strands in front of her face. The deep reddish-brown waves forced her eyes wide open with amazement. Then she noticed her nose poking straight out in front of her face. Her eyes crossed as she reached up to touch it.

The landscape around Luna gradually came into view, causing her eyes to bug out. She whirled her head around to take in the panorama with its extraordinary palette of colours. But the shapes were blurry. She began to wonder if she had regained only her near vision. She strained to focus on the unfamiliar shapes until she realised she was clenching every muscle in her body. Her eyes were dry from keeping them open so long. She moved her hands slightly above her nose and rubbed her eyes. When she lowered her hands, the blurry, distant shapes turned into clear, sharp vision. It was almost as if all she had to do for all these years was simply rub her eyes, even though she knew that was not true.

She couldn't remember a time when she had seen this clearly, even in her youth. She sat there for a few moments, craning her neck and soaking in the sweeping vista of the strange world around her. Some of the newly formed shapes were buildings of all different shapes and proportions: short and wide or tall and thin, boxy or round. Luna quickly began to recall the names of the multitude of colours in her visual field.

"Green," she whispered, pointing to one of the buildings. "No, blue."

Her finger and her eyes moved simultaneously to the next building. "Orange?" she said. "No, that's brown."

Luna stood up slowly and looked around. Behind her was only a sea of white light. She figured it was best to make her way toward the buildings. Luna wrestled off her safety suit and left it in a crumpled pile on the ground. Certainly she did not need it in this new land.

As she slowly stepped forward, the white ground felt soft. It was not quite as springy as the ground on Olfinder, but it felt as if she were stepping on giant pillows. It occurred to her again to wonder if she might be dead. Maybe this was heaven. Luna wasn't particularly religious, but her nan, Knitsy, was a believer, even if she had a habit of taking the Lord's name in vain. Maybe Knitsy knew something Luna didn't.

Luna watched as the colourful buildings grew upon her approaching them. She could make out small, moving dots and a large golden structure. Eager to see more, she broke into a light jog until the edge of the mysterious town was metres . . . inches away. She stopped dead before a road that blended in with the white space all around her. Timidly, she hovered her foot over the stony road and stepped down gently. It seemed safe, so she continued away from the endless white space and toward the commotion.

Luna walked along the road between the buildings, which formed a small alleyway leading to a bustling scene ahead. She could hear various languages that, blended together, sounded like a jumble of general grunts and hisses. Once she reached the end of the alley, she realised what the moving dots were that she had seen from farther away—a town full of creatures. The scene ahead of her was a bustling crowd in a town centre of sorts. There were creatures everywhere, none of which she recognised as she had never properly seen any inhabitants of other worlds first-hand. Some were in a hurry, while others strolled along in pairs or small groups. Luna had to step out of the way so that a skyscraper-sized creature wouldn't step on her.

As Luna navigated through the strange sights all around her, a slithering sound by her feet made her prick up her ears. Her heart raced as she knelt to see the source of the sound. Just an inch ahead of her trainers was a small gelatinous blob slithering slowly forward. Luna spoke to it excitedly.

"Hello! You, the Cipton!" Luna had lived on Cipto, a planet immersed in complete darkness, for seven years, so the sound of the Cipton gait was immediately recognisable. It was the first time she had seen one, however. She marvelled at its translucent, eyeless form. There were some murky streaks in its body, but the creature didn't seem bothered. Knowing Ciptons to be one of the kindest species in the universe, Luna suddenly felt less alone in this strange place.

The Cipton stopped in its wavy tracks and squealed in a flabbergasted tone. It turned around, seeming confused as to why it was being addressed.

"What do *you* want?"

Luna's eyes bugged out at the harsh response. Perhaps this creature wasn't a Cipton.

"Erm, sorry, are you from planet Cipto?" Luna asked.

"Yes, I am. And again, I ask: What do you want from me?" Its blobby body quivered with rage.

"Where are we exactly?"

The Cipton exhaled in annoyance. "You're in the Time Belt, obviously."

The response clicked in Luna's brain as the puzzle in her head began to piece together. "And, erm . . . how do I get out of here?"

The Cipton laughed, bouncing into the air with malevolent glee. "We're stuck in here for the rest of time! This is your new world. Surely you recall how you got here?"

Luna's stomach flipped. She knew exactly how.

"Well, have fun!" the Cipton announced with finality, bouncing and slithering away as quickly as its undulations could move it.

Luna tried not to let the anxiety take over her body. There had to be a way out. She figured a stroll around the Time Belt might yield some clues as to an escape route, if there was one. But the words of the Cipton hung in her brain as she walked.

As she swerved through the bustling crowd, she spotted a colossal spherical structure that was situated in the middle of a giant four-way intersection. The structure's framework consisted of golden pipes encircling the sphere at random angles, like a big ball of yarn. Poking out from between the pipes at various points were objects of sundry shapes, from cubes and pyramids to spheres, toruses, and even more complex forms for which Luna knew no names. They bore strange markings, and many of them had mechanical pointers moving this way and that. Strangely loud ticking noises surrounded the structure. She walked around the sphere, trying to figure out what these objects were. One of them, a flat disc, caught her eye, and it made sense in an instant. It was an analogue clock of the sort with which Luna was familiar, except it had only minute and second hands. A golden inscription on this clock read EARTH.

Next to the Earth clock was a very similar analogue clock with minute and second hands moving at the same pace as those on the Earth clock, except in the opposite direction. The golden inscription above this clock was a bunch of strange symbols, but as Luna focused on it, the microchip embedded in her left wrist translated it, and the strange symbols swivelled into the word HARVINTH.

Luna reasoned that the objects on the spherical structure were time-telling mechanisms from around the universe. She studied them. Some of the clock hands moved linearly, rather than turning. A few moved in complex spline configurations. Some of the clocks ticked at a regular interval, while others ticked at varying intervals. Some even moved in a non-rhythmic fashion. Even across the space–time continuum, time was defined differently everywhere.

At the very top of the pipe ball, where all the pipes converged, was the largest clock of them all. It was a transparent sphere, but it had no ticking hands. It was filled one-quarter of the way with a black liquid and was slowly but continuously being filled with more of the liquid from a main pipe faucet at the top of the sphere. Confused, Luna focused on its inscription: BANK.

Evidently, here in the Time Belt, time worked very strangely. If at all.

CHAPTER 2

CLORINCLADIELLAMORE
LECOMERIELLASTRAIN

L una stood, entranced, listening to the ticking of the pipe ball for what seemed like hours. She was at a loss for what to do or where to go, but the ticking sound calmed her. She gently closed her eyes, temporarily shutting out the overwhelming flurry of colours and creatures around her.

Through the dull roar of the bustling crowd, Luna heard a faint shuffling coming from behind her. She opened her eyes and turned in the direction of the out-of-place sound. She saw a hooded figure, covered in a large black cloak, whose body proportions resembled those of a human. The figure stood stock-still with its hands clasped behind its back and its head down. It was surrounded by a collection of small black orbs. Luna slowly walked over to see if the human, or whatever was beneath the cloak, might be able to help her. As she examined the objects, she noticed they looked extremely fragile. She eyed up the figure, but its gaze was elsewhere under the hood. Luna pointed to the orb in front of her.

No response.

Gritting her teeth from the somewhat awkward interaction, Luna picked an orb up and cradled it gently in her palm, feeling its smooth surface. She could see a distorted reflection of herself in the orb. It was a face she hadn't seen in years. Some minor ageing lines traversed her skin, and seeing her face without a big pair of glasses took her by slight surprise. She tucked a loose strand of her wavy, dark red hair behind her ears and patted down some wild sections. Her nose appeared quite large in the reflection compared to the rest of her face. Her fingers grazed her nose as she sought to connect tangible reality with the reflected image. Then her eyes met themselves in the reflection. It was strange to be looking at herself as if she were facing a stranger.

"Hello," she whispered, half expecting her reflection to reply to her.

Remembering why she had originally walked over, Luna quickly averted her gaze from the orb and eyed up the stoic figure, who was a few inches taller than she. Luna squinted to see the figure's face, but only darkness was visible in the space under the hood.

"What are these for?" Luna asked, holding the orb out in front of her. Her voice trembled, but she cleared her throat and stood up straighter.

The figure replied in a deep, raspy voice: "The key to your travel, to get you off the gravel."

Luna's heart began to beat faster. "Travel? Like getting out of here? Can I take this with me?"

"Oh, dear me! Nothing is free!" wheezed the figure. "You must propose a trade in order to obtain this aid."

"Well . . . what would you take for it?" Luna tried to think of what, if anything, she had to offer. She could only think of the safety suit she left back where she started—although finding it again in the infinite white space would be difficult.

"There are many sorts of objects I collect, but I sadly cannot be so direct."

Luna decided she had exhausted the possibilities with this mysterious figure for now. There were probably many more clues to uncover. She placed the orb back on the ground in front of the figure and walked away.

Without warning, Luna was instantly heaved to her left. Something hard had swiped her side. She grabbed her ribs in pain as her body slammed into the road.

"Hey!" she snapped, shooting a menacing glare at the source.

"Sorry!" exclaimed the attacker, who had been thrown to the ground as well. They had a strangely high-pitched voice.

Instantly Luna's face relaxed. It was a small, frightened-looking boy. He resembled a human child, perhaps three years old at most. But he also had a pair of small horns poking out from under his blond hair, and two sharp claws instead of hands. His eyes were red, but they were kind. He was crouched on the ground, trembling. In front of him was a silvery disc that hovered a short distance above the ground, wobbling as if internal gyroscopes were searching for input. It appeared he had been riding the disc through the massive crowd and lost control of it.

Luna instantly noticed his terrified expression and forced her face into a smile—something she seldom did, as she was a rather tight-lipped, emotionless being, at least in the eyes of her family.

"Don't worry," said Luna kindly. "It was just an accident. What's your name?"

The boy poked his head up from behind the disk and stared at Luna curiously.

"M-my name is Clorincladiellamore Lecomeriellastrain."

Luna suppressed a smile, thinking it funny that such a small boy had such a long name. Then the boy's kind eyes caught hers, and she smiled a more genuine smile. The boy sensed her laughter as a cue to emerge slowly from behind his disk.

"You look like me," he said.

"Sort of," she trailed off, staring at his horns. "Where are you from?"

"I don't know."

"How about your mum? Or dad? Where are they? I can take you to them," Luna offered.

"Uhhh, I don't know where they are," he pouted, a small frown forming on his sweet face.

Puzzled, Luna continued her questioning. "Do you know how you got here?"

"Uhhh," he repeated. "No."

Luna was growing concerned for the young boy. "So you don't know where your family are or how you got here . . . is the only thing you do know your name?"

"Yes," he nodded sharply, with a toothy smile.

"It's a great name," said Luna.

"I made it up," he replied nonchalantly. "What's your name?"

"It's Luna. Quite a bit simpler than yours," she laughed.

"Looner!" the boy howled.

Luna giggled even harder. "How long have you been here for?"

"Erm . . . I don't know."

Luna sighed. Asking him questions wasn't getting her anywhere. "Should we explore together?" she suggested. "And may I call you Clorin? My home planet likes to use nicknames."

Clorin beamed his red eyes at her sweetly and nodded. He pointed to the silver disk.

"Okay, but I'll drive," said Luna.

Luna and Clorin situated themselves in the centre of the disk. When Luna leaned forward to look for a button or lever to start it, the disk lurched, causing Clorin to shake with fear and grip her flannel shirt. Luna took a deep breath and leaned her body to the left slightly. The disk steered left and then slightly forward as Luna carefully balanced their centre of mass.

Clorin laughed delightedly once they settled into a smoother ride. He tapped her back and chimed, "Faster! Faster!"

Luna gave in to his request and leaned farther forward, and soon the two were zigzagging through the densely populated streets of the Time Belt. Other flying disks zoomed above and below them, carrying various creatures past them in a blur. Luna's heart beat faster, and she gritted her teeth as she dodged the oncoming obstacles. Strange creatures caught their eyes at every moment, causing Clorin to exclaim, "Whoa! That one is huuuuge!" and scream at the ones who had one too many large teeth. Luna couldn't help but laugh at each of his outbursts. She had never met anyone who made her laugh so freely—not even her younger sister Elbina, with whom she had the closest connection of anyone in her life.

The extraordinary brightness of the Time Belt caused Luna to squint and shield her eyes with her hand. It was a peculiar kind of brightness that never seemed to let up. They were speeding so quickly through the roads that the colours and sounds of the beasts were starting to overwhelm Luna again, a sensory overload that she was not used to. She desperately needed a break, and she noticed Clorin most likely did as well, considering he was cowering in fear behind her. He yelped as a scraggly-looking beast pawed greedily at him as it flew by.

"Should we stop here?" Luna asked, leaning her head back slightly but keeping her eyes on the busy street to avoid a crash.

"Y-yes," said Clorin as he tucked in closer to her flannel.

Luna steered the disk to the side of the road and hopped off, then helped Clorin down as the disk hovered in the air. A group of Olfinderians took the opportunity to hop on the disk and fly off, singing their enchanting frequencies as they disappeared into the crowd.

Luna and Clorin observed various creatures walking in and out of the colourful buildings. Some were carrying various trinkets, foods, and accessories.

"Shall we try out one of the shops, Clorin?" Luna asked, peering down at him.

He gave her a small smile and nodded.

"Which one?" she continued, putting her arm around Clorin's shoulder.

Clorin eyed up some of the things that the creatures were holding and scratched his right horn in deep thought. Then a beast with an abnormally large head emerged from the shop beside them, carrying a thick book. Stringy nasal appendages curled around the book and held it up in front of its eyes so the creature could read as it walked.

"Let's go in there!" said Clorin, tossing his pointed claw in the direction of the shop from which the beast had come.

Clorin stayed close to Luna as they made their way through the crowd to the bright green door of the book shop and went inside. The shop's interior walls were orange. The place buzzed with creatures of all sizes obsessing over books, strange-looking writing utensils, universal maps, and magazines featuring the hottest universal couples. Two slimy, yellowish creatures with tumbleweed-like hair, each with a single oversized front tooth, were fighting over the last copy of a magazine.

"S89-42, it's *mine*! I saw it first!" one of them whined.

"Ooh, no, X04-16, you know I'm *destined* to end up with someone from Epiton! I took the quiz last month. And *you* got Cipto. So it's mine!"

A third creature, like the first two except with three oversized front teeth, arrived on the scene. "You two are driving me insane. No one gets a magazine this time. Put it down now, or I'll take your legs off again."

The quarrelling pair groaned and followed their parent out of the shop, leaving the magazine crumpled in its holder. Luna picked it up. On the cover were the words *Epiton Stars* and the image of a grinning young Epitonian with razor-sharp teeth and menacing fiery eyes. Luna studied the image closely, then let out an audible gasp.

"Who's that, Looner?" Clorin asked, pointing to the picture.

Luna opened her mouth, but no words came. Her eyes scanned the headline. "APOLLO of the House of Aithne," it read. "The Universe's most eligible bachelor. Take the quiz inside to see if YOU would win this Pyroll champion's heart!"

Luna replied a bit gloomily, "It's . . . erm . . . my brother-in-law. He's married to my sister, Ann Lou. Or I thought he was . . ."

Clorin shoved his nose closer for a better look at the bachelor. "He looks like me," he said, pointing to Apollo's singular horn.

Having never properly seen Apollo before, Luna studied his image intently. He seemed to have lost one of his horns, perhaps to the GeoLapse or a particularly brutal game of Pyroll. He looked terrifying, but Luna knew he must be special to have stolen Ann Lou's heart and vice versa. She didn't want to be as judgemental of him as Knitsy had been.

Clorin quickly lost interest in the magazine and decided to take a wander around the upper level of the shop while Luna scoped out the ground floor. There were many sections of the floor that had very futuristic types of reading, like one section that had floating electronic slabs. One particularly bulbous creature with a hairy head and a hairless body poked its head toward one of the slabs, which then managed to get lost in its many tufts of hair. The creature then sat on a chair, removed the slab from its hair, and poked around on the slab so that digital information swirled around its head. Pictures and videos bounced into frame as the creature continued to read.

Fascinated, Luna continued around the shop until she sniffed something familiar—paper! She browsed the aisles of books that looked just like those on Earth, in awe at just how many books she hadn't read. How had she been so naive to think all authors came from Earth? How spectacular it would be to read books from different parts of the universe! She sniffed deeply, taking in the papery smell. Luna loved books—they brought her into a new world and let her escape her own. She had even managed to write some books during her time on Cipto. Her fingers grazed the spines of the books as she walked along the aisles, sparking a smile. She caught sight of creatures sitting comfortably between the aisles and along the walls entranced in various books. Her body filled with warmth as she felt a newfound connection with all the readers in the book shop. Who knew that mere pages with text on them could capture the imaginations of so many different beings?

She picked an aisle to start her investigation of new books and discovered that she was in the atlas section. Each atlas was a thick, heavy book containing star maps of galaxies and individual planets. There were thousands of them. Luna sat in a chair in the corner of the shop for a while, reading intently about Zwicky's Triplet galaxy. When she replaced it on the shelf and searched for another atlas, she came across a much thinner one hidden between two larger books. It was titled *Atlas of the Time Belt*. She snatched it and was surprised to find that it only had four pages. She read the following passage on the first page:

The Time Belt is located in the fourth dimension, orbiting the circumference of the space–time continuum limitations of various universes. There are four levels to the Time Belt: Vivalok, Mortalok, Galalok, and Focalok.

Luna's heart raced as she searched the other pages for more information, but there was none. The first page showed a map of Vivalok; the second, a map of Mortalok; the third, Galalok; and the fourth, Focalok. Luna's finger traced each map as she tried to identify which level of the Time Belt she was in.

The Focalok map was entirely greyed out except for a black circle in the centre, labelled BANK. Was that where she was? Where were all the shops? The roads? Turning to the Mortalok page, she saw a bunch of randomly placed dots as well as several cave illustrations. A white circle at the centre of this map was labelled BANK also. The Galalok map, in contrast to that of Mortalok, had a tightly packed set of dots organised in a grid formation with one larger dot at the bottom. But there was nothing on the Galalok map labelled BANK, so Luna immediately dismissed that option.

Turning to the Vivalok page, Luna immediately saw a circle labelled BANK, half black and half white, with a tangle of gold lines around it. She also recognised the main road in the centre of town that encircled that Bank, as well as the alley that she walked to find the centre of town. The page was overlaid with colours splashing everywhere. That's where she was. Vivalok.

Luna hopped to her feet and rushed to the till area. To her dismay, the queue was wrapped around several aisles. Clorin was now running between the aisles tossing a ball of fire between his claws, laughing to himself. Luna waved him down, and he paraded over to her excitedly.

"What's that you've got there?" she asked.

Clorin looked up at her, beaming. "A Pyroll!" He held up the Pyroll, which was the fiery ball used for the game of the same name.

"Would you like me to buy it for you?" Luna asked.

Clorin nodded happily. "Yes, please, Looner!"

Luna wondered how she was going to pay for their purchases. Was there money to be made or had in the Time Belt? She figured it was worth waiting in the long queue if it meant she would get some answers.

Luna and Clorin eventually reached the head of the queue and were called to the next available cashier, who looked similar to the creature they had seen walking out of the shop earlier holding a book with its long nasal antennae. The cashier's large head reached over the counter and nearly to where Luna was standing. Luna placed the magazine with Apollo on the cover on the counter in front of the cashier, followed by the atlas.

The cashier took the atlas in his sticky hands. "Back on planet Casper," he said, "we had all the galaxy atlases memorised before we took our first steps." He raised his nasal antennae high up into the air and sniffed loudly.

Luna rolled her eyes. She hated when anyone tried to prove they were more intelligent than her.

The cashier continued in a standoffish tone. "That'll be nine hundred eighty-six Chroniya."

Luna's eyes widened. It sounded like a lot of whatever that was. "Erm . . . I don't have any money, I'm sorry. How do I get money here?"

The cashier suddenly threw his head backward with a gloating laugh. "Newt!" he shouted. "Get this!" Another Casperian across the shop slowly turned its head. The cashier continued, unconcerned by the growing line of customers. "An Earthling who doesn't know what Chroniya is! It's as if they're trying to maintain the stereotype!"

Next to Newt, a Pomberian customer was trying to pull a book down off a shelf. But the book was too heavy for the Pomberian's gelatinous arms, and it landed on top of him, splatting his small purple body uncomfortably against the floor.

Clorin sprang to his feet and helped the Pomberian to its jelly-like knees. He patted the Pomberian's head with a small *squish* and gestured that the two read the book together. They both slid along the wall into a seated position and Clorin started reading the book to the Pomberian with great emotion, although he was holding the book upside down.

"And get this, Tycho!" Newt said through garbled laughter. "A Pomberian who can't lift a mere children's book!"

The Pomberian blushed a bright yellow as the two Casperians laughed at it. Clorin stuck his tongue out and hissed at the Casperians before continuing to read to the Pomberian.

Luna glared at Tycho. "There's no reason to be mean! So it's small and has no bones to keep it upright! I could say plenty of rude things about you if I wanted to!"

Tycho stopped laughing and raised an eyebrow at Luna. "Take your best shot. Take a shot at the most intelligent creatures you will ever meet—the very ones who have solved nearly all the mysteries of the universe!"

Luna huffed. "I'm not taking your infantile bait. Just tell me what Chroniya is."

Clorin sensed her sternness and hushed his reading. He held the book over his and the Pomberian's eyes. Only his small horns were visible from the top of the book.

Tycho rolled his eyes. "Did you see that large Bank structure back in town? The sphere at the top is filled with Chroniya."

Luna stood frozen with confusion. She even looked back at Clorin, hoping he would miraculously understand. But now the book and the small horns were both trembling in fear.

"Okay, but how do I get Chroniya?"

"Augh! Earthlings," muttered Tycho. Then Tycho said, as slowly as if talking to a child: "Chroniya is a measurement of time, and it is how we pay for things on Vivalok and other levels of the Time Belt. Of course, time stands still in the Time Belt, but should you ever leave, the Chroniya you spent here will be deducted from the time remaining in your life. It's a great bargain for most, considering the chances of escaping the Time Belt are one in three hundred omnitillion."

Luna was completely red in the face. "So, how do I get out of here?"

Tycho laughed in her face. "Are you unable to comprehend how small a one-in-three-hundred-omnitillion chance is? The answer is—well, all you need to know is that once the Bank is full of Chroniya, someone gets a chance to escape the Time Belt. Whether they succeed or not, the Bank is then emptied of its Chroniya, and we must fill it up again before another resident can try to leave."

Luna stood in thought for a moment. How strange that even in a timeless place, nothing was free.

"You're holding up the line!" squeaked a voice from somewhere in the queue. Luna peered at the queue to see who was complaining. No one had a particularly unhappy expression and she wondered if the heckler was invisible or just incredibly tiny.

Luna ignored the complaint and asked Tycho, "How do I find out how many Chroniya I have available to me?"

Tycho rolled his orange-sized eyes again. "Only Father Time knows how much we all have."

"But . . . what if I spend my life away without even knowing it? I could get out of here only to find I have used up all my time."

"If you go over the limit, you get chucked into Mortalok, which means you can never escape. Makes people careful about what they buy. You won't see too many elderly buying frivolous things around here. The kids, though . . . they're reckless with their time."

"So if I buy this atlas and this magazine for nine hundred eighty-six Chroniya . . . how much time is that?"

"Wow, you Earthlings really are stupid. In Earth time, nine hundred eighty-six Chroniya is roughly . . . four point nine eight two hours. No, excuse me, I forgot to round up . . . four point nine eight three hours."

Five hours. She could spare five hours.

"Looner?" piped Clorin, slowly making his way back to her, now waving the Pyroll above his head.

"With the Pyroll," said Tycho, "it'll be one thousand one hundred eighty-four Chroniya."

Six hours. Luna was fine with that.

"How do I . . . give you my Chroniya?"

"Hold still."

A buzzer sounded from above. Luna jerked her head up and saw the end of a very wide golden pipe poking out from the ceiling. A beam of light collimated around her body and blinded her for a few seconds. She felt a warming sensation envelop her body. Before she could even fully comprehend what had happened, the light disappeared.

"Did it work?" she asked in a concerned tone.

"Oh, yes. All the beam does is shorten your telomeres by a minuscule amount—in this case, enough to shorten your life by six hours should you ever leave. I don't think you need to worry, though. I don't foresee the shallow capacity of your tiny Earthling brain ever getting you out of here!"

Luna's face glowed red with fury. Just as she was about to erupt again at the smug shopkeeper, she saw Clorin in the corner of her eye and thought better of it.

"Come on, Clorin. Let's go play with your Pyroll." She reached out a hand for him to grab, and the two walked hand in claw out of the shop.

CHAPTER 3

The Jalopy Junkyard

Luna and Clorin roamed the busy streets of Vivalok in search of a new place to explore. Luna couldn't help but stare at every creature she passed, hoping she would recognise someone. A gut feeling told her that her siblings were on the Time Belt somewhere. But she wasn't sure they'd all be on Vivalok. What were the chances of that? Why had Luna landed on Vivalok instead of some other level of the Time Belt in the first place? Her siblings could easily be on any of the other levels for all she knew. She needed more information in order to formulate some hypotheses.

"Something smells yummy!" exclaimed Clorin, tugging on Luna's hand as they walked. His claw dug sharply into her soft hand. Trying not to yelp in pain, she squeezed her eyes shut.

She sniffed the air. It did smell quite flavourful. Nearby, a steady stream of customers flowed from a shop with a bright red exterior. They were carrying and eating strange-looking cuisine with evident enjoyment. Curious (and, she realised, quite hungry), Luna followed Clorin as he pulled her toward the shop.

The aromas of cakes, exotic meats, and something along the lines of gasoline wafted into their noses as they stepped inside. The place was packed with creatures pushing toward the counter, trying to get a taste of the universe's most prized delicacies. A few dine-in tables had been provided near the window, where a lucky few sat and tried to enjoy their food despite being jostled by the crowd that was almost on top of them.

Suddenly someone shouted, "Stop! Thief!" Some in the crowd tried to make way as a scruffy, fanged, manatee–like creature carrying what looked like a raw T-bone in one flipper hobbled for the door. A creature with three wings darted this way and that through the crowd, using its thorax like a rudder, in pursuit of the meat-bearing thief.

This opened up some space for Luna and Clorin to join the crowd. The line led to a buffet with an astounding variety of dishes, continually replenished by chefs of equally varied species. Some of the foods were on fire, others were iced over, and still more were in gaseous form. Some looked like small rocks one would find on a beach; others looked like an average wooden door. There was a beautifully crafted charcuterie board out for samples, and Luna licked her lips as she grabbed a piece of cheese. As she opened her mouth to bite, she caught a glimpse of the description: *Churned Wing Lice – Extra Mature.* Luna quickly replaced the abhorrent food back to the board, trying not to gag in front of the hungry customers. Clorin eyed the churned wing lice and popped it into his mouth, followed by a hearty "Mmm."

The chefs behind the buffet were creating an entertaining ruckus as they juggled foods across the table to hungry customers or piled their dishes with exotic condiments. One furry chef squirted a bluish liquid from its nose into the mouth of a fish-like creature with different-sized green spots on its scaly skin, which then swished in mid-air happily out the door.

A large menu hung on the wall behind the buffet. Luna read the first few items aloud to Clorin with the help of her microchip translator.

"Let's see, they have Polskin from Epiton, Fava cakes from Epiton . . . oh, the Fava cakes are sold out. Erm, there's chocolate cake from Earth. I would recommend that. My sister Elbina made those every so often, and they were absolutely delicious. Unfortunately, she couldn't eat them—she couldn't digest food the usual way—but she was an amazing cook. Erm, they also have Moolweep from Cipto. It's kind of like milk from Earth but a bit grainy, in my opinion, but you might like it. Gasoline candies from Kilo-209 . . . titanium crunchies from Rhothgo . . . ew, cabbaged eggs from Antympanica. I wouldn't recommend those." Here she pinched her nose, making Clorin laugh. "Anything you fancy from those first few?"

"Chocolate cake, please!" begged Clorin.

"Excellent choice. I'll get us each a slice."

Luna waited patiently in the packed line despite being elbowed and pushed around. A metallic-bodied creature nearly fell on top of Clorin after one of the chefs catapulted a pancake at its face, but Luna remained calm and held Clorin closer.

"Looner?" Clorin whispered. Luna knelt down beside him, and he pointed toward the window. "They look like you."

Luna followed Clorin's pointing claw to a table where two customers were eating voraciously. The red hair on the young man caught her eye in particular. Luna sprinted up to his table without hesitation. His teeth were sunk into a hefty Polskin leg. His companion had a slice of chocolate cake in each hand and five more in front of her, trying to shove as much in her mouth as possible.

Joy bubbled up in Luna's heart. "Riff!"

Riff looked up from his food. His eyes bugged out, and then he nearly knocked the table over as he leapt up and hugged Luna tightly.

The chocolate-covered woman joined in the embrace. Luna tried to ignore her and focus on Riff. He towered over her, enveloping her with his warm body. He smelled so strongly of cologne, the one she grew up hating. He always stunk up the bathroom and the hallways at home with it. But at this moment, the spicy, putrid smell was the most wonderful scent she could ever imagine. Finally, they broke off the embrace. Luna stared deeply into his eyes.

"I can't believe I found you," signed Luna. The whole family was accustomed to signing with Riff, as he was deaf.

"I can hear you!" exclaimed Riff with a smile. "Well, not entirely, in this madhouse. Can we find a quieter place?"

"Looner," Clorin whined, still tugging her flannel. "I want chocolate cake."

"Erm . . . right. Riff, we'll meet you outside, okay?"

Just as Luna started to turn back toward the till area, the chocolate-covered woman's eyes met Luna's. Luna's mouth fell open. Her best friend! Never in her sister's twenty-one years of life had Luna seen food splattered all over Elbina's face. She grabbed Elbina, not caring that chocolate cake was smearing all over her flannel. Elbina's bony frame was no different than when they were growing up. Her brown, wispy hair fell over Luna's shoulders as they hugged. The room instantly fell silent to Luna. The commotion in the crowded shop didn't bother her anymore. Just the touch of Elbina felt like home. The last time they'd been reunited, on Harvinth, they hadn't been able to spend nearly enough time together. Luna didn't want to let go.

"Let's not make a scene, now," Riff joked as he pulled Elbina toward the exit. "Elbina's embarrassed us enough for one day with her atrocious table manners. Come on, Elbs, let's wait outside."

Luna paid for her and Clorin's chocolate cake with another hour off her life and swivelled back through the crowd to meet her siblings outside. They found a quiet alley a few paces away from the food shop and sat in a tight square.

"I honestly thought I'd never see you guys again," said Luna, holding her forehead.

"It feels like it's been ages, but it's only been, what? A few days maybe?" Elbina asked in her soft voice.

"A few hours, more like," Luna replied. "The Jalopy dropped each of us off at the individual GeoLapse headquarters, and then I just remember disappearing mid-battle . . . I'm assuming we all did. How were your individual missions?" Luna swallowed hard, knowing that if their missions were anything like hers, it may be hard to discuss.

"Dreadful. Well, at first, successful!" Elbina piped up. "But dreadful at the end," she trailed off in a slump.

Riff nodded and cleared his throat. "Same."

Luna took a deep breath, knowing the subject needed a quick change. "So, Elbs, what is your official sentiment on chocolate cake?"

A smile erupted on Elbina's face. "Brilliant! It's so much better than the Gasser. I'm glad I can be rid of that stupid contraption that makes that horrid buzzing noise every time I'm feeding. But now . . . I can just taste things that aren't a gross, grey gas, and I can chew, swallow, and repeat as many times as I want! *Le gâteau au chocolat, c'est ma vie!*" Elbina said in her best French accent, holding a slice of chocolate cake to the sky in praise.

"What Elbs has neglected to tell you is that along with her newfound sense of taste, she is also a drama queen!" Riff said, cocking his head.

Luna couldn't help but let out a chuckle. "And how about you, then? Back on the heavy metal?"

Riff mimed a quick drum solo in air. "I have been listening to 'Take Flight' on repeat since I've arrived here. This is my favourite place in the universe."

Luna rolled her eyes. The Death Brigade was Riff's favourite band growing up, which meant she had no choice but to listen to them daily on full blast. The band was the heaviest of heavy metal, and their music made her want to rip her hair out, strand by strand.

"And you, Sis? What's it like to see again?" Elbina asked with her mouth full of cake.

"It's different. Great, but different. I feel like you move around with a different perspective. It took me a little while to get used to all the colours again. But seeing actual words in books has been interesting. I just want to read everything."

"Well, nothing's changed in that regard," Elbina winked.

"Who's the shadow, Luna?" asked Riff as he eyed up Clorin stuffing his face with chocolate cake. "Looks like he and Elbina will get on swimmingly."

"His name is . . ." Luna's hands sprang to her temples as she tried to remember. "Clorincladiellamore . . . Lecomeriellastrain. But you can call him Clorin."

"Ah, well that clears it all up," said Riff.

"He ran into me shortly after I arrived. He said he doesn't know where his family is. I couldn't bear to leave him alone."

"He's probably just confused. He's not the only one," Elbina said. Her voice was muffled by her last big mouthful of chocolate cake. "Luna, what is going on? Where are we? One second I was setting off a grenade to fend off the GeoLapse outside Hayden's dormitory—" she swallowed in fear at the horrific memory, or perhaps it was the cake "—and the next, I walked right through his door like a ghost, and he couldn't even see me."

"You seem so concerned that you've nearly lost your appetite there, Elbs," jested Riff, prodding Elbina's shoulder.

"Shut up, Riff," snarled Elbina, with bits of chocolate spewing out of her mouth. "At least *I* didn't cry!"

"I never said I cried!" huffed Riff, folding his arms and turning away.

"Are you two done being childish?" asked Luna, with one eyebrow raised.

She often found herself being the most mature out of all the siblings, which made sense as she was the oldest. As close as they all were, they very often bickered. Even though Riff was twenty-three, Luna still found him consistently acting like a young teenager.

Neither of them answered, but Luna knew they were eager for answers.

"Here's what I hypothesise. Remember in the Time Belt on our way to Harvinth when Nan told Father Time she wanted to essentially swap places with Mum?"

Her two siblings nodded.

"And remember how Father Time said messing around with the dead was foolish, so he punished her? Well, we thought that punishment was her dying. But I think it was more complicated than that."

Riff's eyebrows furrowed. "How d'ya reckon?"

"There's this old story told on Cipto called 'The Tale of How Cipto Lost its Light.' It's about a Cipton named Connie who was the planet's shining star, you might say. Everyone loved and worshipped her. One day she grew very sick, and the only way for her to get better was to travel past the Time Belt. That way, time could be reversed, and she could go back to Cipto so that she could be treated early, before she got too sick. So Connie and Rodney, her father, flew past the Time Belt in a Jalopy. The legend says that the reason Cipto is so dark is because a similar thing happened to Rodney. His answer to Father Time must have also been foolish, because it erased all existence of Rodney *and* his descendants— which included Connie. Do you see where I'm going with this?"

Elbina spoke up. "So you're saying . . . we don't exist anymore?"

"That's my assumption," said Luna, clasping her hands together. "We're in a whole other world full of creatures who also don't exist any-more. But we'll have a chance to escape as soon as enough Chroniya is built up."

"That black stuff in the golden statue thingy in the centre of wher-ever we are?" inquired Riff.

Luna nodded and stifled a laugh at his vagueness.

"Why can I hear, though? And you, see? And Elbs . . . eat like a creature from Kilo-209?" asked Riff, dodging a swift slap to the skull from Elbina.

"Well, since we don't really exist, I guess we're just sort of soul versions of ourselves. Our old bodies don't exist anymore. Here, we can do whatever we want."

"So what's the plan, then? How do we get out of here?" asked Elbina, a worried look growing on her face.

"Here's all I know," started Luna, holding out the atlas of the Time Belt. "There are four levels to the Time Belt. We're on Vivalok. We need to explore the other areas to see if we can find clues on how to escape."

"Do you think Nan is on one of the levels? And Ann Lou?" asked Riff.

"Yes," replied Luna. "Any descendant of Nan who was alive when she was taken away is probably stuck here, along with Nan herself. We need to start somewhere. I say we explore as much of Vivalok as we can, and along the way we can investigate how to get to the other levels. I'm going to head back to the book shop to do some more reading and see if there's anything there."

"I'll come with you!" piped up Elbina.

"I'll have a wander around Vivalok," said Riff. "We can all meet at the Bank statue later."

"But when do we meet up? Those weird clocks at the Bank are no help," said Elbina.

"Just use the clock on your microchip, duh," Riff said smartly.

"Not working, Einstein," Luna said, holding her left wrist up. Where a digital display should have been, the output only showed ?? : ??.

"Maybe we can meet up before dark," Elbina suggested. "Clorin, does the sky ever get dark here?"

"Uhhh, I don't know," Clorin shrugged.

"Let's just use a different form of time, like how long it would take to eat a big meal in the shop," Elbina said.

"In that case, we're talking ten seconds for you," Riff jested.

"How about however long it would take to read a short novel?" Luna proposed.

"I've never done that in my life," said Riff. "How about the time it would take to listen to *Anvils Ablaze*, The Death Brigade's first album? I transferred you guys each an album on ChipMusic before we all left home all those years ago."

Luna flicked her left wrist to find The Death Brigade on ChipMusic. "I have *Anvils Ablaze*."

"It's a wicked one. I hope you listened to it often on Cipto," Riff said with a happy sigh.

The album shone on a digital display on Luna's forearm. The album art showed an angry man holding up an anvil that was engulfed in flames. The rest of the band in the background were also in flames as they posed with their instruments.

"Yeah, I listened to it . . . all the time," Luna said, sarcastically. "I never thought I'd say this, but good idea, Riff," she added, squeezing her brother's shoulder. "Just put your music volume all the way down and check every so often how far through the album you are."

"Um, actually, I recommend volume on full blast. But to each their own," Riff said. "Clorin, want to come with me? We can get you another slice of cake while we walk." Riff smiled and held out his hand.

Clorin sat close to Luna and looked up at her, his red eyes full of worry.

"You don't need to be afraid of Riff," said Luna. "He's my brother. He'll keep you safe." Luna encouraged him. "And, Riff," she whispered, burrowing her stare into his own, "be careful what you spend from now on. We can't be wasting too much of our time."

"I'd say chocolate cake is an excellent use of my time," Riff said. It got a small chuckle out of Clorin.

Once Clorin had gathered up the courage to wander with Riff, Luna and Elbina started for the book shop. The sisters finally had some alone time to talk about things that Riff would have pretended to gag at.

"So, Sis," started Elbina, fidgeting with her fingers. "I have some girl talk I desperately need to get off my chest."

Luna wasn't a huge fan of girl talk, but she made the exception for Elbina. "Let me guess . . . Hayden?"

"Yes!" Elbina bounced with a skip in her step as they walked. "After all these years, he and I kind of . . . sparked something back on Harvinth. It was amazing. I'd never had anyone interested in me *ever*! I felt like . . . like Ann Lou, for once in my life!"

Luna felt bad that Elbina always felt like a shadow to Ann Lou, even though Ann Lou was the youngest of the siblings. "Well, don't romanticise Ann Lou. You're perfect the way you are. It doesn't matter who's interested in you, or not. But I'm happy for you anyways, Elbs."

"I'm not romanticising Ann Lou! But it doesn't matter now, does it? Just when I get myself an interested boy, I go and vanish from existence! I have to get out of here and back to my life. Well, we all do."

"Another sibling wedding in our future, then?" said Luna playfully.

"Oh, let's not get too ahead of ourselves. But . . . wow, that would be something." Her smile broadened as she imagined a possible future with Hayden. "Enough about me, though. What about you? I don't think you've ever told me about anyone you've liked. Was there ever anyone in school? Or even on Cipto?"

Luna couldn't help but laugh out loud. "Me? Elbina, I have no interest in dating. I just want to do my own thing. And for you to be happy. That's all that matters to me."

"There's no one? Like, in the whole universe? No one who ever made your heart, you know . . ." Elbina clasped her hands over her own heart. "Sing?"

Luna shook her head. "Immersing myself in a good book makes my heart sing."

Elbina blushed. "Fair enough."

As the sisters entered the book shop, Tycho saw Luna and let out a growl.

"Just ignore that melon-headed moron," snarled Luna, glaring sidelong at him.

The sisters prowled the cramped aisles of the shop, looking for books about the Time Belt. Finding nothing, they split up and started riffling through books hoping to find even the merest mention of the Time Belt. After what seemed like several fruitless hours, Luna decided to look for books about planets that lie beyond the Time Belt. She found a book on Harvinth and curled up in the corner of the shop, reading studiously.

While she was focused on a chapter about Harvinth's early planetary origins, Luna heard a familiar slithering sound just in front of her. A Cipton was reading a book and fidgeting around trying to turn the page, with little success.

"Need some help there?" asked Luna, reaching forward to help.

"No!" squawked the Cipton rudely.

Luna recognised the creature's voice. "Hey, you're the Cipton I ran into earlier. By the Bank."

The Cipton seemed caught off guard and began to squirm uncomfortably. "Oh, yes. You're that Earthling. Don't let me interrupt your reading." The Cipton turned and tried to beat a hasty retreat, but by human standards it was at best a slow slither.

"Actually," said Luna, "I was just trying to find some information on the Time Belt. Maybe you could help me."

"Help you? Oh my, I would love *nothing* more," droned the Cipton sarcastically as it continued to slither away, directly over the book it had left lying open on the floor.

"Wait, I didn't mean to offend you. I'm sorry. Can I have your name? So I can address you properly if I run into you again?"

The Cipton continued to squirm. "Constance," she replied darkly. Without another word, Constance rushed out of the book shop as quickly as her slithering body could take her.

Luna scratched her head in confusion. It was such a strange conversation, and ill-mannered Ciptons were exceptionally rare. Luna picked up the book the Cipton had been reading. Along with text, the book had raised markings on each page, similar to Braille, which allowed Ciptons to read by touch using their slithery undersides. Luna noticed the title: *An Anthology of Poems*, by E. Bowser III. She recognised the author's name, but with all the thoughts swirling around her head she couldn't think where from. So she placed this book and the one on Harvinth neatly back on the shelf.

Luna found Elbina, and they both concluded that there was no information on the Time Belt to be found anywhere in the book shop beyond the atlas Luna had picked up on her first visit.

"Is *Anvils Ablaze* finished yet?" Elbina asked in a hopeful tone.

Luna checked ChipMusic. "Merciless Souls," the final song of the album, had thirty seconds remaining.

"Just in time. Let's go," said Luna, and the sisters exited the book shop.

As the sisters neared the Bank, Luna spotted the mysterious hooded figure again—the same one she had seen before, just standing motionless with orbs all around. As before, the figure seemed to have no business at all; it just stood perfectly still with its hands clasped behind its back. Perhaps all the Vivalok creatures were just as puzzled by the presence of this figure and its mysterious orbs.

The sisters spotted Riff and Clorin playing catch with Clorin's Pyroll. Luna smiled as she saw Clorin squealing with glee every time he caught the fiery ball in his claws.

"This little guy has a future in Pyroll!" said Riff enthusiastically, causing Clorin to squeal even more. "He might give Ann Lou a run for her money! Or, should I say, her Chroniya!" Riff tossed the Pyroll high into the air, and Clorin sped underneath its arc, leaping with great power into the air and catching it firmly.

"Did you guys find anything at the book shop?" asked Riff.

"No," said Luna. "Did you two find anything interesting?"

"Well, Clorin and I came across a very curious place quite a ways away from the hubbub of town. Want to tell them, little man?"

Clorin came running at full speed, waving his claws around in excitement. "Spaceships!"

"Where?" asked Luna. She opened the atlas to the map of Vivalok and showed it to Riff.

Riff pointed to the southeast corner of the map. The spot under his fingertip was empty white—no shapes or colours at all.

"I hope you missed that ruddy old Jalopy," said Riff.

"No way," Elbina pushed his shoulder.

"Come see for yourselves," Riff said as he started walking away.

They walked through the crowds until they were less and less dense. As soon as they reached a point where there was no one else around them, Riff pointed to what looked like a small, dark dot on the horizon. They were bathed in white light, their only sense of direction being the shrinking colours of Vivalok behind them and the dot ahead of them.

Gradually, the dot grew into a group of irregular shapes, which then evolved into angular mounds—miles of them. Slowly it became recognisable to Luna as an enormous junkyard. It was filled with haphazard piles of manufactured objects ranging from the size of a skyscraper down to pieces that would fit in the palm of a human hand. Some of them were very clearly pieces of vehicles: engines, hulls, windscreens, wings, and wheels, most of them battered beyond repair. The rest were of indeterminable origin: control panels (some still smoking), gauges, greasy machine parts, and jagged pieces of metal.

As they walked through this landscape of wreckage, something caught Luna's eye, something that stood out because it wasn't nearly as battered as the rest of the objects.

Clorin ran up to it and pressed his face against the curved sides of the object, trying to see inside.

Riff said to Luna and Elbina: "There. Look familiar?"

Luna gasped. It was an hourglass Jalopy, the same kind that she and her siblings had ridden from Cipto, to Olfinder, Antympanica, and Harvinth. "Is that . . . ours?"

Elbina inspected the Jalopy closely from all angles, looking for any discernible differences between it and the one they had ridden in before. "It's tough to say. There could be more than one. But how?"

"Let's try it out," said Riff giddily.

He pushed against the side of the glass, trying to tilt the glass up from its hinged stone base. He had forgotten how heavy it was. Leaning into it with as much of his weight as possible, he managed to push it up far enough for someone to crawl in. Clorin imitated him by pushing on the bottom half of the hourglass.

"Good job, little man," panted Riff, smearing his forehead along the glass to wipe the sweat off. "One of you hop in now, before I keel over."

Luna stepped forward and crawled into the bottom half of the hourglass. As gently as possible, Riff lowered the glass around her. He, Elbina, and Clorin watched Luna intently.

Inside, Luna waited for the Jalopy's usual greeting and its green light. She waited for what seemed like several minutes, but neither of those events occurred.

Riff eventually helped Luna out of the hourglass. They found a few other Jalopies of different models but similar size, but none of those activated either.

"If they're here," Luna said, gesturing at the acres of broken machinery around them, "maybe they're broken."

"Do we have to fix one?" asked Riff. "I wouldn't even know where to start."

Clorin ran and jumped behind Luna. He gripped her flannel and began to tremble.

"What's making that sound?" Elbina said, catching on to his sudden fear and turning her head to find the source.

The three siblings listened closely, and Luna instantly recognised what Clorin was hiding from. It was a faint slithering sound—and it was coming from a few metres away, close enough for Luna to recognise the little blob hiding behind one of the Jalopies.

Luna strode over to Constance, the Cipton whom she had now run into twice since arriving in Vivalok. Constance appeared shocked upon hearing Luna's approaching footsteps. Luna noticed that she had a dark object in her stomach. Constance was already slightly murky in colour, so Luna couldn't tell what exactly it was.

"You again? Can you quit following me?" Constance quivered in frustration.

"Constance, why are you hiding from me? I'm not trying to hurt you," pushed Luna.

"You're invading my personal space, you annoying, pestering Earthling. I'm just trying to enjoy a nice, quiet slither around Vivalok."

Luna didn't buy the excuse. She tried bargaining. "Look, Constance, is there anything I can help you with? I have a feeling we're both looking for the same thing. Maybe we can work together."

Constance positively writhed at this suggestion, her normally blank face twisting in fury. "I order you to stay away from me! I'll . . . I'll tell someone to take all your Chroniya if you come within another metre of me!" She bounced away from Luna as quickly as her gelatinous body could go.

Luna took this as her cue to quit trying with Constance. She walked away from the Cipton, who by now was out of earshot, and went back to her siblings with a new plan of action. "We should go back to the book shop. I think I know where we can find a clue."

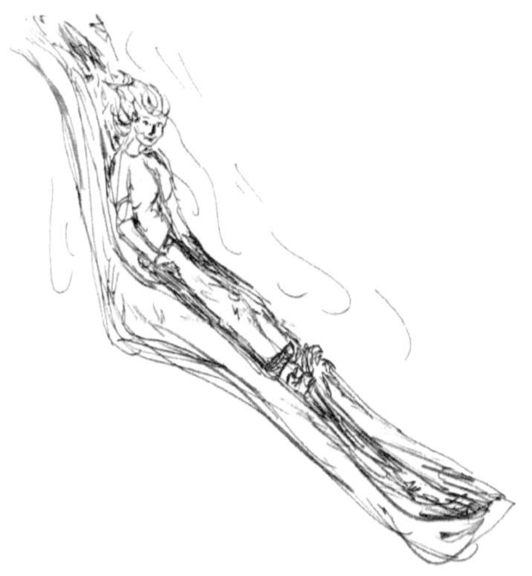

CHAPTER 4

A Treasure Hunt in Vivalok

Luna swiftly led her siblings and Clorin back to the book shop without another word. After a few awkward glances from Tycho, who was still tending to a long line of customers, Luna guided the group to where she had been previously reading. She grabbed *An Anthology of Poems* by E. Bowser III from the shelf and began furiously flipping through it.

"Um, Sis?" piped Elbina. "Not that we don't love watching you read, but why are we here? We looked everywhere in here for information on the Time Belt, and we didn't find any."

Luna said, without looking up: "That Cipton I was talking to at the junkyard has been acting very suspicious around me. I saw her reading this earlier. I think she knows something about the Jalopies. I just have to figure out what she knows."

"A Cipton was *reading?* With what eyes?" asked Riff.

"What can we do to help, Luna?" asked Elbina. "We're not completely useless, you know."

The three siblings cosied up around the book while Clorin played with his Pyroll in the next aisle. Luna could see the fiery ball appearing over the shelf, disappearing, then reappearing as Clorin played catch with himself.

They pored over several pages of E. Bowser III's anthology, unable to detect any sort of easily discernible clues right away.

"Is there anything written in the page margins?" suggested Elbina.

Luna flipped through the rest of the book. "No. Nothing."

"Maybe the Cipton was enjoying the feel of the pages under her blobbiness and just wanted to get away from you," proposed Riff, still pondering the subject of Constance's reading abilities.

Luna snapped, "Riff, you are absolutely no help. Just go play with Clorin before you drive me completely mad."

Riff shrugged and went to play with Clorin.

"Luna, when the Cipton was slithering away, did you see how far she'd gotten into the book?" asked Elbina. "Maybe there's, I don't know, a smudge or something on one of the pages. It looks like hardly anyone has ever touched this thing."

"Good thinking," said Luna. She opened the book a little less than halfway through, then turned the pages one at a time, carefully inspecting the condition of each one. Before long, she saw something. "Look," she said, running her finger along the bottom edge of the page. "It's crinkled."

"What's on that page?" said Elbina.

A poem on the page was called "The Next Levels." Luna read aloud.

In order to move about,
You must become a master scout.
If you decide to persist,

You can reach the place where the dead cease to exist.
This is the same way to get to the place of the inmate,
As well as the place to change the date.
Start each time at the collective sphere,
And first head to midnight for a place to soothe the ear.
Next, find your way to three with a prance,
May your taste buds start to dance.
Off to six down a long lane,
You'll find a place to fill your brain.
Lastly, toward nine a few lengths,
To the place where one may show off their strength.
Bring to me all that drains your pockets,
For which I will give you a chance to fly in your rocket.
Find me, the only townsfolk
Dressed in the oversized black cloak.

Luna paused, pondering the riddle and silently piecing together her assumptions. Elbina didn't dare say a word for fear of interrupting her thoughts.

Clorin and Riff peeked around the end of the aisle. Riff, for once, kept silent.

Clorin whispered, "Is that a puzzle, Looner?"

"Kind of," replied Luna. "I think I know what we have to do."

"Talk us through it, please," said Elbina.

"It's basically a sort of treasure hunt around Vivalok. The beginning of the poem mentions the other three levels—Mortalok, Galalok, and Focalok. I'm assuming 'Where the dead cease to exist' is Mortalok because it has the same root as the Latin word *mortem*, meaning death. 'The place of the inmate' is probably Galalok because the Middle English word for jail was *gaol*. And Focalok . . . I'm not too sure about that one, but by process of elimination, we can assume Focalok is 'the place to change the date.'"

"But what does that all mean? 'Where the dead cease to exist,' 'the place of the inmate,' 'the place to change the date . . .' I don't understand," Elbina continued.

Luna shrugged. "I don't have all the answers, Elbs. But the root words match up. We just have to take it as a clue for now."

"So, what else?" asked Riff.

"Well, it says we have to start at the collective sphere. That one is obvious."

Luna glanced at her siblings to give them a chance to help solve the riddle. She was met with two blank stares.

"The Bank, guys. Come on."

"Ooh," said Riff and Elbina simultaneously.

"We follow the directions to the four locations," explained Luna, "and apparently we're going to find objects there, although it doesn't say what. And then . . ." Luna re-read the last several lines again. "Then we can exchange the objects for a chance to escape Vivalok. Then we give those objects to that strange, cloaked figure in front of the Bank. I bet the dark orbs are the key to the Jalopies."

"Brilliant," said Riff. "Let's get started."

The four of them hopped up and were about to head to the Bank when Tycho cleared his throat loudly. Luna paid three more hours off of her life so that they could take the book with them.

* * *

The group gathered at the Bank and awaited their first direction. Luna read aloud: "'And first head to midnight.'"

"What does 'midnight' refer to?" asked Riff. "There's a bajillion clocks here."

"It might not refer to a time. It's probably a direction," suggested Luna. She pulled out the atlas and opened it to the map of Vivalok. The map showed the Bank in the centre of town. It was the intersection of four main roads, one north, east, south, and west.

"So, midnight is north, three o'clock is east, six o'clock is south, and nine o'clock is west?" guessed Elbina.

"Correct," said Luna. "The four objects we need are on each of these main roads. First we need to find 'a place to soothe the ear.'"

They walked north from the Bank, grasping each other's hands tightly so as not to get separated in the crowd. Starting on the east side of the road, they stopped at each of the shop windows and peered inside, looking for something that might match the description in the poem. They reached the end of the road, looking away from Vivalok and into white space, without any further insight.

"I don't know about you guys, but my ears would have been soothed at that shop halfway down the road where everyone was sticking their tails in the fire," said Riff.

"Let's cross here and check the other side," said Luna.

The group swivelled through the crowd to the west side of the road and started checking those shops. About halfway back to town, Riff was the first to peek into the window of a shop with a white exterior.

"Hey, there's a drum set in there! Way in the back! Can we please go in for a second?"

Luna stared at him blankly. "This is it, you idiot. 'A place to soothe the ear.' It's a music shop!"

They rushed inside. Riff made a beeline for the drum set while the rest of them looked around the shop. It was filled with different instruments, most of which they had never seen before. Sounds echoed from every area of the shop as customers tried out different instruments. In the children's section, Clorin grabbed a small megaphone emblazoned with a colourful logo that read "Sound like an Olfinderian!" When he spoke into the small end, hypnotising sounds came out of the large end. Luna immediately shuddered, remembering the horrifying Olfinder Chorale Concert where a GeoLapse attack occurred during the Olfinderians' entrancing song.

Elbina immediately recognised her sister's distress and knew what was triggering it. "It's okay, Sis," she said kindly.

They heard Riff's drumming in the background as they strolled through the aisles, looking at flutes with spikes instead of holes, rubbery horns, and geometrically complex metallic shapes with hundreds of keys to push and pull.

"What do you think we need to find?" Elbina asked quietly.

Luna propped open the anthology again. "The fourth to last line says, 'Bring to me all that drains your pockets.' Sounds like we should look for the most expensive item in the shop." Elbina saw Luna's disheartened expression and quickly understood what that meant: they would be sacrificing a large amount of their time.

"We can split the cost. We're looking for four objects from four different shops . . . so we can take turns paying," suggested Elbina, trying to remain in good spirits.

The sisters walked over to where Riff was drumming. They smiled as they watched him, his eyes closed and his moppy red hair flapping about. He was in his own world, finally hearing the music again, the very thing he lived for. Clorin was hopping up and down in front of the drum set and flailing his arms and legs in every direction, clearly enjoying Riff's impromptu concert. Luna and Elbina laughed as other customers joined him and danced in each of their own planet's styles. Some bounced on their heads, others whipped their limbs in a circular motion, and one small beast with waxy skin and a singular toe started happily darting into all the shelves with glee, knocking everything about. The shopkeepers hurried over to the creature and restrained him before any more damage was done.

Once Riff had tired out the dancing customers, he got up, set Clorin on the drum stool, and handed him the sticks. Clorin's legs were too short to reach the pedals, but he was nonetheless delighted by the chance to bang out rhythms on the snare, toms, and cymbals.

Riff rejoined Luna and Elbina. "Sorry, got a bit carried away there. What've I missed?" he asked, full of energy.

"Well, the poem is alluding to four shops. We think it's saying that we have to buy the most expensive object in each shop. Only then can we trade the objects for the orb and try to escape Vivalok," responded Luna.

Riff nodded solemnly, also understanding the consequences. "Right. Well, let's shop."

The siblings approached the cashier, who was grooving to the cacophony of the shop by swaying back and forth in smooth, wiggly movements. Several of its pink and purple tentacles hung in the air, also bouncing back and forth to the offbeats.

"Hooow can I help you?" it asked in a sing-songy voice.

"What's the most expensive thing you sell here?" asked Luna.

The cashier looked bewildered. "My myyyy, got some time on your hands? That would be the instrument of planet Minag, my home planet. It's called the Gliedelfrop."

The cashier pulled a tiny glass case from behind the counter with the tip of one of its tentacles. It carefully opened the case and showed them the Gliedelfrop, which was snugly fit in the plushy innards of the case. It looked to be the size of a pea.

"*That?* That's the most expensive thing in the shop?" groaned Luna.

The cashier looked taken aback. "How dare you speak so disdainfully about the Gliedelfrop? The planet Minag is host to the universe's most enthralling music events. Don't think I haven't been warned about you from Tycho at the book shop!"

"Can I give it a try?" asked Riff curiously.

"Of course," the Minagian replied, placing the tiny instrument in Riff's cupped hands.

He stared at it with an eyebrow raised. Unsure of what to do, he juggled it around in his hands.

"Stick it somewhere. Anywhere," the Minagian clarified.

Riff's eyes bugged out. Fortunately, he succeeded in containing his amusement. He stuck the Gliedelfrop under his tongue and waited for something to happen.

"Sing a note. Any note," the Minagian urged.

Riff hummed a middle C, which immediately triggered a wave of what sounded like electronic dance music in the key of C. The music sounded as if it was coming out of Riff's nose and ears. He quickly discovered that he could open and close his mouth to make the music louder and softer, and that forming different shapes with his lips changed the timbre of the music. He even tried closing his mouth and pinching his nose shut, dampening the music so that it sounded more bass-like.

"Very good! Now sing another note!" shrieked the cashier.

Riff decided to go for a high A, immediately causing the music to nicely transition into the new key. He hummed all sorts of notes while the Gliedelfrop quickly adapted. The customers of the shop again surrounded Riff, dancing along to his intensely captivating music.

He spat the Gliedelfrop into his palm and smiled a huge smile. "I love it! How much does it cost?"

"Eight million seven hundred nine thousand five hundred forty-eight Chroniya," replied the cashier.

All of their jaws dropped. Even Clorin, who had stopped playing the drums, was astounded. "Biiig number!" he exclaimed.

"Eight million?" said Riff. "How much time is that?"

"I'm not from planet Casper, so my maths are a bit rough, but in Earth time . . . that's probably just over five years."

The siblings looked at one another in despair. No one said a word until Riff plucked up his courage. "Look, we have to try to get out of here, guys. I'll take this one."

"You can't possibly do that. I will not allow it!" said Elbina sternly.

"It's the only way, Elbs! Someone has to take one for the team!" Riff eyed up the cashier bravely. "I'll pay."

The golden pipe above their heads flashed a beam of collimated light over Riff. Once the light disappeared, Riff coughed and struggled to maintain his balance for a few seconds. Luna and Elbina supported him by the arms until his dizziness had passed.

"Enjoooy!" sang the Minagian, waving out the McHubbards with one tentacle while beckoning the next customer forward with another. Its remaining seven and a half tentacles grooved to the music that reverberated throughout the shop.

"Riff, I'm sorry. I never wanted you to do that," said Luna.

"What's five years?" he said sweetly. "Keeps me from living a sad life as a grumpy old man," he added, winking at her. "Besides, I felt really guilty when I went into hiding back on Antympanica. It caused you, Ann Lou, and Nan so much hurt. And Matt and Joe. I had to step up this time. For them."

Luna sighed deeply. "Let's just look for the next shop."

The four started back toward the Bank, and Riff kept them all entertained with dance music from the Gliedelfrop. He and Clorin skipped ahead of the sisters, dancing in the street without a care. Their exuberance provoked giggles from creatures in the crowd, and Luna and Elbina hung back, not wanting to be associated with the two embarrassing boys. Once they reached the Bank, they all then headed east, toward three o'clock.

"What are we looking for next?" said Riff.

"'May your taste buds start to dance,'" recalled Elbina. "Isn't the food shop on this road?"

"You're right, that must be it," said Luna, and they set off to where the wonderfully pungent aromas of the universe's cuisines were wafting from.

"Chocolate cake!" shouted Clorin with glee, running ahead of them.

The siblings met him in the shop, which was still filled to the brim with customers, as it had been at their last visit. They made their way into the queue, which was curled tightly around the shop through many aisles.

"Ooh, the dishes I could make with these ingredients!" Elbina said, closing her eyes and taking in the exotic aromas. "At least I can eat food and taste it now."

"What do you think the most expensive item is?" Riff asked. He was peering into a nearby display case and licking his lips at a bundle of rocks covered in something that looked like strawberry jam.

"Whatever it is, they probably don't sell much of it," said Luna. "No one would spend years of their life on one meal without a motive behind it."

As soon as they reached the cashier, a large furry beast with giant teeth, they asked for the most expensive item once again.

"Aghhh," it replied in a monstrous voice. "That'd be the Fava cakes from Epiton." The cashier began to lick its lips like Riff, but the cashier had more saliva dripping from its mouth, forming a small pool on the counter.

"One Fava cake then, please," said Luna.

"Looner, I want chocolate cake," Clorin said, tugging on her.

"Not now, Clorin. We can't spend too much on stuff we don't need."

"But I need one *noooow*!" he whined, pulling harder.

"No!" she snapped, waving a finger.

Clorin began to throw a fit, screaming and crying, and trying to kick Luna's leg. Luna stepped back, but not quickly enough to dodge his attack. He landed a kick on her shin. He was surprisingly strong for a creature his age, and she nearly fell to the ground.

"Get that ill-behaved creature out of here, I'm starving!" shouted someone further down the line.

Luna dragged Clorin out of the shop by the horn, holding him away from her body so his kicks couldn't reach her. For the first time since she had met Clorin, she was furious at him.

"You cannot speak to me that way! Nor can you hurt me. That isn't nice!" she scolded, still holding him away from her.

Clorin's red eyes glared ferociously at her as he huffed, screamed, and kicked the air.

Riff came out then and knelt down next to Clorin. "Hey, little man. I got you this," he said, holding out a slice of chocolate cake.

Luna angrily eyed up Riff while Clorin leapt at him, trying to reach the cake.

"You can have it on one condition."

Clorin froze.

"You need to be nice to Luna. And you have to listen to her. Understood?"

Clorin looked at the ground, embarrassed.

"Understood?" Riff repeated sharply.

"Yes, Riff," Clorin replied in a soft mumble.

"Now say that you're sorry," continued Riff, holding the cake just out of his reach.

Clorin looked apologetically into Luna's eyes and let out a soft "Sorry."

"That's all right," answered Luna, letting go of his horn.

Clorin meekly took his cake from Riff and sat in silence as he munched on it.

"Thought you were going against my parenting skills there for a second," Luna said grumpily to Riff.

"Kids shut up when you give them food. Still works on me, too," Riff quipped.

Elbina emerged from the shop, not carrying anything. "They're sold out of Fava cakes," she sighed.

"Damn it," Luna muttered, forming her hands into fists.

"We can just come back later," said Elbina.

"Next shop?" suggested Riff.

They returned to the Bank and started down the main road south toward six o'clock.

"The poem says, 'You'll find a place to fill your brain,'" said Luna.

"I think I saw a school down the road here," said Elbina.

"What would you buy at a school?" asked Luna.

"A kid, what else?" said Riff.

"Any other places?" asked Elbina.

"Maybe the book shop?" suggested Luna.

"Possibly a more sensible idea," said Elbina.

They walked into the busy book shop, and Luna led the group straight to the till. Tycho groaned, "Oh, not this crazed lunatic again!"

Luna despised his arrogance, but she maintained a pleasant demeanour. She politely asked, "We need the most expensive item in here, please."

Tycho goggled at her. "Do you remember when I explained the whole Chroniya concept to you? Do Earthlings understand things as the opposite of what they are told? Because spending *more* Chroniya is kind of a *bad* thing."

"We know," replied Luna. "We still want whatever it is."

"All right, then," said Tycho. As he turned away, Luna heard him mutter, "Dull-witted Earthling." She closed her eyes for a moment, suppressing the urge to bark at him.

Tycho came out from behind the counter and led them to a nearby shelf. On the lowest shelf were some of the largest books any of them had ever seen, even Luna. These books were thicker than Clorin was tall. Tycho pointed to the thickest one and left them to figure out how to carry it. Riff knelt down and managed to wrangle the heavy tome off the shelf and into his arms. He huffed and puffed as he carried it to the till. He dropped the book on the counter and proceeded to sit on the floor to catch his breath.

"What is this book even about?" Elbina asked Tycho.

"It's the traditional 'baby's first book' on Casper. It's in every Casperian household," sniffed Tycho. "It contains most of the languages in the universe, as well as basic black hole theory and so forth. Most children have it memorised in their first week of life. I'm not sure why you Earthlings want it, given that even the first page exceeds your brain capacity."

"We'll just have to muddle through," Luna said. Riff and Elbina were in awe of Luna's self-control under the circumstances.

"That'll be ten million four hundred ninety-nine thousand nine hundred ninety-nine Chroniya. It's on sale today."

Before they could discuss who should take the loss for this purchase, the gold pipe sent down its wide beam and the light collimated around Riff. He looked up in horror as the beam completed the transaction.

"Hey! We didn't even get to decide who should pay!" said Luna.

"I can ring up a second copy just for you if you'd like," Tycho rudely replied.

Riff winced and held his head, then collapsed, just barely managing to catch himself on the edge of the counter. Tycho's face broke into an evil grin as Luna and Elbina helped Riff to his feet. Luna glared at the chortling Casperian as she wrapped her arms around the book and struggled to lift it up. She ended up just pushing it on the floor and out the door, settling it just beside the shop window. Elbina came out next, supporting Riff, which was no small feat considering he was over twice her weight and a head taller. Elbina pushed him down to sit on the massive book, and he slouched over and held his face in his large hands.

"Riff!" squealed Elbina, who was also catching her breath. "Are you all right?"

"Yeah, just dizzy," Riff said with the tone of a sick child. "I might hang back from our last stop, if that's all right."

"Sure, take it easy." Elbina hugged him.

"Clorin, why don't you stay here and keep Riff company," Luna suggested. Clorin leapt for joy.

The girls headed back to the Bank and then took the road to the left, where, according to the poem in Bowser's anthology, they would find their final clue. About three-quarters of the way down the road, Elbina made a suggestion. "'A place to show your strength' could be in here," she said, pointing through the window of a shop with a purple exterior. "There's a lot of big rock creatures in here. I can see some flexing their muscles. It looks like a gym of sorts."

Elbina and Luna walked in and entered a spacious interior where the floor and walls were made of a material similar to marble. A long corridor led to an arena space. A variety of creatures were entering and exiting the arena, but none compared to the size and ferocity of the giant boulders with muscly arms and a single angry eye. The lobby was ringed with identical floor-to-ceiling banners that featured a boulder creature with particularly muscular arms striking a menacing pose.

Luna whispered to Elbina, "I don't see anything for sale here, but let's ask." Luna hoped they wouldn't attract attention for being small and weak amid the overwhelmingly brutish clientele.

They tiptoed to the main desk, where a creature of the same boulder species was sitting.

"Yes?" asked the boulder suspiciously raising his single eyebrow. His voice was impossibly deep by human standards.

"What do you sell here?" asked Luna.

The creature's expression did not change. "We don' sell anything here. Yer in the wrong place."

Just then, another boulder creature rolled up and said, "Oi, Brick. Four games o' Luge Crash."

"Sure thing, Wrench," said Brick.

Immediately the golden pipe above them sent a beam of light over Wrench, who then rolled away down the corridor. Quite a few boulder creatures seemed to be congregating there.

"Um, excuse me . . . Brick, is it?" said Luna. "You said you don't sell anything here!"

Elbina held Luna's shoulder, fearful that her sister might challenge Brick to a one-on-one brawl.

"We don'," Brick replied. "Yeh pay ter play Luge Crash here. It's the planet game on Rhothgo. Very competitive. Only the strongest o' the strong win."

Luna calmed herself down, although she was starting to have a bad feeling about this place. "And, erm . . . do you get anything for winning?"

"Yeh get a medal made o' the most precious metals o' planet Rhothgo. That's if yeh can beat the top Rhothgo Luge Crash player in Vivalok." Brick pointed to the Rhothgan featured on the banners behind them. "Don' happen too often, though. And she only gets beaten by other Rhothgan players, if it does happen. Yer welcome ter take a look at the course and start in the beginner class if yer interested."

Luna and Elbina held off on payment and decided to take a look around the gym. Wanting to see what the excitement was in the corridor, they joined the growing crowd there and followed them. As they moved down the corridor, the shouts of players grew louder and louder until they turned a corner to the right and found themselves in a huge circular arena. Hundreds of players were running this way and that in seeming chaos. Around the perimeter of the arena were fifty numbered decks. It soon became apparent that the players were jostling for the chance to get through a deck while trying to block others from doing the same. Above each deck were scoreboards that displayed a number from 0 to 1000. The grunts and shouts of the players echoed around the domed arena, accompanied by clanging metal sounds against a constant background noise of faint rumbles and booms.

Luna and Elbina moved to the centre of the arena, which was the safest place to look around without getting in the way of the players. Above the decks and scoreboards was a single 360-degree panoramic video screen that went all the way around the arena. The girls turned around slowly, taking in the action on the screen. At first it was disorienting: players on the screen seemed to be flying away in all directions. Gradually the girls began to match the action in the arena with what they were seeing on the screen, and they realised that the view on the screen was looking not out, but *down*. The floor on which they stood was in fact a platform near the ceiling of an absolutely cavernous cylindrical space below. Each of the fifty decks led to the top of a gigantic metal slide similar to those used in the sport of luge, and each player who managed to reach a deck was jumping onto one of the slides, which were very steep, and sliding down. Luna and Elbina watched the game in amazement. The Rhothgan players in particular, being round and heavy, rolled down the slides with incredible force and speed. This was the source of much of the clanging noise that filled the arena.

The fifty slides intertwined in a complex web that stretched down so far one couldn't see the bottom. The space around the web of slides was lined with concentric rings of wooden blocks. As soon as the players entered the depths of the web, they were lost to darkness. Intermittent booms and crashes could be heard in the distance below. There were many flying creatures around, including some Antympanicans, who appeared to be repairing the wall of blocks that encased the web of slides.

Wrench rolled into place at the top of a slide and flexed his muscles for a few moments. Luna dashed up to him.

"Excuse me, Wrench? What's the object of this game?"

Wrench broke his pose and looked around angrily for the creature who interrupted his pre-game routine. "Huh, what, where . . . an Earthling?"

"We're interested in playing," Luna continued.

"Yeah, right." Wrench resumed his muscle flexing.

"We want to learn from the best of the best. There's no one better for us to learn from," Luna continued, putting on a hopeless tone.

Wrench flexed harder and met Luna's eyes with his one giant eye. His anger seemed to subside slightly. "Yer absolutely right, Earthling. So Luge Crash is simple. Yeh slide down one o' these," he gestured to the winding slide below him. "Once yer at the bottom, yeh leave the slide in a sort o' projectile motion. Yeh crash into the wall o' blocks and knock down as many as possible. The more blocks yeh knock down, the better yer score. Then those little winged flyers pick up the fallen blocks and put 'em back in ter place for the next slider."

"Sounds simple enough," said Luna, nodding to Elbina.

"Watch me," continued Wrench, as he held his rocky body in the air with a handstand above the slide. He then hurled himself down the slide and clanged every which way, shaking the entire webbed structure of slides. A few moments later after Wrench was out of sight, a shudder of falling blocks resonated throughout the arena.

The girls backed away from the start of the slide to let other eager Rhothgans have their chance at knocking down the blocks.

Just then, Elbina caught a flash of yellow in the periphery of her vision. A human around her size was running around the arena trying to find an open slide to ride down, but she kept getting pushed out of the way by Rhothgans wanting their turn. Her blonde hair whipped every which way as she searched for an opening. As soon as Elbina saw the girl's deep blue eyes, she pulled Luna forward in a lurch.

"Luna, look! It's Ann Lou! ANN LOU! OVER HERE!" Elbina screamed at the top of her lungs, trying to overpower the loud clanging of the slides and the booms as players crashed into the block wall.

Ann Lou whirled around, shocked at having heard her name. Upon catching sight of her sisters, she shrieked with excitement, abandoned her search for a slide, and ran straight into their arms.

"Ann Lou!" cried Luna. "I can't believe we found you!"

"It figures we'd find you here," laughed Elbina, "hanging around a bunch of ferocious creatures playing a dangerous sport, just like you did on Epiton!"

Luna breathed in her youngest sister's scent with relief. This reunion felt almost as sweet as the time they had reunited on Cipto, one of the most memorable days in Luna's life. Luna could sense that her other two sisters felt similarly about this reunion from their intense and prolonged embrace. They decided to find a quieter spot in the lobby to sit and catch up.

"You guys have no idea how relieved I am to see you," said Ann Lou. "I've been so confused about what's going on. One second I was hugging Apollo on Mount Cameroon, and the next . . ." Her eyes welled up with tears. "He—he couldn't touch me, or hear me, or see me! It was so scary. And then I got warped *here* somehow—"

"It's okay. That's exactly what happened to us," said Elbina. "I was just about to make sure Hayden was all right after the GeoLapse attack in the hallway outside his dormitory, and then I vanished the same way."

Luna rolled her eyes at their mentioning boys. She needed to change the subject. Her gaze fell upon Ann Lou's left arm, which was fully biological instead of the usual prosthetic. The realisation caused Luna's mouth to fall open. She grabbed Ann Lou's arm and pulled it up to her eyes to get a close look at it.

"Your arm! It's back."

"Yeah! Haven't had both of these guys in a while," she said, flapping her arms. "Based on your careful inspection, I'm assuming there's good news on your side as well," she added.

"I can see, yeah. And Elbina can finally enjoy food. And Riff can hear again."

"Riff's here?" Ann Lou gasped. "Where?"

"He's hanging back with our new little friend, Clorin. You can meet him later."

"Even more of a relief," said Ann Lou, sitting back against the wall. "So, what's going on here?"

Luna caught Ann Lou up on the concept of Chroniya, and on what they had learned so far from the atlas, the anthology, and about the Jalopy junkyard and Constance. Ann Lou listened intently through it all.

"So what is it you guys need here then?" asked Ann Lou.

"I'm guessing we need to win that medal against the top Rhothgan player. The metals it's made of must be worth a lot of Chroniya," said Luna.

"Is that the last object you need?" Ann Lou asked.

"No, we still need something called a Fava cake," replied Elbina.

"Well, you can check off the Fava cake," Ann Lou said as she pulled one from her pocket. It was a small, icy sphere with a reddish glow in the centre. "I never particularly fancied them on Epiton. They're freeze-dried lava cakes. They burn if you eat the middle, I'm warning you now. But they remind me of Apollo. I just wanted to have a piece of him with me."

Luna's eyes lit up. "Fantastic! So that just leaves Luge Crash. Quite possibly the hardest task of them all."

"Well, to drown out the sadness of losing my husband about two days after the wedding, I have been learning how to play Luge Crash. It's quite similar to Pyroll in the sense that there really are no rules, and you crash into a lot of walls."

"Do you think you can beat the top player?" asked Elbina.

"Please! You're looking at the top Pyroll player in the universe," Ann Lou bragged, flicking her long blonde hair behind her shoulders.

Luna and Elbina rolled their eyes and laughed.

"Well," said Luna, "if anyone can do it, it's you, Ann Lou. Ready to give it a go?"

"You bet I am."

The sisters hopped up and walked up to Brick at the front desk. "One game with the top player, please," said Ann Lou with the utmost confidence.

Brick sized up Ann Lou and shook his head. "If yer payin', I can't stop yeh."

Ann Lou stood directly below the golden pipe and watched as the light surrounded her and took away four and a half years of her time.

Brick handed Ann Lou an orange challenger's vest. "She'll meet yeh in the Champion's Arena. Go down the corridor and turn left. Good luck . . . yeh'll need it," Brick added with a chuckle.

"I'll meet you there. I just have to grab some things first," Ann Lou said to her sisters as she marched off.

Luna and Elbina made their way down the corridor and this time made a left at the end instead of a right. This led them to an arena similar in size and configuration to the other one, but instead of fifty decks, there were only two. The two slides still managed to tangle between each other at an extreme depth, making it nearly as difficult to see the bottom as the other arena.

A loudspeaker sounded with an announcement from Brick. "Versus Luge Crash game now taking place in the Champion's Arena! A must-see if yeh want a laugh!" Brick couldn't help but start going off in a laughing fit before hanging up the loudspeaker.

A crowd started to pour in from the other arena. Many were Rhothgans, curious about who was taking on their planet's champion. Shortly the crowd parted to make way for a Rhothgan about three times the average Rhothgan's size. She pushed her way angrily through the clearing of smaller Rhothgans and took her place at one of the slides. Luna gulped, hoping this was just a mere bystander, but she soon recognised this Rhothgan as the one featured on all the banners in the lobby. Luna began to worry whether Ann Lou's confidence would be enough to carry her to a victory.

"Who dares take me on without warning?" bellowed the champion, quickly quieting the audience of the arena.

Luna and Elbina slumped against the wall, hoping no one would notice them.

Ann Lou swaggered into the arena, chest puffed out, carrying her Pyroll stick in one hand and holding a Pyroll high in the air with the other. No one noticed her walking in until she took her place at the other slide across the circle from the champion. When the crowd realised she was the challenger, they burst out in laughter. Ann Lou just smiled a huge smile and waved ostentatiously at the champion with her stick. Luna and Elbina's jaws fell open at her display of hubris.

"You sure we're related to her?" whispered Elbina.

The champion growled and flexed her boulder-like muscles.

The loudspeaker sounded again, and Brick announced, "Champion Ignea of Rhothgo, yeh can go first."

The champion bellowed into the air generating reverberations that seemed to shake the entire gym. Ignea forcefully jumped into the air and slammed down onto the slide, sending a clanging echo in conjunction with the previous bellow. Everyone's gaze followed Ignea as she started her roll down the slide. She took its complex twists and turns with tremendous skill, creating such an incredible amount of momentum on her way down that she was out of sight almost immediately. Her exit from the slide was confirmed only when a second bellow echoed from the depths of the arena, quickly followed by a loud crash and a massive collapse of the block wall surrounding the slides. Luna and Elbina's eyes bugged out when they saw over three-quarters of the block wall go crashing down. In the other arena, even the largest Rhothgans were knocking down maybe a quarter of the blocks at a time, and many of the non-Rhothgan creatures hadn't knocked down even one block.

Luna watched the scoreboard above Ignea's slide. The digits rolled up and up, finally stopping at 802 out of 1000 possible points. To Luna's surprise, Ann Lou didn't look bothered.

"A personal record *and* a gym record!" hollered Brick from over the loudspeaker.

The spectators erupted in cheers and shouts. The loudest were the Rhothgans, who bellowed and crashed into each other to show their planetary pride. After a rather lengthy pause while the Antympanicans and other flying creatures returned Ignea to her slide deck and repaired the wall, finally it was Ann Lou's turn.

Brick's voice again filled the arena. "Challenger Ann Lou McHubbard of Epiton, yeh can give it a go now." He chuckled a deep laugh before hanging up the loudspeaker.

The crowd snickered as Ann Lou walked to the edge of her deck, carrying the Pyroll and her stick. She stood with her heels on the edge of the deck and her toes in mid-air. She bent down and placed the Pyroll between her feet, then took her Pyroll stick in her right hand and stood up straight and tall. Luna watched with a lump in her throat as Ann Lou placed her left arm behind her back, closed her eyes, and took a small jump and gracefully began to fall feet first down the first steep section of the slide, her blonde hair flying behind her. Luna and Elbina gripped the edge of the chasm of the arena and held their breath as they peered down. As Ann Lou fell, she lifted her legs up slightly, keeping her knees straight and the Pyroll held between her feet. Just where the steep section of the slide was beginning to scoop forward, Ann Lou's body met the slide with barely any noise or loss of momentum. She zoomed down the slide at great speed, holding the Pyroll stick horizontally and moving it to counter the lateral forces whenever she was getting too close to the edge of the slide. She entered the densest part of the web and was quickly out of sight.

The crowd continued to sneer, and even Ignea joined in with them once Ann Lou had been out of sight and out of hearing range for a few seconds. Luna had no idea how her sister was going to knock down enough blocks to pull off a victory against Ignea, considering Ann Lou was probably one-tenth the weight of a single block.

"Come on, Ann Lou," Luna whispered. She could feel her heart pounding from beneath her shirt. She could barely breathe, not knowing whether her youngest sister was all right.

Shortly Luna heard a faint crackling noise from below, and an Antympanican flew up from deep within the chasm bearing a smiling Ann Lou on its back. The Antympanican glided low over the platform, and Ann Lou hopped down and ran up to her sisters with an even bigger smile than before. The crowd fell silent, confused by the lack of crashing noises. All the blocks appeared intact. There was no indication that Ann Lou had even exited the slide.

"Wh—what happened?" asked Luna.

"I set the wall on fire," whispered Ann Lou. "I hit the Pyroll mid-air as I flew off the slide and managed to wedge it between two blocks."

Sure enough, the crackling noise grew louder, and as the spectators peered down into the chasm, they saw a glow at the bottom that grew and grew until the block wall was completely ablaze. Before their eyes, it erupted into flames. Ignea and the rest of the Rhothgans watched in horror as the block wall slowly fell into ashes and disappeared, along with their pride.

An Antympanican flew by and wiggled its wings to get the attention of the other block-builders. "Let's get some new blocks. Earthlings always seem to ruin everything." It fluttered away with the rest of its flock.

But the Rhothgans lacked disdain toward Ann Lou for this extreme act. They stared at her in awe.

The crowd watched the scoreboard on the ceiling update with Ann Lou's score.

1000/1000.

In her entire career, Ignea had never come close to a perfect score. She rumbled past Ann Lou without acknowledging her. The crowd sat in stunned silence as Ignea exited the arena. The other Rhothgans stared at Ann Lou with their big menacing eyes as Ignea's angry rumble faded away down the marble corridor. As soon as Ignea was out of earshot, the Rhothgans surrounded Ann Lou and roared a triumphant chant that shook the entire gymnasium. They now had a new star Luge Crash player to idolise.

Immediately Ann Lou was surrounded by new Rhothgan fans, all trying to get a word in with her to help them train, including Wrench. She practically had to fight her way through the crowd to get to the corridor to retrieve her medal.

Back in the lobby, Luna watched as the banners updated to feature Ann Lou's confidently smiling face instead of Ignea's fierce glare. Ann Lou stepped up to the desk and held out her hand presumptuously. Luna couldn't help but smirk as Brick stared at the banners in disbelief, then looked back and forth between the banners and the young Earthling in front of him. Finally, he grumbled and handed Ann Lou her medal. Ignea's fierce body formed the medallion's circular shape. When Ann Lou took the medal from Brick's rocky hand, it was so shockingly heavy that she nearly dropped it. She carefully put it around her neck, which was now hunched slightly from the added load.

As the sisters exited the gym, all the Rhothgans and other gym-goers pressed to the inside window of the gym trying to catch a glimpse of Ann Lou before she disappeared into the busy streets of Vivalok.

"How do you do it, Ann Lou?" asked Elbina, shaking her head as they walked. "How does literally everyone fall in love with you?"

"Not *everyone*. Don't be so dramatic," replied Ann Lou, still wearing a sly smile on her face.

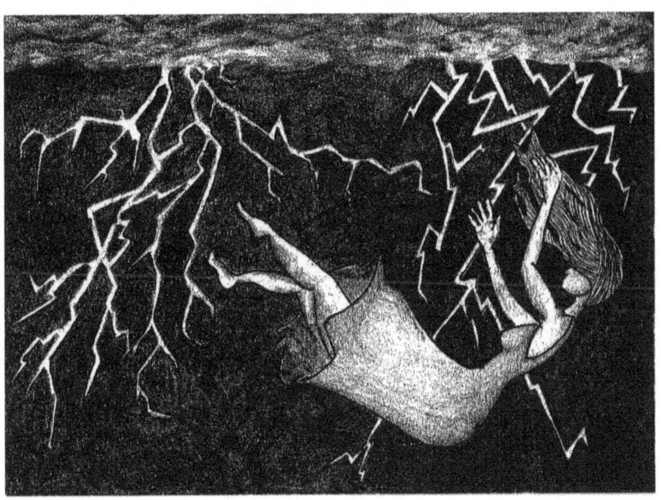

CHAPTER 5

CLORIN'S WORST MEMORY

The sisters, now three in number, went to collect Riff and Clorin. Riff was still sitting on the Casperian dictionary. He and Clorin were tossing Clorin's Pyroll back and forth. Riff still looked exhausted from the hefty time drain he had endured earlier. But when he caught sight of Ann Lou walking alongside Luna and Elbina, his face lit up.

"Ann Lou is here too? No way!" Riff exclaimed, spreading his arms wide as Ann Lou ran up to him. "The Pyroll champion is here!"

"And now also the Luge Crash champion," added Luna.

Ann Lou gave Riff a huge hug, then showed him her medal.

Riff gasped and clapped her on the back. "Well done, Ann Lou! That's brilliant!"

Ann Lou then pulled the Fava cake from her pocket. "Luna and Elbina told me about the poem. I've got a Fava cake. You've got the . . . the . . ."

"Gliedelfrop," said Riff.

"That," said Ann Lou. "And we have the Casperian dictionary, and I won the medal. That's everything. We're ready to go, bro."

Then Ann Lou's eyes met Clorin's. "Who's this?" she whispered to Riff.

Clorin ducked behind Riff. Ann Lou poked her head around the dictionary to make sure Clorin was all right. Riff leaned back and patted him on the shoulder.

"Hey, little man, don't be afraid. This is our sister, Ann Lou. She actually plays Pyroll—like, for real. Ann Lou, this is Clorin."

"Clorincladiellamore Lecomeriellastrain," corrected Luna. "He made it up," she added, proudly.

Ann Lou walked to where Clorin was hiding, bent down, and gently extended her hand. "Nice to meet you, Clorin. I like your horns. My husband has similar ones. Well, had. He lost one of them to some bad guys."

Clorin didn't budge. He stayed behind Riff and clung to his shirt with his small claws.

"Clorin takes a little while to warm up. Don't take it personally," said Luna. "We should be off to the Bank anyways. Riff, let me help you up."

Luna supported her brother as he got up from his seat on the dictionary and made sure he was stable on his feet. Then she led the group toward the Bank. This time Ann Lou carried the Casperian dictionary. Riff insisted on holding the Gliedelfrop beneath his tongue, producing poppy beats as they made their way through the bustling crowd. Minagian passersby wriggled their tentacles to the beats as Riff paraded past them.

Luna could see the hooded figure through the dense crowd as they approached, and unsurprisingly, the figure hadn't moved. No one in the vicinity seemed particularly interested in the orbs either. This caused Luna's heart to sink a little. She wondered if she was wasting everyone's time by harping too much on this figure and his precious orbs when no one else seemed to care.

No, Luna thought to herself. *You're on to something. The poem says so.*

She broadened her shoulders and took in a deep breath.

Once they reached the hooded figure, Luna gestured for her siblings to present the objects of their trade. Riff took the Gliedelfrop from under his tongue and wiped it on his shirt, and Ann Lou placed the dictionary on the ground and held out the medal and the Fava cake.

The hooded figure nodded. "Some excellent finds; to what I was searching for, this certainly aligns. I present to you now an orb, which allows you many places to explore." The hooded figure carefully picked up one of the orbs with grey, skeletal hands and held it out. The siblings gasped in unison at the skeletal features that appeared to be like human bones.

Containing her nerves, Luna gently took the orb from the figure's metacarpals. "Thank you."

"A warning before you travel," the figure added as the siblings started to turn away. "The orb is really quite fragile. Should it break, a most horrible memory will awake. Do keep it safe from shock, or else you will land back in Vivalok."

Luna nodded, and she and her siblings darted toward the Jalopy junkyard in the southeast corner of Vivalok. They each pushed through the heavy crowds until they found themselves first running in blank white space darting toward a small dot in the far distance, and then finally arriving in the Jalopy junkyard. Luna immediately noticed that the hourglass Jalopy that they had previously seen was missing.

"That's odd," she remarked. "Do you think someone took it?"

"Can't imagine who," replied Riff. "How many creatures do you think know about this place?"

Luna opened her mouth when Clorin exclaimed, "This one, Looner!"

He ran and pointed to a clear, glassy, roundish vessel that looked like a crystal with many facets. It was small, but it appeared large enough to hold two people, if a bit uncomfortably.

Luna counted the number of sides. "It's a dodecahedron. There's twelve sides."

Elbina raised her eyebrows. "You sure?"

Luna was already formulating an indignant retort as she turned to look back at the vessel. Instead of a dodecahedron, it was now a pyramid. Before Luna could say anything, the vessel began to shimmer, and they all watched, spellbound, as its edges bulged, split, swirled, and recrystallised into an icosahedron.

"A shapeshifting Jalopy!" exclaimed Riff, with a boyish awe that rivalled Clorin's.

"What shape would you call that?" asked Ann Lou.

"I suppose I'd call it . . . an apeirotope," said Luna. "An infinitely sided polyhedron."

"It's not very big," said Riff. "Why don't we find a bigger one we can all ride in?"

"Most of them look completely ripped to shreds," said Luna. "This one has only one little ding in it." She pointed to a small nick in the glassy surface near one of the upper vertices of the now cuboidal vessel.

"Well, I'm getting in," Ann Lou said as she trotted toward the Jalopy.

"And me!" added Riff, skipping after her.

Luna groaned. "Hold up, you lot!" Her siblings stopped and stared at her. "Well, no offence, but none of you knows what you're doing. I'm the one who can logically decipher these poems. Besides me, it looks like only one more can fit."

"I'll clean your room for a month," said Riff.

Luna rolled her eyes. "That bargain won't work anymore, I'm afraid."

"I'll read you every book in the book shop," said Ann Lou.

"I can read them myself, thanks. Wow, I never realised how rubbish your bribes were."

Elbina just looked down at her feet, hiding her eyes behind her hair. Luna knew this was Elbina language for "Please don't pick me."

Suddenly they heard scratching sounds and grunts behind them. They turned and saw Clorin easily scaling the glass body of the Jalopy with the tips of his extremely sharp claws. As he reached the top of the vessel, it morphed into a spherical shape, and Clorin squirmed inside through a small hole.

Luna looked back at her siblings and shrugged. "Looks like Clorin's going."

"Oh, come on!" whined Ann Lou, tossing her two fully functional arms into the air.

Riff pouted.

"You guys stay right here while we go," Luna ordered.

"Where will you be going?" asked Elbina.

Luna stopped and scratched her chin. "That's a good question. Which level of the Time Belt do you think we should go to?"

Riff perked up. "Ooh, ooh! Go to Mortalok. It sounds creepy."

Elbina shot him a disgusted look. "And why on Earth would she want to go there?"

"No, I think we will go there," said Luna. "I'm interested to see why the Bank structure appears empty of Chroniya," she said, pointing to the Mortalok page in the atlas.

Luna went up to inspect the Jalopy, now an octahedron, while Clorin hopped around inside it waiting for her entrance. She tapped the glass of the apeirotope a few times with her index fingernail, then tried pushing her way in, without success. She furrowed her brow as it continued to change into new shapes every few seconds, but no hole revealed itself. She laid her hands on the cool glass as it continued to bulge and retract into new shapes, thinking she might feel a hole instead.

"A hole, just there!" shouted Ann Lou, pointing at the top of the apeirotope, which for the moment was a sphere again.

Luna dove awkwardly into the hole, holding the orb close to her chest as she tucked into a somersault. She landed in a ball, curled within the spherical body of the apeirotope. Clorin clapped and squealed with glee.

Riff, Ann Lou, and Elbina surrounded the apeirotope. They all waited patiently for it to change shape again, but it seemed to have frozen in its spherical form. Clorin gasped as the inside of the apeirotope lit up green.

"Hello, Luna McHubbard and Sulien of the House of Ann Lou," said the vessel in its soft monotone. "The Jalopy is ready to depart. Please state your destination."

Luna's face blanched. Sulien of the House of Ann Lou? That would mean . . . Luna eyed Clorin, who was waving his claws excitedly in anticipation of take-off.

Luna shook her head. There had to be something wrong with the Jalopy. His name was Clorincladiellamore Lecomeriellastrain, not Sulien. And Ann Lou . . . what could she possibly have to do with Clorin? Luna shifted her gaze to her youngest sister, who, being outside the Jalopy, hadn't heard the greeting.

Luna's siblings watched and waited. Elbina looked concerned, as if she wanted Luna to get out of there and stay safely with her on Vivalok. Ann Lou and Riff, still miffed at not being able to go, pointed into the air and shrugged.

Whatever the Jalopy's greeting meant, Luna knew she had neither the time nor the information to stop and figure it out right now. "Mortalok," she said.

"Enjoy your trip," replied the voice.

The Jalopy accelerated upward. Luna and Clorin watched through the glass as the siblings below waved to them, Elbina's face full of worry, and then became small dots among the endless landscape of Jalopies in the junkyard. From this height, the true extent of the junkyard became clear. Vivalok was a dot in the centre of a landscape of white space about the size of a marble in one's palm. Vivalok, which had seemed so vast when they were crossing it on foot, was minimal in comparison to the junkyard. In the southeast corner, the junkyard extended farther than the eye could see. What were all these Jalopies doing here?

Clorin became bored of the sight and tapped the orb, bundled with care under Luna's arm, with his small claw. Luna figured he needed something to keep him busy, so she reasoned with him.

"Do you want to hold it?" she asked.

Clorin nodded his head with enthusiasm.

"Okay, but you must be *very* careful. Here, wrap it in my flannel and hold it close to you." Luna slipped off her flannel with care, bundled it on Clorin's lap, and nestled the orb into it.

Clorin's red eyes lit up at his very important job. He held his face up close to the orb and laughed at his distorted reflection.

Slowly, the junkyard disappeared from view. Clorin grew bored and dozed off, curling his body securely around the orb bundle. Luna started to feel the Time Belt's calming effects, and she watched as bright white light gradually enveloped the Jalopy until it seemed as if she and Clorin were floating freely in space, suspended in a warm blanket of light. The first time she had experienced it, she, Ann Lou, Riff, and Knitsy were travelling to Harvinth, and it was unnerving watching their grandmother being taken away from them. Now the experience felt familiar, and she felt no fear. But her joyous feelings started to dim as the bright light began to turn grey. A clap of thunder startled her and woke Clorin, and before Luna could muster up any reassuring words, violent winds began pushing the Jalopy back and forth. The remaining light dwindled to black, leaving only flashes of lightning as the thunder grew louder and a torrential rain began hammering against the glass. Luna held tight to Clorin, who was trembling and whimpering as the storm shook them. She was determined to stay calm for his sake, even though she was filled with anxiety as she thought again about the junkyard and wondered what mechanical flaw had landed this Jalopy there.

Then a simultaneous thunderclap and lightning bolt caught them both off guard. They yelped, Clorin flailed his arms, and the orb went flying. Luna's face froze with fear as the dark orb hit the glass wall of the Jalopy.

"Nooo!" she cried, reaching out, but she could not possibly have reacted fast enough. The orb cracked open, releasing black smoke that filled the cabin.

Luna felt herself falling through the storm, no longer supported by the sturdy glass of the Jalopy or shielded from the rain. Cold and soaked, she tried looking around for Clorin as she fell, but the darkness and her hair in front of her eyes impaired her view. She flailed her arms and legs about, hoping to feel Clorin falling alongside her, but she was alone. She closed her eyes, waiting for either an impact or an end to the storm, whichever came first.

A sudden absence of sound filled her ears, and she opened her eyes in confusion. There was no storm, no Jalopy—just hard ground under her and a strange roof above. Beads of sweat ran down the sides of her face. She began to pant from the intense heat. Looking around to investigate the sudden rise in temperature, Luna found herself in a circular hut made of clay. It had a metallic roof with a hole at the top. Luna propped herself up on her elbows and looked around. All around her on the floor of this place were giant slabs of overcooked meat. They were all burnt to a crisp and the smell of charcoal overwhelmed her nasal passage. Luna's face twisted in disgust. Where was she? Was she about to become one of those slabs of meat?

Shuddering as she struggled to her feet, Luna noticed that there was a baby crib by the wall of the hut. She tiptoed over to the crib, looked inside, and gasped. It was Clorin in the crib. He looked to be about the same age as she last knew him to be—about three. He was sleeping soundly, his small chest rising and falling with each breath, his tiny claws resting on his stomach. His sandy hair was soaked with sweat and sticking to his forehead, although he didn't seem bothered by it. Instinctively, Luna reached in the crib with a gentle hand to tuck his hair behind his ears, but she quickly pulled it back when it went through Clorin's head as if she were a ghost.

Petrified, Luna glanced around the hut and gasped yet again when she saw a small bed behind the crib with someone sleeping in it. It was a girl with unkempt and tangled blonde hair. Ann Lou.

Luna covered her mouth, afraid she might scream. When she had regained her composure, she noticed that this version of Ann Lou appeared to be a few years older than the Ann Lou whom Luna had just been with on Vivalok. Her previously chiselled face was fuller, and a lot of her muscle mass appeared to be diminished.

Maybe I should try to talk to them, Luna thought. It seemed at least possible that they might know what was going on. Luna certainly had no idea.

"Clorin?" asked Luna softly and cautiously.

He lay there, quiet and still.

"Ann Lou?"

Ann Lou continued to sleep.

"Clorin?" Luna tried to jostle the crib gently, but her hands went through the bars. Clorin snoozed soundly, unperturbed by Luna's presence.

Luna rushed over to where Ann Lou was sleeping. Luna could only think to wave her hand in front of Ann Lou's nose, hoping she'd sense that someone was there.

Nothing.

Then a bang on the ceiling jolted both Clorin and Ann Lou awake. An Epitonian dropped in through the hole in the ceiling, carrying something and fuming visibly. Luna froze when its piercing red eyes glared in her direction until she realised they were in fact focused on Ann Lou. The Epitonian huffed and puffed, curling its claws inward as if trying to hold back an attack. Luna faced the Epitonian squarely, imagining for a moment that she could protect Ann Lou, but of course she could not. The Epitonian ripped away its glare from Ann Lou and set what it was carrying on the floor. It was a cluster of ice balls that resembled the Fava cake that Ann Lou had shown her earlier.

Ann Lou sat up in bed and growled at the sight of the Epitonian, and it hissed at her in return. The Epitonian's hisses turned into threatening shouts. She backed up behind Clorin's crib to get a full view of their angry conversation.

"You're still in bed? You should've been up hours ago!" yelled the Epitonian, whom Luna now recognised as the one-horned Apollo from the magazine cover she had picked up earlier at the book shop.

"How the hell do you expect me to do everything around here?" fired Ann Lou, gesturing angrily with her arms, one of which was prosthetic.

"Not everything. Just something!" he barked at her. "I come home to find Sulien unchanged and unfed, the leftover Fava cakes melted, and three Polskin on the roof! I mean, come *on*, Ann Lou!"

Apollo kicked one of the newly acquired Fava cakes across the floor and shook his head in disgust. Clorin, or Sulien, popped his head up from the crib to take in the conversation. His two small horns were just visible above the top of the crib.

"Need I remind you what you did to me?" shouted Ann Lou. She yanked the bedclothes off herself, and Luna shrieked at the sight. Ann Lou's legs were blackened from what looked like dead tissue, and they were skinny, and limp. "I was the epitome of health," she screamed, her face turning purple. "The Pyroll Champion of the Universe. And now I'm nothing!"

"You blame me for something I couldn't control? You always claim to be the person who embraces adversity. You're such a manipulator," he shot back, now grabbing a strip of Polskin off the floor and slicing it in little pieces with his big claw.

"I can't play Pyroll because of you. I can't do anything because of you!" Ann Lou was trembling now.

Clorin crouched down in his crib but still glanced at his mother and father as they each spoke.

"Ann Lou, I can get you back into shape if you'd just be willing to do one damn thing—"

"Let me grieve, Apollo!" she wailed.

"It's been three years! It's time to get up!" Apollo brought the sliced Polskin over to Clorin and fed him piece by piece. Although Clorin was scared, he cautiously took each piece from his father's claw and chewed it ravenously.

"Look at him. He's famished," Apollo huffed. "My poor boy . . ."

"He was sleeping just fine," Ann Lou growled, curling her hands into fists. "There was actually some peace and quiet in here until you came along."

Apollo looked at her inquisitively. "Until I came along? With food for our stomachs? Having fended off the rumours being passed around town? My mother refuses to even come here anymore. Same with Egan, who needs every bit of support after Fintan sacrificed himself trying to save *you*." Apollo brandished a piece of Polskin toward Ann Lou with his last word.

Ann Lou grimaced. "I didn't ask Fintan to save me that day. I'd give anything to change that now."

Apollo sighed, his menacing face softening slightly. "Ann Lou, I'm sorry about what happened during your pregnancy. But you can't keep blaming it on me. We couldn't have known the baby's birth would cause the paralysis and stop the oxygen flow to your legs. But you're alive. You can still live a good life here. Remember how you got on with just one functioning arm when you first played Pyroll? Where's that woman? Where's the woman I fell in love with?"

Clorin pinched off a piece of the Polskin in his father's claw as he turned his head to his mother.

Slowly and with great effort, Ann Lou pushed herself to a seated position and reached for her Pyroll stick, which was beside her bed. It had acquired a layer of dust, but she brushed it off and held it firmly in her right hand.

"How would you like to live with one functioning limb?" she asked stoically.

"Ann Lou, I'm not saying that it's easy. But I'm saying you need the willingness to try. I'm here. I love you! I want you to get your fiery passion back! Do it for Sulien, at the very least!"

Clorin paused upon hearing his name, then reached for another piece of Polskin. His eyes were darting between his mother and father. Out of the corner of her eye, Luna saw Ann Lou slowly raise her stick. Luna stumbled back into the wall as Ann Lou drew the stick backward.

The Pyroll stick hurtled through the air and struck Apollo in the arm, sending bits of Polskin onto the floor. Clorin let out a small scream and ducked down in his crib, clinging to the bars with his claws.

"You almost hit the baby!" Apollo roared, his voice reaching a new level of fury.

Ann Lou snatched a Pyroll from the pile by her bedside and threw it at Apollo with brute force, striking him in the ankle. Fired up by her direct hit, she threw the remaining Pyrolls with a steady rhythm, striking him repeatedly in the same leg, causing eelich to spew out into a hazy cloud. Apollo roared in pain as Clorin covered his eyes with his claws and trembled.

Ann Lou heaved herself to the floor and crawled with just her two arms toward Apollo, grabbing hold of the Pyroll stick that had landed beside the crib. She swung it at his eelich-diffusing leg, and he stumbled to the floor, gripping his ankle in pain.

"I hate this life!" She struck Apollo again and again. "I hate my body! And I hate you!"

Clorin screamed for his life. "Daddy!" he bawled. He huddled in fear at the far end of his crib.

Luna screamed and dove to Clorin's rescue, attempting to wrap her arms around him and shield him from the horrifying sight of his mother's attacks on his father. But Luna's arms just went straight through Clorin. She couldn't help him.

Ann Lou, seeming utterly crazed, swung her stick, bashing everything within reach. *This isn't Ann Lou,* Luna thought as she sank to the floor and hugged her knees. This wasn't her sister. She had to have gone mad, finally letting loose all her pent-up feelings over the past couple years since the pregnancy.

One swing, directed toward the base of the crib, nearly caught Clorin's claw, which was reaching down toward Apollo. Apollo kicked the stick from Ann Lou's hand, then managed to get up and grab Clorin. Ignoring the pain in his ankle, he dodged Ann Lou's final swing and jumped up to the ceiling hole.

"You've lost your privilege as a mother," said Apollo, his voice trembling and weak. "We're out of here!"

Ann Lou lay on the floor with her four limbs outstretched. Tears flooded her eyes as she realised what she had just done to her family.

Apollo met her eyes for one last glance. "I guess you were right. It *is* possible to hurt someone you love."

Luna watched as Apollo and Clorin disappeared from view, the last glance from Clorin being one of pure terror at the scene he had just witnessed. No wonder he was so scared all the time.

Ann Lou tried to move, but her limbs lay at awkward angles. She cried hysterically, gasping for air as tears poured from her eyes and dried quickly on her face from the immense Epitonian temperatures. She knew she had done wrong. Years of frustration unloaded all at once. In that moment, Ann Lou lost everything.

Luna wasn't sure how to feel about her sister. Rage filled her at Ann Lou's brutal treatment of her husband. And yet the Ann Lou she knew would never hurt someone physically. Never would she have believed that Ann Lou could be capable of such a hurtful attack. Yes, she could be condescending, annoying, and stubborn, but never violent, at least not to Luna's knowledge. Sympathy and rage collided, creating a storm of conflicting emotions in Luna's body. She almost wanted to take the Pyroll stick and hit her sister back, but compassion won out and she instead rushed to Ann Lou's side. She tried to place a loving hand on Ann Lou's head, but her hand went right through.

The scene faded to black in front of Luna's eyes. When light reappeared, she and Clorin were back at the junkyard, sitting in the apeirotope Jalopy while her curious siblings peered in through the glass. Clorin gaped at Luna with his now tear-filled red eyes. His mouth trembled, and he released a cry and gripped Luna tightly. Luna couldn't help but cry with him. This was her nephew. Her family. And if she could help it, she would make sure he wouldn't ever feel that scared again. The two held each other for a few moments before Riff knocked on the glass, catching their attention as he made a funny face, hoping to get a giggle out of Clorin.

"It's okay, Clorin. You're safe with me." Luna pretended to laugh at Riff's changing contorted faces through the glass to reassure Clorin that he didn't have to be scared anymore. Clorin started to giggle with her and wiped away his last tears with a small claw.

Once he had stopped trembling, Clorin hopped up onto Luna's shoulders and out through the hole in the top of the sphere. Riff greeted him and helped him down. Luna shakily removed herself from the Jalopy with Elbina's help. Luna couldn't help but shoot an angry glance at Ann Lou.

The Jalopy resumed its old shape-shifting form, now turning into a pyramid.

"Did you make it to Mortalok?" asked Riff as Clorin ran circles around him. Luna was relieved to see he seemed already to have forgotten the horrors he had just relived.

"No," Luna replied with a frustrated sigh. "We have to try again. We need another orb."

The rest of the siblings sighed with grief at the realisation that they would need to spend another hefty amount of time collecting more objects. This loomed in their brains as they sluggishly made their way back to the town centre of Vivalok.

CHAPTER 6

A Mystery Donor

While on the slow walk back to Vivalok, Luna held her tongue every time Ann Lou said something. She couldn't help but glare at her every so often. Luna couldn't possibly ignore that Ann Lou had just attacked her husband and terrified her child about whom she didn't yet know.

"Chocolate cake, anyone?" Riff announced, catching Clorin's attention.

"I'm not in the mood," Ann Lou groaned. "I need to go to the gym and release some steam. Someone come with me? Bet it'll be funny to face Ignea again," she said with a menacing grin, looking strangely Epitonian in nature.

"I'll come with you," Elbina offered. "I need some Hayden advice."

"You know, you should be thanking me that you guys are together in the first place. I was the one—"

Luna interjected, suddenly furious. "Will you just stop talking, Ann Lou?"

Ann Lou stared at her oldest sister in confusion. "Luna, I was joking. I'm—"

"Just go. I'm . . . stressed is all," Luna replied, looking away.

"All right. Elbina, let's go. What do you want to know about Hayden? Ask away."

The girls quickly disappeared into the crowd and out of earshot.

Riff caught Luna's attention. "You all right?"

Luna sighed. "I just need to sit down and clear my head."

Luna, Clorin, and Riff settled down at a table by the window at the busy food shop. Clorin was happily munching on some gasoline candies while Riff and Luna each sipped on a cup of tea with Moolweep.

Riff wrinkled his nose at Clorin's breath. "Man, this kid is built like a tank. Even I wouldn't eat those."

Luna sat quietly and looked out the window at the bustling crowd, all of whom were regularly entering and exiting the shops on the colourful street.

"What's bothering you?" asked Riff in a serious tone. He could tell Luna wasn't in the mood for his jokes.

"It's just . . . what I saw. It was really horrible," she replied, covering her eyes with her hands.

"Tell me," he urged.

She shook her head.

"You have to trust someone, Luna."

"That's the problem, Riff. I don't think I can." Luna lowered her hands and blinked intently at Riff. Clorin let out a powerful belch.

"Little man, that was awesome," laughed Riff, clapping him on the back. Clorin laughed and continued munching on his candies.

"Luna," he continued, lowering his voice. "Please trust me. We're the oldest. We have to do what we can to help each other. Mum would want us to stick together."

Luna relaxed her tense stance and sighed. He was right. Any mention of their mother was an easy way to convince her. "Okay, but you can't tell Elbina or Ann Lou."

"Pinkie swear," promised Riff, holding out his hand.

Luna rolled her eyes and wrapped her finger around his. They both leaned in closer to one another so the rowdy table of Antympanicans next to them couldn't listen in.

"So this one"—Luna glanced quickly toward Clorin—"accidentally broke the orb mid-flight. That strange hooded figure, through its speech poems or whatever they are, said something about a bad memory awakening if it were to break. So, I got to see what Clorin's worst memory was. But . . . it was in the future."

Riff rubbed his chin. "How do you know?"

"Because . . ." She gulped, and her voice fell to a whisper. "Well, he's Ann Lou and Apollo's son."

"What?" Riff exclaimed, gripping the sides of the table and catching the nosy Antympanicans' attention close by. Clorin looked up at him as well, and Riff patted his arm to reassure him.

"Their *kid*?" Riff continued in a harsh whisper.

Luna nodded.

"But how—what—I don't understand," Riff stammered.

"Ann Lou must have gotten pregnant when she and Apollo reunited on Harvinth. Since Clorin was technically . . . inside her, he also came to the Time Belt as his future self."

"Do you think it was before or after the wedding?" joked Riff, making a dramatic shocked face.

"Shut up," Luna said.

Riff eyed Clorin lovingly as he shovelled the remainder of the candies into his mouth, stuffing them in his cheeks like a hamster.

"He gets that from his Uncle Riff," he laughed, pointing at Clorin's giant cheeks.

"But that's not all," Luna whispered. "Ann Lou had, or I guess will have, a really difficult pregnancy. It causes her to lose function in her legs. She snapped and got really abusive toward Apollo. Apollo eventually took Clorin away and left Ann Lou behind. That's when the memory ended. Oh, and Clorin's real name is Sulien."

"Sulien?" Riff repeated. Clorin looked up, and his eyes filled with tears.

"Let's call him Clorin. I think there's bad memories associated with S-U-L-I-E-N," Luna said, gritting her teeth.

Riff sat back and took several deep breaths. "I just don't believe it. There's no way."

"Love does strange things to people," Luna said.

"It's a good thing girls don't talk to me, then," remarked Riff with an exaggerated sigh of relief. He then leaned back in and whispered, "She has a right to know it's her kid, though."

"This is exactly why I didn't want to tell you!" Luna barked at him, slamming a fist into the table. "Just pretend I never said anything."

"But he obviously has memories of her," said Riff, gesturing to Clorin. "He can't be around her. It's causing him a lot of stress and anxiety. Every time he looks at her, he remembers!"

Luna looked at Clorin's innocent face, which was now covered in grey liquid. He had managed to get gasoline in his hair and on his horns as well. She felt badly for him.

"Why is he the age of a small child, though?" Riff added. "Why isn't Ann Lou still pregnant with him?"

Luna could see the Antympanicans at the next table leaning close to listen in. Luna held up her hand so they couldn't watch her mouth movements.

"As I said before, I don't think we're in our true bodies here. I'm guessing since he was technically inside Ann Lou before she disappeared on Mount Cameroon, he counted as a descendant of Nan. He had to be present here in some way. So he must have come here at the age of his worst memory."

Riff nodded and patted Clorin on one of his horns.

"I just don't know how we can fix this problem," Luna continued. "But the bigger issue is that we're no closer to getting out of the Time Belt than we were before. We have to buy everything again."

Riff had been contemplating this for a few moments when Elbina and Ann Lou walked in. Luna and Clorin both grimaced at the sight of Ann Lou; Clorin practically looked sick to his stomach. Ann Lou, unaware of the reason, approached Clorin and knelt in front of him holding a small football. "A peace offering for you, little guy. This is something we'd play with back on Earth."

Clorin batted the ball away with his claw and leapt into Riff's arms trembling. He gripped Riff's shirt collar in his fists and buried his face in Riff's neck. Ann Lou stood up, confused, looking at the ball for signs of anything scary.

"He just has an upset stomach from the candy," Riff lied. He saw Luna turn away from her sister and stick her nose in the air.

"How about we all take a walk together and give Luna some time to think. Another round of *Anvils Ablaze*?" Riff said.

Luna nodded solemnly and Riff patted her shoulder.

"Are you okay?" Elbina asked, a yearning in her eyes for her sister to confide in her.

"I'm okay, Elbs, I just need some time with my books. I miss them," Luna said, managing a weak smile.

Elbina nodded and left with Clorin and her other two siblings. Once they were gone for a few minutes and Luna had finished her tea, she strolled outside and found a bench near the Bank. She watched the passers-by. Some stopped to look at the clocks or sat and talked. Small children played or whizzed around on silver disks. Luna wondered what their stories were. What led to their untimely arrivals in the Time Belt? How long had each of them been here? Had any of them tried to escape? And how was the universe being impacted by their disappearances?

Luna looked up at the Bank's gleaming pipe ball. She noticed that the sphere at the top was nearly full of Chroniya. A load of black liquid was pouring into its bowl as she stared. It seemed strange to her that so much would be poured in at once. Luna pulled out the anthology and rifled through Bowser's poems. As she began flipping through the pages, she caught sight of the hooded figure to her right, standing still like before in front of all the orbs. She decided to walk over to get more information.

"Excuse me," she said.

The figure looked at her. "Yes, what question have you? About your orb, is that true?"

"Yes," Luna answered. "What if we, erm . . . broke it and can't afford a second one? Can we get another?"

"I see your careless blunder," replied the figure. "Has caused your hopes to turn asunder. Clearly were you warned, and now a memory you have mourned. No trade, no orb; though the price may sting, to try again, four objects you must bring."

It was the answer Luna had most feared. She walked back to the bench and sat down, distracting herself by watching the crowd for a while.

"Looner!" shouted Clorin in his sweet voice.

Luna looked up to see Clorin, Riff, and Elbina riding up on one of the silver disks. Behind them was something heavy that seemed to be dragging the disk down a bit.

Elbina and Clorin hopped off, and Riff steered the disk carefully up to Luna. "We've got it. All of it."

Luna raised an eyebrow at him as Clorin ran into her for a hug. "What do you mean?"

"Well, we decided to go into the book shop to see if the Casper dictionaries were on sale, which of course, they weren't. But that obnoxious cashier told us that everything had been prepaid for us, and he just handed us a set of everything! The dictionary, the Gliedelfrop, a Fava cake—even the medal!"

"How is that possible?" asked Luna. "Who would do that? And why?"

"Are you really going to question people's intentions at a time like this?" asked Riff. "Let's get the orb!"

The four of them ran over to the hooded figure and presented the objects. The figure nodded. "I am most impressed at how quickly you completed this quest. Take this orb as your key to levels one, two, and three."

Clorin reached for the orb, but Luna gently pressed his claws down. "I'll hold on to this one, all right?"

Luna tucked the orb securely in her flannel shirt pocket and led them to the disk that would take them to the Jalopy junkyard. Once they arrived, they found the apeirotope in the place they had left it.

"I think someone else should come with me instead of you-know-who," Luna suggested, pointing her head toward Clorin.

"I'll come!" Riff piped up.

Clorin hugged Riff's legs tightly. "No, Riff, no!" he whined.

"You can have some time with Auntie Elbina!" Riff said freely. Elbina looked a bit puzzled. "Did I say 'Auntie'? I meant 'Chanty.' Boy, does she love to sing!"

Clorin eyed up Elbina cautiously while staying glued to Riff. Elbina wasn't exactly thrilled, either.

"Just take him to the gym or something," suggested Riff. "I saw Ann Lou going back in there earlier. I'm sure Clorin would enjoy watching her demolish the Rhothgans at Luge Crash. Maybe it'll help him soften toward her."

"Well, all right, then. Come on, Clorin," she said sweetly. "Let's take a walk into town." She held out her slender hand, and Clorin gingerly took it and walked with his head hung low toward the hustle and bustle of Vivalok. He looked back at Luna after a few steps with tear-filled red eyes.

"Elbina's safe," Luna said, smiling at Clorin. Clorin managed a weak smile and continued walking with Elbina.

"Ready?" asked Riff, who assumed a ready stance as he waited for the apeirotope to change to a spherical form.

Cube . . . square pyramid . . . ellipsoid. *SMACK!* Instead of jumping inside the apeirotope, Riff had hit it hard and bounced off.

Luna eyed him confusedly. "Are you that thick? That's an ellipsoid, not a sphere."

"If you'll remember, I never got to take my geometry A-levels," groaned Riff.

"Sphere!" shouted Luna, taking a graceless leap and plunging her body through the small hole at the top of the Jalopy. Riff waited for the next occurrence of the spherical form, then sprang toward the hole. Only his head went in, and he had to wiggle himself through the rest of the way.

Riff and Luna managed to sit side by side in the cramped space. The apeirotope froze in its spherical shape and lit up green.

"Hello, Luna McHubbard and Griffin McHubbard. The Jalopy is ready to depart. Please state your destination."

"Mortalo-o-o-k!" sang Riff.

"Enjoy your trip."

The Jalopy accelerated upward. Luna shielded the orb with her hands, and Riff pressed his face against the glass, watching the vibrant view surrounded by many thousands of Jalopies.

Just like last time, Luna watched the dazzling colours of Vivalok blur into a rainbow as the siblings sailed away. Gradually the white light and its warming sensation took over. Then, as abruptly as before, the white shifted into grey clouds and thunder preceded a terrifying darkness. The storm whipped the Jalopy with its winds. Rain pounded on the hull as deafening thunder and flashes of lightning surrounded them.

"Bloody hell!" shouted Riff. "You didn't mention the killer storm!"

A hard jolt caught them off guard and banged their heads together. Luna was starting to wonder if the Jalopy would hold together. Riff held out his arms and pressed his hands against the glass to steady himself, and Luna curled her body around the orb to cushion it. A shear wind knocked the Jalopy into a freefall—at least, it felt as if they were falling; they couldn't see anything through the curtains of rain pelting the glass. Luna wrapped her arms and body around the orb like a cage, trying desperately to protect it without crushing it.

With terrifying force, the Jalopy landed on a hard surface. Riff held Luna, and Luna held the orb tightly to her chest as the Jalopy rolled them around and around until finally it came to a stop. When Luna opened her eyes, the surroundings were not familiar. The rain pattering on the Jalopy was nowhere near as hard as what they had experienced during their flight. They heard a few claps of thunder followed by the glow of distant lightning through the clouds, but there were no visible bolts.

Riff gently prodded his right shoulder with his fingertips. "That was awful. I wonder if there's a chiropractor on Vivalok."

"At least it's better than reliving a bad memory," Luna said. "Where should we go?" she asked, flipping to the page in the atlas for Mortalok.

Riff took the atlas from her and scanned the page with intensity. Mortalok was quite different from Vivalok. There were no roads or shops. There wasn't much to it except for the visual depiction of the terrain ahead of them with the smear of dots in a disorganised fashion. And the Bank.

"What do you think these little dots are for?" Riff asked, circling a group of them with his fingertip.

"I dunno. Let's just head for the Bank. It should be somewhere around here, according to the map." Luna pointed to the Bank feature on the map.

"Okay."

Riff wriggled his body through the hole and helped Luna out as she cradled the orb. The ground on which they had landed was uneven and stony. It reminded Luna of the ground on Cipto. She then noticed the strange feeling of raindrops falling on her face. Earth was the only planet she had ever lived on that had a possibility of being rained on, but she had never known a time when the Earth's environment was safe enough for rain to even exist, since the atmosphere had been completely destroyed. The cool water felt nice on her skin. She wondered why the drops didn't hurt since they were falling from so far up. She held out an arm and watched the raindrops fall on it, noticing how some of them bounced off her skin while others rolled down the side of her hand. She saw that Riff was enjoying himself as well, jumping in a nearby puddle and sticking his tongue out to catch raindrops in his mouth.

Mortalok was uncomfortably quiet. With no shops, there were no clamouring crowds. The only sound was rain and distant thunder. It seemed to Luna and Riff that they were the only creatures around. They stood and looked out at the landscape, a vast rocky plain ringed with cliffs and mountains. The rain was letting up, and fog blanketed much of the plain.

"The Bank is that way," said Riff, pointing to a distant rise.

They started walking. As they descended into the fog layer, strange shapes loomed in the distance.

"Those must be the dots on the map," said Luna.

"Maybe they're rock formations," said Riff.

At that moment the wind strengthened, and the shapes drifted slightly.

"I don't think so," countered Luna. "They're moving. See that? They're, like, waving." A faint howl rose up from the plain. "Maybe they're trees."

"N-not any kind of tree I've ever seen," said Riff, shuddering.

"Should we go see?"

Riff looped an arm through one of Luna's and nodded slowly.

Luna took the first step, trying to be the confident oldest sibling Riff needed her to be at this time. Together they walked toward one of the strange shapes. As they got closer to it, they realised that the shape was floating, tethered to the ground by a rope. It was round like a balloon, but sort of misshapen and grey.

They approached and walked slowly around it. They gasped simultaneously when they saw that it had an eye. It was closed, but it was definitely an eye.

"Oh, bollocks," said Riff.

"It's . . . a Rhothgan," said Luna.

It was indeed a Rhothgan. It was a bit faded from the usual Rhothgan colour and looked less menacing with its one large eye closed. It was not moving, other than to drift gently when the wind pushed it.

"Let's go back," whispered Riff, hiding his neck in his collar.

"No, Riff," said Luna. "We need to know what this place is all about."

A gust of wind came along, and they heard the howling sound again. But this time it was accompanied by a distinct rumble, like a faint Rhothgan voice, from directly above.

Riff let out a small shriek and started pulling Luna in the direction of the Jalopy. "Luna, we should definitely go!"

"We have to get to the Bank. Pluck up some courage, for heaven's sake."

"I don't want to," Riff whined.

"You sound like Clorin. Just keep behind me if you're that scared," she said, tossing his grip off her arm.

Riff and Luna kept walking. The strange floating shapes were scattered everywhere. Each one they stopped to inspect was a different creature from one of the many planets of the universe. Like the Rhothgan, they were all inert, faded, just floating, attached to the ground by a rope. Whenever the wind picked up, they made a sound. Some groaned, others hissed or buzzed or squealed. Each sound was a faint shadow of what the creature's voice had been in life. There was no way to get to the Bank except through this macabre field of creatures, these floating shells of their former selves.

"Now," said Luna as they trudged on, "what do we remember about Mortalok?"

"That it's creepy as—"

"Riff!" said Luna, annoyed.

"Didn't the poem say something about dead people?" said Riff.

"Right!" exclaimed Luna, pounding Riff excitedly on the shoulder. She pulled out the anthology and opened it. "'The place where the dead cease to exist.' That's what the poem says. Tycho at the book shop also mentioned that you get sent to Mortalok if you spend all your Chroniya. I bet loads of these creatures spent all their time on Vivalok."

"S-so are w-we the only . . . alive creatures on Mortalok right now?" Riff stammered.

Luna turned in a full circle to encapsulate a panoramic view of the landscape. "Looks like it, I'm afraid."

"Right," said Riff in a resigned tone.

As they reached the crest of the rise, the Bank came into view. It was about the same size and shape as the Bank on Vivalok, but this Bank had no golden pipes. It was just a transparent sphere, and it was completely empty. Luna wondered if it was some sort of metaphor for the amount of time that these creatures had left.

"Let's just walk and see what else we can find," Luna said cautiously.

The two continued their slow stroll through the endless sea of creatures on ropes. Luna tapped her left wrist three times, hoping her microchip might be able to translate some of the hisses and other strange voices, but it could not. A drizzle of rain started to fall again, getting heavier as they continued forward.

Riff shouted over the now heavy rain. "Let's go into that cave!"

They ran toward a notch in a nearby cliff face, zigzagging through the floating creatures as the rain pelted them—first in sheets, then seemingly by the bucketload. They reached the cave and ducked inside. The cave was shallow but sufficient to protect them from the downpour. More of the tethered creatures were floating inside the cave, but the rain didn't appear to be subsiding, so Riff and Luna huddled together to wait out the storm. Lightning flashed as ear-splitting crashes of thunder intensified. Riff and Luna looked into one another's eyes with fear.

Between the claps of thunder, Luna heard a cry from somewhere behind them. As she whipped her head around, the next flash of lightning revealed a mane of wild grey hair surrounding a pale human face. Luna screamed. Riff jumped, then matched her scream.

It was their mother.

CHAPTER 7

THE TOWERS OF SOULS

"What in the bloody hell is Mum doing here?" yelled Riff, pointing a trembling finger at his mother's floating figure. The rope that tethered her to the floor of the cave was protruding from her stomach, like an umbilical cord.

"I don't know!" bellowed Luna, just as terrified as Riff and shaking just as violently.

"I'm leaving! I've had enough!" screamed Riff. He clambered to his feet and started for the cave entrance, despite the pouring rain outside. Luna lunged toward him and grabbed his ankles, causing him to fall into a rope and pull a floating Olfinder down toward his face.

"Arghhh! Get off me! You're awakening them all!" Riff sounded absurd, but then Luna was having a difficult time finding words herself.

"Just-j-just stay here! For a minute!" Luna pleaded with him. "We need to figure out what's going on!"

Riff looked into Luna's eyes and swallowed hard. They took a few moments to catch their breath.

"Okay," said Luna. "She's creepy, but she's our mum. Let's try to listen to what she's saying. Maybe that'll help."

Riff's eyes bugged out, and he vigorously shook his head. His red hair swished into a blur, sending droplets of water flying from the tips. "No. I can't look at her. This is too much." His eyes welled up with tears.

Luna thought about how much he looked like Clorin had when they had just returned from Clorin's worst memory.

"I'll do it. You stay there," she signed to him over the heavy sounds of the storm.

Luna's breathing was ragged and her heart pounded as she slowly walked toward their mother. She fought back tears. Luna always imagined reuniting with her mother, and every scenario she'd imagined had been a happy one. Her mother's arms would be outstretched for an embrace; her rosy face would bear a twinkling smile. Around her, there would be smells of aromatic foods. There would be laughter. And a warm hug would wrap the sensations all up.

But this was the complete opposite. The gloomy weather, the darkness of the cave, the deathly pallor of her mother's skin—it was as if a crack of thunder had shattered Luna's hopes for a happy reunion.

Henrietta floated as freely as if she were underwater. Her wild, curly grey hair bobbed up and down. Even though her eyes were closed, her face still wore its usual sweet expression. Her face had lost all of its rosy colour, but that was to be expected from a supposedly dead person. Luna also noticed the clothes her mother was wearing, particularly the apron. She couldn't remember a time in her few visual memories when her mother hadn't been wearing her apron.

Henrietta was whispering something. Luna cupped her hand around her ear, but over the noise of the storm she couldn't make out what her mother was saying. Gingerly, Luna grasped Henrietta's rope in her shaky hands and pulled it, bringing her mother down in slow stages as the rope started to pile up on the cave floor. She caught a glimpse of Riff, whose eyes bugged out even farther than they had before.

Henrietta's soft lips were close to Luna's ear. Luna couldn't help but remember the last time her mother had kissed her: it was the final goodbye before Luna had boarded the bus for Cipto all those years ago. Now, whispers in Henrietta's voice surrounded Henrietta's entire body as if encapsulated in a bubble around her. But the whispers weren't coming from her mouth. They were coming from a hole in her neck. Luna forced herself to look at the hole. It wasn't revealing any internal anatomy; it was just black. Still unnerved, Luna scrunched her eyes shut and put her ear up to the hole, her stomach turning with nausea. Still she could not understand the whispers. They were sweet-sounding, like the way her mother used to sound when she would fret about Luna not being able to prepare her breakfast, or when she would insist on making her a tea. But Luna could not make out any words in the whispers. It was as if they were in some unfamiliar language.

Luna groaned in frustration. "Riff, come here and listen. I can't tell what she's saying!"

Riff shook his head no.

"Riff! Come on! It's her voice," Luna said in a reassuring tone.

"Okay, oookaaay." Riff held up his hands in surrender and slowly got on his feet. He took a deep breath, held his head low, and slowly walked to Luna's side. He, too, slammed his eyes shut as he inched closer to Henrietta. He listened, but the whispers were nonsensical. He shook his head again.

"Nothing," he said quietly, backing away and folding his arms in discomfort.

Riff looked directly at his mother's face. Tears filled his eyes and a whimper uttered from his throat. He instinctively reached out a trembling hand and touched her face. Her cheeks were cold. Luna released the rope, and they watched their mother gracefully float back upward to her resting place. Riff grabbed Luna's arm and pulled her in for an emotional embrace. Luna, seldom one to cry, started to sob along with her brother. It was the wake they'd never had. This was the first physical evidence that their mother was in fact dead. Not just a rumour that the GeoLapse had killed her. Not just an ERA video of her explaining that she would be dead soon. Actual, tangible evidence.

The two released their embrace and signed to one another over the noise of the storm, which hadn't even begun to subside. Riff still signed, "Remember that time Mum almost set the house on fire?"

Luna choked back tears as she laughed at the memory. "I think that was the day Elbina started to enjoy cooking. She knew someone had to step up in the kitchen."

Riff smiled and glanced up at their mother quickly, as if she might be listening in. "What was it she burned again?"

"I think it was Ann Lou's birthday cake. She'd left it in the oven for ages. I've never heard Nan swear quite that much," Luna replied with a chuckle and a smile. A tear rolled down her cheek.

Riff nodded and started to sign with more joviality. "I think that was the start of Nan's new language—swearing every other word."

Luna thought about the incident, which, at the time, was a bit scary. If their house had burned, they'd all have been exposed to the outside environment, which would have killed them instantly. But now, looking back on it, the memory was bittersweet. In her head Luna could hear Knitsy waking up from her nap in the living room to the smell of smoke in the kitchen adjacent. She had marched up the stairs, swearing the entire way, and banged her cane on everyone's doors. In the end, the funniest thing about it was that Knitsy had seemed more angered that the cake was delayed than about her life being at risk.

Then Riff's expression turned sombre. "So why is Mum here?"

Luna pondered that for a few moments. It was a good question. Their mother hadn't been with them when they all went through the Time Belt. But Knitsy's unfavourable response to Father Time's question when they first travelled through the Time Belt a month ago meant that her descendants could no longer exist, and that included their mother, along with the siblings and Clorin.

Luna raised her hands to sign. "Mum was dead before we got sucked into the Time Belt. So she went to the place where all the dead go. It's for anyone with no time left."

Riff blinked away a tear.

They stood there a while longer, looking up at their mother as a slew of memories passed through their minds. Eventually Luna signed, "Should we get back to the Jalopy? I don't think the storm is letting up."

Riff frowned. "Now I don't want to leave."

Luna placed a hand on his shoulder and smiled as their eyes met. "We can come back."

Riff nodded. They walked to the cave entrance, then simultaneously looked back at their mother. Riff gave her a small wave and dashed into the teeming storm.

As they ran back to the Bank, the rain slowly diminished into a sprinkle, and they were able to slow their pace along the way, although they were still drenched. From the Bank, they went up to the top of the rise.

"There it is," Riff said, pointing to the Jalopy off in the distance.

Once they reached the Jalopy and had nestled themselves safely inside, it illuminated with its green glow and recited its usual script, prompting them to choose their desired destination.

"How are you feeling?" Luna asked.

Riff exhaled, his breathing laboured. Luna remembered he must still be having a difficult time physically since losing so much Chroniya from the first orb's spending.

"I'm all right. Just . . . difficult to process something like that." Riff fidgeted with his fingers.

"I know," said Luna, her voice croaking as she tried pushing away the scare they had just endured. "We can take a break if you want. Should we go back to Vivalok?"

"I dunno. Where else could we go?" Riff replied.

Surprised at his potential interest in continuing on, Luna said, "Well, either Galalok or Focalok."

Riff nodded. "Focalok has a cooler name. We've come all this way, let's just go there."

"You don't want to tell Elbs and Ann Lou what we saw?" Luna inquired.

"We're the oldest two. We should protect them. You know how much guilt Ann Lou felt about Mum after she left for Epiton."

Luna saw the exhaustion in Riff's face. She understood his not wanting to burden their younger sisters. But she also knew they would have to be told eventually. She nodded. "Okay. We don't have to tell them this instant. But after Focalok, we'll go straight back to Vivalok to fill them in. It's only fair."

"Deal," Riff agreed.

"Focalok," Luna replied to the Jalopy's inquiry.

"I apologise," said the voice of the Jalopy, "but you cannot travel to that destination via Jalopy. Please state your destination."

Luna and Riff eyed one another with hesitation.

"Erm, Galalok, then," stated Luna.

"Enjoy your trip."

The Jalopy zoomed away from the stormy land of Mortalok and farther into the depths of the Time Belt. As the Jalopy exited the violent storm's path, the rain and thunder stopped and the craft stabilised. Gradually the grey light around them dimmed to a dark shade reminiscent of nightfall. As the Jalopy descended to the land of Galalok, Luna pointed out three moonlike bodies that reflected a bit of light from some distant source. Had it not been for the moons, Galalok would have been as dark as Cipto. The Jalopy landed with a small bounce, before slowly rolling to a stop. Luna and Riff waited a few minutes to let their eyes adjust, then tumbled out of the Jalopy.

Riff pulled Luna to her feet, and they looked up in uneasy awe at the strange city before them. Hundreds of incredibly tall, pointy towers poked through the Galalok sky. These cone-shaped towers varied somewhat in height and proportions, but otherwise they had an eerie sameness. Each tower had a single dim light at its tip. The air around them was chilly. Every so often one of them would get shivers up their spine, as if a ghost were near. It was also a creepily silent night.

Luna pulled out the atlas and held it close to her face. The Galalok map showed a precise grid of dots that appeared to denote the towers. Toward the bottom of the map was one larger dot, about ten times the size of the others. This large dot connected to some sort of passageway that led to the bottom of the map and then disappeared.

"Let's just head through the centre of town toward this big dot here," said Luna, pointing out the big tower to Riff on the map.

"Yeah, all right," said Riff quietly. He and Luna started walking, but then Riff stopped and quickly turned on his heels.

Riff craned his neck forward and squinted. Then he pointed back toward the Jalopy. "Luna, look. We're not alone this time." A few yards away from the apeirotope was an hourglass Jalopy. It looked like the one that had gone missing from the Jalopy junkyard.

Luna scratched her chin. It certainly appeared that someone had arrived here before them, but she couldn't see or hear anyone around. "Let's see if we run into anyone, then. Maybe they can help us."

The siblings set off down a cobblestone path between a pair of towers. Luna felt a shiver tickling her spine and she looked over her shoulder.

Nothing was there.

Suddenly, a piercing cry from above shattered the silence. Luna shot her head upward with a deep gasp as she dug her fingernails into Riff's forearm. Her eyes darted back and forth across the dark sky, looking to see if something was there. There was nothing.

"What was that?" Riff whispered.

"I don't know," Luna whispered back. "Let's keep going."

Luna held her firm grip on Riff's arm as they continued. As they passed the next two towers, another cry sounded, and the two siblings jumped again. Luna's gaze made its way to the dim light at the top of the tower on their left. Could someone be in there? Trapped?

"There," Luna said, pointing to the dim light. "We have to get up there and save whoever is in there!"

"Erm . . . we do?" Riff asked, but Luna had already run to an opening at the base of the tower. The opening was about half Luna's height. It seemed to lead to complete darkness, but Luna crouched and went in. Riff followed behind her, swearing under his breath. Luna instinctively felt around the dark room to see if she could comfortably stand, which she could. Before their eyes, a torch on the wall lit up, revealing a larger opening ahead of them that led into another dark room. The opening behind them began to rumble, and they swivelled on their heels to see a stone slab emerging from the top of the opening. It moved down until it met the ground with a thump, shutting them inside the tower.

Riff whined softly. Luna stepped up and reassured him by saying, "I'll go first."

She tiptoed through the opening in front of them, and another torch lit up, revealing a circular room. Skeletons of strange creatures lined its periphery. A spiral staircase made of stone led from the centre of the circular room to a wooden landing about fifty metres above their heads.

"Let's go." Luna beckoned to Riff as she started jogging up the steps, and he reluctantly followed.

"Those skeletons had better be decorations," Riff muttered. The spiral staircase was very steep, and it was a struggle trying to keep up with his sister.

They were less than halfway up when the steps began to rumble and shake, causing Luna to fall onto her knees and Riff to shriek. Some external force was pulling stones from the stairway and throwing them toward the wall, creating gaps in their path.

"Run!" shouted Luna.

Luna leapt to her feet, and the siblings bounded over the gaps in the stairs as they continued upward. Then a stair was pulled out from under Riff's foot just as he stepped on it. He fell through the gap, barely managing to catch the stair above him with the tips of his fingers.

"Luna! Help!" Riff cried.

Luna whirled around and gasped at the sight of her brother's struggle. His fingertips could not hold for much longer by the looks of it.

"Argh! Riff!"

Luna crouched down and held her balance with a steady arm on a stair.

Please hold, please hold . . . Luna's internal narrative pleaded with the stair.

She held her other arm out to Riff. "Grab on, now!"

He lunged with strain and missed, almost falling this time.

"Careful!" Luna shouted, a bead of sweat dripping from her forehead.

Riff lunged again and caught a hold of her outstretched hand. Luna pulled with all of her strength, and Riff hooked his elbow on the stair, allowing him to pull himself up. The stair started to rumble.

"Move!" Luna urged, pulling him toward her.

Riff scrambled to his feet and hopped to the next stair up just before the one he had been stuck on whipped to the side of the wall and crashed into pieces.

"Almost there!" Luna shouted.

The two raced the rest of the way to the top, highly motivated by their desire not to fall to their deaths or be squashed by flying stones. Luna leapt onto the landing, which, though rickety, felt more stable than the stairs. Riff dove just after her, stumbling to his feet. Luna grasped his shoulders to steady him.

Riff was wheezing. "Erm, remember when I said . . . we should keep going instead of . . . going back to Vivalok? Never listen to me again."

"Noted," Luna replied.

The wooden landing on which they stood was not so much a floor as a skinny catwalk. It led to a tall, narrow opening in the wall opposite. Riff and Luna inched sideways across the walkway until they reached the opening and squeezed through it. Riff had a bit of trouble fitting through, but Luna helped him by tugging on his jumper.

A torch lit up the scene in front of them. This room was even taller than the first one had been. The ceiling, probably a hundred metres above them, had what looked like stalactites several metres long hanging from it. Riff pointed to the very top of the room. There, amid the stalactites, was another opening with a very slender landing just in front of it.

"How in the bloody bollocks are we supposed to get up there?" Riff asked.

Luna surveyed the scene around them. On the floor in the centre of the room was a small circle that looked like it was drawn in chalk. More skeletons of strange creatures were scattered around the room, as well as a pile of rusty old shields tossed in the corner.

"Why do I feel like we're going to need the shields?" asked Riff.

Luna walked over and grabbed one of the shields from the pile. It was dented in several places and extremely heavy. She dragged it behind her toward the centre of the room. When she neared the chalk circle, she took small, careful steps toward it and stopped at the edge, allowing the tips of her trainers to just touch the chalk. She lifted one foot and looked back at Riff, who shrugged. Holding her shield tightly, she stepped inside the ring.

The moment her foot came to rest, Luna's entire body was forced upward toward the ceiling. She heaved the shield over her head as protection from the rapidly approaching stalactites. The shield smashed into the stalactites, and Luna's head banged against the shield. She proceeded to fall back down. Upon landing, she tried to bounce herself at a different angle but instead hit the stone wall and slid down it onto a pile of bones.

Riff ran over to help her up. "You all right?" he squawked.

"I'm . . . fine," Luna replied breathlessly as she dusted herself off. She traced an arc in the air with one finger. "Just have to . . . land in the right place. You give it a go while I . . . catch my breath." Luna doubled over and put her hands on her knees, sucking in air and releasing big breaths.

"Okay . . ." Riff was not keen to have a go.

He awkwardly held his shield and tried a different tactic: a running start followed by a jump into the circle. Luna watched him fly high into the air, falling short of the thin landing by about two metres. He fell down, then bounced upward toward the stalactites.

"Shield, Riff!" shouted Luna.

Riff lifted the shield just in time to smash right into the stalactites. He fell straight down and landed on his feet, pushing his body down into a crouch upon contact with the ground. This propelled him upward again, directly toward the landing. He let go of his shield to maintain his momentum, and he managed to catch the ledge with his fingertips. He gracelessly pulled himself upward and secured himself on the ledge.

"This is so high!" he shouted to her, his echoes filling the room.

Luna followed his lead. On her way up, her body was flung into a horizontal position. She managed to cover her face with the shield, but her right leg smashed into the stalactites. One of the tips pierced her skin. The pain mounted as she fell back toward the ground. She landed on one foot and managed to bounce up toward the landing. She let go of the shield, as Riff had, and managed to reach the landing. Riff caught her in his arms and put her down gently.

"Your leg!" he squealed. "Can you walk?"

Luna nodded and stood up, but immediately collapsed to all fours on the landing. "Just hold me up."

Luna's brain swirled with adrenaline. The pain was only starting to settle in. They hobbled together through a wide opening that was already lit on the other side. A series of torches were aligned in a circle on the wall around the small room. Opposite the siblings was a small window that showed a view of the ghostly cityscape of Galalok. But the most curious part of the room was a tiny bottle, small enough to fit in the palm of one's hand, filled with a mysterious gold-flecked potion. The bottle was hovering at their eye level. Even more peculiar was the sound coming from the potion. It sounded like it was crying.

"Bring me closer," Luna ordered Riff, who kindly helped her forward toward the bottle.

Luna saw that the label on the tiny floating bottle had raised bumps on it. She reached out a finger to the bottle. An electric shock made her jerk it back.

"Ouch!" she cried, looking confusedly at the now quaking potion.

Swirling flames emanated from the bottle as the floor around them began to shake. Riff gripped Luna's arm just as the floor fell from beneath their feet. They slid down the entire height of the tower, tumbled out of the first opening they had entered, and landed in a pile on the ground. Luna pushed Riff off of her and sat up.

"Well, *that* was a waste of time!" Riff spat. "I'd rather die from one of those stalactites than a stupid potion. Much better story for the grandkids!"

Luna rolled her eyes at Riff's oxymoronic joke. Just then, she heard a familiar slithering sound nearby.

"Constance!" she called.

The Cipton halted, looking slightly astonished.

"Did you get it?" Constance asked with intense curiosity.

Luna and Riff blinked at her. "Get what?" Luna replied.

"N-nothing. Nothing at all!" The Cipton started to slither away as fast as she could.

Riff leaned forward and picked up the squishy Cipton in his hands. He held her in front of Luna. "Talk to her."

Constance growled. "I do not like to be picked up like this!"

"Talk to her!" repeated Riff.

Constance gulped loudly. "I'm not sure what you're talking about, you bumbling Earthling."

"Constance," said Luna, "you're not really exemplifying Cipton values by being sneaky. We're all here for the same reason. We can help each other."

Constance slumped in Riff's hands. "I need that potion."

"And we'll help you get to it," piped Luna, ignoring Riff's glare. "You just have to help us out."

Constance let out a deep sigh. She drooped still lower, and Riff had to squish her tighter so she couldn't escape. "Okay, I'll help you," she said, seething with anger. "I have a hard time trusting anyone, let alone two obnoxious Earthlings."

"Trust us, we feel the same way about you," said Riff. He put her down and sat down beside Luna.

Constance faced them and spoke. "Father Time asks a question of every creature that passes through the Time Belt. Can you recall this happening to you?"

Riff and Luna simultaneously replied, "Yes." Riff gestured for Luna to elaborate.

"Our Nan had to decide an event in her life to change. She chose to switch places with our dead mother. Father Time wasn't too keen on that answer. He—he took her away in some vortex." Luna lowered her head and Riff tenderly patted her on the shoulder.

"I didn't particularly care to hear the details," groaned Constance. "Anyways, when a creature answers incorrectly to Father Time's standards, it is sent to Galalok and becomes a prisoner, and all its descendants go to Vivalok. We must collect the potions that belong to the creature that is the prisoner."

"So Nan is a prisoner?" Riff asked with a horrified expression.

Luna nodded.

"What are the potions?" Riff continued.

"They are parts of the prisoner's soul. We must collect all the soul fragments in order to put them back together again. Only then can you get access to Focalok. But after that, I do not know what happens."

"So why couldn't we touch the potion we saw in that tower?" asked Riff.

"The creature's soul who resides in that potion is not your prisoner. You can only take what belongs to you," Constance said.

"But how do you know which one belongs to you? There are hundreds . . . thousands of these towers," said Luna.

"I can't give you all the answers!" Constance blubbered. "Can't you mindless Earthlings figure out one thing for yourselves?"

Luna exhaled a deep sigh. She was getting tired of all the creatures defaming her intelligence.

"So we need to just get Nan's soul out of one potion bottle?" Riff asked.

"There's three. That one in that tower is the last one I need. But I cannot get to it by myself," Constance said, drooping.

"We'll help you," said Luna. "But come back to Vivalok with us. We need a stronger team if we're to do this successfully."

Constance started to quiver with anger but quickly stopped herself, took a deep breath, and nodded. Luna knew that they needed Constance and Constance needed them. If they put their heads together, perhaps more than one family could be saved from the clutches of the Time Belt.

CHAPTER 8

A Second Rain Cloud

"So Knitsy's soul is stuck in a bunch of potions?" Elbina spread her fingers through her hair and held that pose. "And Mum," she continued. "Wow. Just . . . wow."

Elbina was still struggling to piece together what Luna and Riff had told her upon their return to Vivalok. They all were sitting in an alleyway and talking.

"Looner, look!" called Clorin. He and Constance were tossing his Pyroll back and forth. Constance would catch it in her mouth and then spit it out into a high arc, and Clorin would catch it floppily in his claws.

"Good job, Clorin!" Luna smiled brightly, holding out a thumbs-up. She started to twist her body to sit in a more comfortable position but winced when she moved her leg.

"Does that still hurt?" said Elbina, jumping up from her seat. "I can go get more medication. Or change the gauze."

"I'm fine," groaned Luna. "You're starting to sound like Mum."

Elbina blushed. "Sorry."

Riff called out, "Good catch, little man!" And then, carelessly: "Just like your mum and dad!"

Elbina eyed Riff from the side. Luna tensed up and glared sternly at him.

Riff, realising what he had said, began stammering. "Oh, well, uh, you know me, not lots going on upstairs. Just ignore me. I don't have a clue half the time—"

"What is going on?" Elbina asked her siblings. "You both are acting so weird lately."

Luna sighed and peered at Riff, still frustrated with him. "We might as well tell Elbs."

"Tell me what?"

Riff shrugged.

"It's about Clorin," said Luna. "He's . . . Ann Lou and Apollo's child. You can't tell her, though. It'll break her. It's a long story."

Elbina's jaw hung open. She looked at Luna, then Riff, then Clorin—innocent little Clorin, playing catch with his new Cipton friend. Elbina put her hands to her heart and smiled. "He's family?"

"Yeah, he sure is."

"But how?"

Riff popped up in his seat and clasped his hands. "When a daddy Epitonian and a mommy human love each other very much—"

Luna dropped her face into her hands. "Riff, can you not? Now is not the time."

"Speaking of Ann Lou, where is she?" asked Riff.

"Haven't seen her," said Elbina. "Clorin and I checked the gym while you lot were gone."

"Strange," said Luna. "Well, I'm sure she'll be along. We need to figure out how to find Knitsy's soul."

"Should we ask the strange hooded lad by the Bank?" proposed Riff.

"Your first good idea of the day," Luna replied.

The group set out to the Bank, where the hooded figure stood ominously among the dark orbs.

"I see you are back again, though surely most of your Chroniya has drained. The redhead looks a bit weak; is it actually another orb you seek?"

"Not an orb this time," began Luna. "We know about the potions. We want to know which towers to go to in Galalok."

The figure tossed its head back and chuckled in a husky tone, then regained composure and cleared its throat with a few raspy coughs. "I have given you everything you need; you've clearly not taken heed. But it has been some time since the last success—that is quite disappointing for me to confess. If a clue sets you on a path, you still must deal with the aftermath. Now listen closely—or don't listen at all; that is entirely your call. Those who cannot wake, hold the answers that you must take. To locate their domain, you can follow the rain. The key to understand is already at your command."

"What do we do after we get the soul back together?" asked Elbina. Luna stood next to her, quietly calculating.

"You are fully grown, so you must figure that out on your own. On that, my friend, I cannot bend."

"Why do you talk like that?" Riff spat. "Just give us a straight answer!"

The figure cocked its head. "Why is it I speak with words that sound alike? Simple: I have spoken thus since a wee tyke. Why does the Cipton not see and the Olfinder sing with glee? Why is it you're here and not there, nor in fact anywhere?"

Riff pursed his lips, slightly embarrassed at his outburst, and said nothing more.

"Thank you," concluded Luna. "We won't waste any more of your time."

"Ah," croaked the figure, "I have nothing but time. So I choose to fill it with rhyme."

Luna led her family and Constance around to the other side of the Bank, away from the figure. "We have to go back to Mortalok. I think whatever Mum was whispering is the key to knowing which towers to go to."

"But—we had no clue what she was saying," said Riff.

"This time might be different. We have this," said Luna, holding up the orb. "'The key to understand, is already at your command.'"

Her siblings nodded. Clorin just looked at her in awe with his sweet, red eyes.

Luna then turned to Constance with a glare. "You already knew about this, didn't you?"

Constance drooped where she sat. "I can't give you too much of an advantage . . ."

"Well, remember, your success is dependent on us," Luna told her sternly. "We'll take two Jalopies to Mortalok. Riff and Clorin, you go with Constance, since she already has an orb. And keep an eye on her. Elbs, you'll come with me."

Elbina's face brightened up. Riff saluted, and Clorin mimicked Riff. They made their way to the Jalopy junkyard, where Riff performed the now familiar duty of lifting the stone lid of the hourglass. Clorin and Constance slipped inside, followed by Riff. Luna and Elbina took the apeirotope.

The two Jalopies valiantly fought their way through the turbulent storm. Elbina wrapped her arms around Luna for the entirety of the ride, and Luna hugged her back, all while keeping a firm grasp on the orb. She couldn't help but wonder if her mother was watching her be a mother figure to her siblings—and, now, to her nephew. But then Luna thought of Ann Lou and how she hadn't been there to keep an eye on her. If anyone could take care of themselves, thought Luna, it was Ann Lou.

The Jalopies landed in the drab grey land of Mortalok, and the group assembled and set off to see if the orb would decode Henrietta's whispers. Luna and Riff led the way. Clorin wrapped himself firmly around Luna's leg upon seeing the scary floating creatures and their sinister whispers. Elbina and Luna managed to peel him off, and they each held one of his hands to reassure him. Riff carried Constance so she was on pace with the rest of the group and so he could keep an eye on her.

Riff and Luna led the party to the Bank and from there to the cave where they had seen Henrietta. Luna leapt into the cave and ran to Henrietta's location. When she looked up at the figure above her, she gasped.

A yellowish creature with spikes all over its body had taken their mother's place.

"She's gone!" exclaimed Riff.

"You sure this is the right cave?" questioned Elbina.

"Positive," said Luna, visibly agitated. "I don't understand." She looked around at Constance. "What are we missing here?"

Constance straightened up and babbled in a frustrated squawk, "I don't think it's fair that I should have to tell you everything when I had to figure it out all by myself!"

Luna groaned loudly and tossed her fists against the cave wall.

"Ahhh!" screamed a squeaky voice, followed by small, quick footsteps.

Luna whipped her head around to see Clorin darting out of the cave as quickly as his little legs could take him. Luna started after him but then stopped. A strange dark cloud was forming immediately above Clorin's head. It was raining on him, and only on him. The farther Clorin ran, the larger and darker the cloud grew, and the heavier the downpour became. Clorin ran headfirst into one of the ropes and screamed again, then dashed off in another direction. Now the cloud above his head grew smaller and brighter, and the rain from it slowed to a gentle shower. Luna's head buzzed with an epiphany.

"'To locate their domain, you can follow the rain'!" she announced to the group. "Riff, grab Clorin. Elbs, follow me!" Luna raced out of the cave and immediately acquired her own personal raincloud. It rained heavily on her as she ran to the spot where Clorin had collided with the rope. From there, she ran slightly forward, and the rain eased slightly.

"To the left!" she called, squaring off in that direction.

Luna continued her maze-like steps, going wherever the rain intensified. Miniature thunderclaps and lightning bolts affirmed that she was headed in the correct direction. It was getting terribly difficult to see in front of her. Then a loud crash of lightning caused Luna to jump backward and fall directly onto a rope. The creature tethered to it plunged downward as Luna quickly tugged the rope. It was their mother.

Elbina screamed, then immediately clapped her hand over her own mouth and just watched, horrified.

Luna positioned her ear next to the hole in Henrietta's neck. Being so close to her dead mother was no less stomach-churning this time than the last, but Luna squeezed her eyes shut and listened. The rest of the group stood frozen, watching her do what none of them had the stomach to do.

The whispers continued to be unintelligible, just as she had anticipated. Still listening, Luna took the orb out of her flannel pocket and turned it every which way, looking for any marks or changes in its appearance. Nothing. Luna then picked up the rope and felt along its entire length from the ground upward, focusing all her attention on her sense of touch as the rain impeded her vision. Still nothing. Luna squinted as she peered again at the hole in her mother's neck and pondered. It was approximately the same size in diameter as . . . the orb.

Luna placed the fragile orb in the hole in Henrietta's neck. Upon contact, the orb latched itself into place, and the rope, the orb, and Henrietta all began to glow and spark.

Henrietta's eyes opened, and her mouth fell agape. Staring straight ahead, she began to speak in a loud voice that was easily heard over the rain. "A-three-five. Zed-zed-three. J-one-five-two. A-three-five. Zed-zed-three. J-one-five-two. A-three-five. Zed-zed-three. J-one-five-two."

"Remember those!" shouted Luna toward Elbina and Riff. They seemed to be coming closer, but Luna could barely see their faces through the sheets of pouring rain around her. She wasn't sure if they could hear her.

"A-three-five. Zed-zed-three. J-one-five-two," Henrietta repeated. Her voice sounded more like Luna remembered it, except more of a monotone. "A-three-five. Zed-zed-three. J-one-five-two. A-three-five. Zed-zed-three. J-one-five-two. A-three-five. Zed-zed-three. J-one-five-two."

"I think I've got it! Let's go!" Luna called. She took the orb out of their mother's neck as gently as possible, with trembling fingers. She released the rope and ran back toward the cave until the rain above her had decreased to a drizzle.

"Why's she there? It's s-so horrible!" sobbed Elbina, her chin trembling. Then she dug her head into her hands and wept loudly.

Riff and Clorin remained quiet. Luna's stomach continued to lurch. She hated handling her mother that way with the rope, but she tried to remind herself that they needed the clue to continue.

"Should we head to Galalok?" Luna proposed. There was no way she could reminisce on sweet memories this time around.

Riff cleared his throat and then asked hoarsely, "What do we do with that clue?"

"I dunno yet," said Luna in a low voice, "but we should at least get out of here. I don't think it's doing any of us any good."

The siblings and Clorin nodded. Even Constance, who had been to Mortalok once already, looked as if she had the creeps.

Luna scanned the horizon. "Which way to the Jalopy?"

"I think it was this way," said Riff, pointing to the left.

"No, it was definitely that way," cried Elbina, pointing to their right with a shaky finger.

"Elbs, I've been here twice now. I think I know the way," Riff said in an annoyed tone.

"Don't speak to me that way!" Elbina sobbed, her voice choked with anger.

Riff would not let up. "What's got your knickers in a twist?" he prodded.

"Stop it," demanded Luna. "We shouldn't be fighting by our mother's dead body."

"Geez, Luna, *that's* dark," Riff shot back.

Clorin, who was riding on Riff's back, covered his eyes with his claws.

"Well, I'm going this way," sighed Elbina, heading to the right.

"And you're daft, so we're heading this way," said Riff, heading left with his chin up in the air.

Luna sighed. Personally, she thought the way back was straight ahead, but she didn't have the emotional energy for a fight. She decided to wait for Riff and Elbina to come crawling back, begging her to lead the way.

Luna watched Elbina as she walked away, hands clenched into fists by her sides. Then she turned her head in the opposite direction and watched Riff as he strutted off, looking the very picture of hubris. Then Luna looked back at Elbina, and she noticed that a cloud was forming above Elbina's head. The cloud was growing bigger and darker with each step that she took. Elbina was nowhere near their mother anymore. Why would this be happening again?

Elbina, feeling the rainstorm intensifying, stopped walking and peered up at the cloud.

"Riff!" called Luna, "Come back for a minute!"

Riff and Clorin turned their heads simultaneously. Even Constance, still situated under Riff's arm, perked up. Riff's haughty expression turned to confusion when he saw the roiling dark cloud above Elbina's head. Riff and Luna walked toward her cautiously. Once they had caught up to her, they all followed the storm until, once again, the rain was pelting them at all angles. Thunderclaps started to sound, and lightning flashed in the cloud. The rain was so intense that it stung their faces.

"What's going on?" boomed Riff. Clorin was crying loudly and pounding on Riff's back to turn around.

A lightning bolt cracked beside them, causing them all to jump in one swift motion. Even Constance quivered and huddled more securely in Riff's arm. Heeding the signal, the group looked up at the nearest rope. They all screamed and clutched each other. The blonde hair was unmistakable; the Pyroll stick floating nearby only underscored what they already knew. Ann Lou was now one of the soulless bodies floating in the sea of the dead on Mortalok.

CHAPTER 9

An Old Poem

Elbina fell to her knees and sobbed. Luna felt an emotion she had never quite felt before: the devastation when uncertainty is ripped away and disaster is revealed. Her questions couldn't even be strung together; they flew in meaningless directions within her brain. As the rain fell into her eyes, refracting the image in front of her, she felt as if she were drowning. She wished she were drowning, in fact. Anything that could have taken away the pain of seeing her youngest sister lifeless, Luna would have accepted gladly. She wondered if this was how Ann Lou had felt that day she departed Earth for Epiton, leaving their mother behind, alone and defenceless. Luna knew she would hold this nightmarish memory inside her forever. She felt she had failed one of her siblings. She should have kept her eyes on her. How reckless! Their mother would be furious. Perhaps the storm around them was her mother's wrath. She deserved it. She was the oldest, after all.

Yet Luna couldn't shake the thought that Ann Lou was here on Mortalok for a reason. Mortalok, to Luna's knowledge, was only for people who were already dead when the rest of their family entered the Time Belt, as well as for those in Vivalok who had overspent their Chroniya. But Ann Lou was neither of those. How could she be in Mortalok? It didn't make sense—there had to be some other reason.

Luna couldn't help but remember her talk with Tycho when she and Clorin had visited the book shop for the first time. Tycho's words echoed in her brain now. "The kids, though . . . they're reckless with their time." Fast-forward to the mysterious objects that had been obtained and left for them to trade for a new orb. And how they hadn't seen Ann Lou since she and Clorin came back from their first failed journey. Could it have been Ann Lou who paid for everything?

No, thought Luna—that's not possible. She shook her head. Her eyes were bloodshot, and her entire body was drenched and cold. But she deserved it, so Luna stayed put. It was better than what Ann Lou was living through, or not living through. Luna had to pay the price.

Luna tried to imagine what Ann Lou would have been thinking, if she indeed was the one who had paid for the new set of objects. It was like Ann Lou to do something heroic. But it was quite unlike her not to seek recognition for her actions. So why else might she have sacrificed her Chroniya? Maybe out of embarrassment—to remove herself from society and end the shame of having done something wrong. Luna recalled Ann Lou's outburst on Cipto from a few months back. She had pushed her best friend, Hayden, out of her life for seven years because she felt guilty over their mother's passing. But what would Ann Lou feel guilty about this time?

Had she lost in Luge Crash? Unlikely, and even if she had, she wasn't that much of a sore loser. Could she have run into Hayden or Apollo?

No. Possibly Clorin? Had Ann Lou learned that she was Clorin's mother and would eventually snap, causing Apollo to take Clorin and run away? There was no feasible way she could know that. Well, unless Riff blurted it out to Ann Lou—but he hadn't seen much of her lately either. Had someone else told her?

Luna robotically turned her head to Elbina, who was still prostrate with grief.

No.

Clorin?

Not a chance.

Constance?

Not out of the question. But Constance didn't even know Ann Lou.

Luna shut her eyes. Maybe the information had not come from them directly, but could it have done so indirectly? Luna remembered her secret conversation in the food shop with Riff. She began to piece together her recollections. The table next to them had been occupied by a party of Antympanicans. Although they were the most silent of beings, living on a planet with no sound, they were renowned gossips. They could have listened in. From them, the news could have travelled to Ann Lou.

But if that were the case, would Ann Lou have sacrificed herself?

Luna nodded to herself. Yes. If Ann Lou learned she would one day cause distress to her husband and future child, she would disappear at all costs. Ann Lou had given herself up to spare the rest of them a disastrous future. It was noble but highly unnecessary. Surely the siblings could have balanced out the costs. Then again, Riff had already sacrificed a huge amount of his time.

Luna wanted to hug Ann Lou. Without thinking, she gripped her sister's rope and pulled it downward, bringing Ann Lou to her eye level. Her blonde hair floated around her face, making her look much more peaceful than her drenched siblings. Luna noticed her two perfectly intact arms. It was strange to see her that way; she'd had a prosthetic arm for so long. Even after all Ann Lou had been through, Luna thought she was braver than anyone she had ever known—besides their mother, of course. Then one last possibility crossed Luna's mind. Had Ann Lou overspent her Chroniya to avoid a future in which she could no longer use her legs? Even as much as Ann Lou loved sport, that seemed impossible. In Luna's eyes, Ann Lou's sacrifice had nothing to do with that, and everything to do with not wanting to be less than what their mother was.

It all made sense, but at the same time it felt like a horrible mistake. Ann Lou was such a lively girl, one who loved and was loved. She broke barriers, physically and mentally. She was loyal, if a bit stubborn. If only Luna could have gotten to Ann Lou sooner and stopped this all from happening . . .

Luna gently kissed Ann Lou's forehead. Tears for her fallen sister streamed down Luna's cheek and merged with the falling rain.

Finally, Luna straightened her back and started to loosen her grip on the rope. She noticed that Ann Lou wasn't whispering, nor did she have a hole in her neck like the other dead on Mortalok. Apparently Ann Lou held no secrets for them. Luna could see a bulge in Ann Lou's left sock, however. She gripped Ann Lou's leg so she wouldn't float away and pulled out a crumpled bit of paper. It was starting to get wet, so Luna tucked it into the pocket of her flannel shirt. She then let go of the rope.

"Let's get back to the Jalopies!"

Constance obeyed and snuck out of Riff's grip. She began slithering out of the intense rain, but Riff and Elbina stayed put. Riff's moppy red hair was flopped in front of his eyes. His face was pouting and trembling. Clorin was still wailing and beating on Riff's back. Elbina's face bore the blank stare of one traumatised.

"We have to go," Luna begged, trying to herd her siblings toward the Jalopies. She wanted nothing more than to alleviate her siblings' pain in the face of this added loss. But she wasn't sure if she could cope with it herself. She wished desperately that their mother could be with them.

Finally, Luna grasped Elbina's and Riff's arms and started dragging them. They looked up one last time as Ann Lou's body slowly floated upward, then reluctantly started to run for the Jalopies.

The siblings and Constance ran all the way to the Jalopies without a word. The rain now fell at a light sprinkle. Luna noticed her siblings' and Clorin's faces looked quite pale.

"You all right?" asked Luna.

Elbina's head hung low.

Riff's top lip trembled. "D-did s-she . . ."

Luna nodded. "She's the reason we're able to use the Jalopy."

"What did you pull from her sock?" Elbina asked, still looking down.

Luna gingerly pulled the crumpled paper from her pocket and unfolded it. There were no marks on it. Puzzled, Luna carefully flattened it out with her hand. Then her fingers felt the familiar raised bumps of Braille that filled the page. Luna gently ran her finger over the footer of the page. It read Property of the University of Oxford. She then started reading the Braille from the top. Luna instantly recognised it as the poem Ann Lou had read at the Storytelling Ceremony on Cipto, right before the GeoLapse attack.

"It's a poem from the Oxford textbook I gave to her," Luna said.

Riff leaned over her to read along. His eyes scanned the page in confusion at first. "I can't read that. Oh wait, my chip translates it." His eyes feverishly swept the poem. "Oi," he said with a slight hint of excitement in his voice. "It's the same author as the lad who wrote the poem about finding the objects."

Luna's eyes bugged out. Riff was right.

"Read the poem!" Clorin gleefully chirped. He seemed to have forgotten already the horror they had just endured.

Luna cleared her throat. "It's called 'Slicing the Fourth Dimension.'" She began to read aloud.

Time comes in all sizes.
A dimension so thick and thin
That it passes us with many disguises.
Time is always maintained.
You can lose it, you can find it,

But none is ever truly lost or gained.
Time works so precisely on its clocks,
For you cannot be both lost and found,
Only one suits the father of ticks and tocks.
Time is a lasting gift.
If you decide to change it,
Be prepared for its lasting rift.

"It's talking about the Time Belt, right?" asked Elbina shakily.

Luna didn't reply. Her eyes raced through the lines again.

"Sis?" Elbina finally looked up and stared at Luna. It seemed to Luna that there was nothing in Elbina's eyes. No light. No spark. Just a need for her sister to reply.

"Is there something in there?" asked Riff, furrowing his brow as he read alongside her.

Luna pointed at a section of the poem and read it aloud again, "'Time works so precisely on its clocks, For you cannot be both lost and found, Only one suits the father of ticks and tocks.'" Luna looked around at the group and smiled with delight.

Riff, trying to regain his sense of humour, said, "You've known us for long enough to realise that we have no idea what you're talking about."

Luna said, "I think Ann Lou gave us a clue about how to escape the Time Belt."

Constance perked up. "You—you know how to get out of here?"

Luna glowered at her. "You don't?"

Constance bobbed left and right. "No. I only know about the potions. I obviously haven't gotten that far in the escaping process. I've been a bit held up by a pack of distasteful Earthlings!"

"Well, see then? You have to stick with us and not keep things hidden," Luna ordered.

Constance drooped until she looked like a puddle on the ground.

"Can you elaborate? I'm still lost," Elbina confessed.

Luna said, "Those lines are basically saying we can't exist both here *and* in the real world. We have to find a way to make ourselves exist in the real world. We're basically in a different dimension here."

Elbina waved her arms in frustration. "And how are we supposed to do that? I feel like that's the problem we've been dealing with the whole time we've been here—trying to get out!"

Riff raised his eyebrows at his younger sister. "Do I need to tell you to chill again?"

Elbina shot him a look of disdain.

"Quiet down, you guys, seriously," Luna begged. "I have a hunch that it's something to do with Focalok. It makes some sense: we have to get Knitsy's soul back, since she's the reason we're all here. Then we can have a go at escaping in some way."

They all pondered Luna's hypothesis for a minute. Then they agreed with her. It was a plausible answer to their predicament.

"So, should we go to Galalok then?" asked Riff.

"Not yet," said Luna. "I think there's something more about this E. Bowser the Third that we need to find out. Whoever they are, they wrote all these poems for a reason. I need to go back to Vivalok and do some research."

Constance groaned. Luna knelt down to her. "Constance, I know this is frustrating for you. But there could be something here. I have a gut feeling about it. It may be beneficial to all of us."

"She's right," said Elbina. "You can trust Luna on this one."

Constance growled softly but nodded her blobby head in surrender.

Riff, Clorin, and Constance boarded the hourglass Jalopy, and Elbina hopped into the apeirotope when it became a sphere. Before Luna got in, she looked back to the field of the dead in Mortalok, specifically in Ann Lou's direction.

"Thanks for the help, Ann Lou. We couldn't have solved this part of the puzzle without you."

THE ORIGIN OF THE TIME BELT

Luna rushed to the book shop while Riff, Elbina, Constance, and Clorin took a stroll to the food shop to refuel on hopefully cheap items.

Luna barged through the door, much to the dismay of Tycho, who appeared to be on break. He was in a comfortable chair normally reserved for customers, relaxing over a book titled *Complex Quantum and Theoretical Physics of Parallel Universes (So Easy an Earthling Could Do It!)*. The Casperian sighed and moved the book higher in front of his face with his wiggly, long nasal appendages. Luna waved her hand over the top of the book.

"Oh," moaned Tycho, rolling his eyes. "Didn't see you there. What could you possibly want this time?"

Luna swallowed hard. She knew she had to say something that would get his attention. She had to praise him and bribe him for his knowledge. She cringed at the thought, but it was the only way to get his help.

"I need your expertise on something. Because . . . well, my tiny little Earthling brain couldn't possibly understand on its lonesome." She gritted her teeth as she spoke.

Tycho sat up and slowly lowered the book. "Well, at least you're not too dense to admit that. What may I inform you of today? Would you like me to explain the concept of Chroniya for the third time? Or perhaps I could lead you to the children's section."

Luna took a deep breath before responding. "Not today, thanks. But, do you know where I could find a book on someone named E. Bowser the Third?"

"Well, Earthling, this book shop is much too small to contain biographical archives of every single creature of the universe and beyond. But I do know that in aisle sixteen you can find E. Bowser the Third's *An Anthology of Poems*—"

Luna opened her mouth to speak.

"—which I remember you purchased recently. For eight hundred fifty-four Chroniya."

Luna closed her mouth.

"However," continued Tycho, "you have come to the correct Casperian. Although my only knowledge of E. Bowser the Third is that her poetry is annoyingly pedestrian, I do have some historic knowledge of her grandmother, Ernesteen Bowser Senior."

Luna's eyes grew wide. "Her grandmother?"

"Yes. Ernesteen Bowser Senior is not quite an Earthling, but probably the closest you can get. She's rather like you, actually."

"How so?"

"As you can see," said the Casperian, gesturing toward the large book with his nasal appendages, "I've been doing a bit of light reading on some basic principles of parallel universes. Ernesteen Bowser Senior was a resident of the parallel version of Earth in one of these parallel universes. Her planet is called Thera."

"Parallel universes? Those exist?" said Luna, astounded.

"Ugh. Another reason Earthlings are among the most infuriating creatures in all the universes—your utter incapacity to open your minds to anything you haven't seen. It's so very tedious."

Luna inhaled slowly, determined to keep her cool. "So, did Ernesteen Bowser Senior exist on Earth as well? Since it's parallel to planet Thera?"

"No," replied Tycho, "but theoretically, given the vast size of the infinite universes, there surely are infinite versions of Ernesteen Bowser Senior. But let's not confuse you more for the moment. A parallel universe is simply one that works almost exactly like ours but simply exists in a different space–time continuum. Planet Thera shares many of Earth's characteristics, but there are subtle differences, including the people, some events, et cetera."

"Okay," Luna pondered. "How do you get to other universes, including parallel universes?"

"Our universe, which is referred to as Coloratura, is quite new compared to most of the others. Planet Thera is in a universe called Reprisa, which is also quite new considering it's a parallel universe. Anyways, Coloratura's Universal Union hasn't yet developed the technology to safely travel to other universes. That's not to say that certain communities in other universes don't visit Coloratura. But most are technologically incapable. Theoretically, though, one could access any other universe through a black hole."

Luna's mouth fell open. "A black hole? Are you mad? Black holes crush everything that enters them."

Tycho gasped, along with his co-worker Newt and even a few of the customers in the queue. "Again," said Tycho, "just because it looks scary from the outside doesn't mean it's entirely dangerous."

Luna realised she was getting side-tracked, so rather than pursuing that subject, she just nodded. "So," she asked, "why is Ernesteen Bowser Senior important?"

Tycho goggled at Luna in disbelief, called over to Newt, who was hustling customers through at the next register. "Newt! Get this one! The Earthling asked why Ernesteen Bowser Senior is important!"

Newt burst out laughing. "Why is she important! She only . . ." But he was laughing too hard to speak. Customers glared as Newt wheezed hysterically and slapped the counter with his nasal antennae. Finally, between gasps, he said: "She only . . . she only solved some of . . . some of the greatest mysteries of the multiverse!"

Luna looked at Tycho and, summoning all her strength, gave him a sweet smile.

Tycho wiped a tear of laughter from his eye with his nose and continued. "You Earthlings crack me up! Even on Casper we hold Ernesteen Bowser Senior in the highest esteem. She was the most brilliant Therian ever to have lived. She built the first working time machine."

Luna could not hold back a small snort. "Do you mean no one on planet Casper ever managed to make a time machine?"

Tycho sneered. "Oh, so you think building a time machine is easy? I'd love to see how you get on even starting a project such as that. In any case, we Casperians were much too busy writing the astrophysics textbooks that Ernesteen Bowser Senior used to develop her invention. So, naturally, I give my community the bulk of the accolades." Tycho waved his nose up high in the air. "Although, considering the relatively tiny size of the Therian brain, I do concede that Ernesteen Bowser Senior deserves a little credit."

Luna pondered Ernesteen's accomplishment for a moment. "It's funny, isn't it, that E. Bowser the Third, granddaughter of the woman who developed the first time machine, wrote so many poems about time and the Time Belt."

"Perhaps she was proud of her grandmother," Tycho suggested.

"But how would her granddaughter have known about the Time Belt? And have a book of poems distributed all over different universes, including the Time Belt?"

Tycho opened his mouth to respond but quickly realised he didn't have an answer. "What are you saying?"

"I don't have an answer, but do you think E. Bowser the Third could have had something to do with the creation of the Time Belt? How long has it been around?"

"Unfortunately, there is no known record of the origin of the Time Belt, as those on the physical plane barely know of its existence at all, and I've never heard of anyone within the Time Belt who has been able to escape," Tycho explained.

"But Father Time must know about it. Surely someone has had some sort of interaction with him while in this domain. He could be behind the origin, correct?"

"Father Time speaks to those who pass through the Time Belt. But no one has ever seen him."

"Do you think there's a way to destroy the Time Belt?" Luna asked.

"My, my, you ask a lot of questions. Is there anything you do know? To answer your question, I must delve into beginner space–time physics. Are you familiar with the concept of different dimensions?"

Luna shook her head in embarrassment, patting the flannel pocket where she'd put the poem from Ann Lou's sock. "Not entirely."

"Tragic," said Tycho. "No matter; I can keep this simple. You'll only need the first few dimensions anyway. Let me draw you a picture."

The Casperian poked his long nasal antennae in the air and then withdrew it, leaving a single black dot that hung in mid-air. "Dimension zero. A point in space."

"Now, we must give our point a direction. If you put a bunch of points together in a row, what do you get?"

"A line?" said Luna.

"Precisely." Tycho drew a horizontal line through the dot. "Dimension one. A line."

Tycho continued. "This line can exist in only one direction: horizontal, as you Earthlings would say. Now, we must give it room to go in another direction. This brings us to dimension two." Tycho waved his nose and the line disappeared. He then drew a wiggly line.

"The line can now move up or down as well as horizontally. Are you still with me?"

Luna nodded.

"Now, dimension three. The line needs another direction to move in. Where else could it go?" said the Casperian, testing his student.

"Erm . . . like, outward and inward. Toward me," Luna replied. It had been a while since she had studied linear algebra back in school.

"Correct." The Casperian reached up and turned the squiggly line so that it was pointing toward Luna. It resembled a ramen noodle frozen in mid-air.

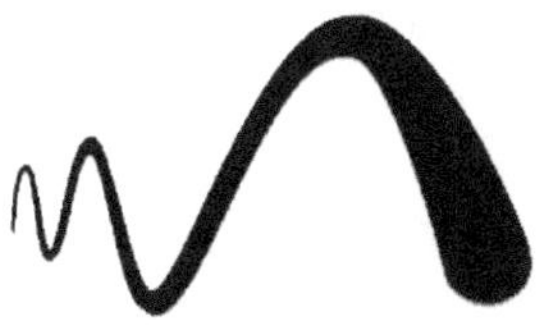

"That line can exist anywhere in three-dimensional space. Can you think of a way we might implement a fourth dimension?"

Luna thought about this. "So, currently, the line exists in three-D space." She exhaled a large puff of air. "But now it needs to move another way."

Tycho nodded. "And how will we make it move?"

"Over time?" Luna guessed.

"Correct! If we give this line some life"—here Tycho waved his nose, and the freeze-dried noodle began to undulate like a snake—"it can move, but this kind of movement happens through time. So there you have it. Time is the fourth dimension." With a flick of Tycho's nose, the undulating line disappeared.

Luna rubbed her chin. "So, the Time Belt is in the fourth dimension?"

Tycho nodded. "It is theorised."

"And without time, there's no life or any sort of existence, and vice versa?" Luna continued.

Tycho nodded again, proud that he had managed to teach a human basic physics principles. Luna looked away from Tycho, then paced around slowly, lost in thought. She peered through the window at the never-ending bustle of the crowd outside.

Then she mused aloud: "If we destroy time, we destroy the Time Belt."

Tycho replied sharply. "Whatever you're thinking about, Earthling, I'm not sure you have the brain power to bring it all to fruition. Besides, the Time Belt isn't such a bad place to be. I can read books and eat

Casperian food here. I'd rather be in this dimension than worry too much about the problems of the universe."

"But your time will run out eventually," Luna remarked. "Anyways, speaking of time, I'd better get going." As she headed to the exit, she added, quite sincerely: "Thanks for teaching me quite a bit." She bowed her head and stepped through the door.

Tycho called after her, "Always a pleasure to share my immense, overwhelming knowledge," but Luna was already out of earshot.

Luna made her way through the busy crowd outside the book shop to a quiet alleyway. She took out E. Bowser III's anthology and began paging through it, looking for words such as *destroy* and *universe*. Nothing immediately caught her eye, until she flipped to the title of the poem on the last page of the anthology, "My Chroniya." She scanned through it slowly with her eyes, absorbing as much of the poem in one go as she could. It read:

My Chroniya, oh the treasure you hold,
Deep, deeper in the depths of the gold.
Not only are you my sustenance,
But your existence would cause utter dissonance.
Should you ever have an untimely drain,
All inhabitants who have paid would exit my domain.
Although their memories of their time here would be the same,
They would instead exist on a physical plane.
How unfortunate for me that would be,
Although I consider myself lucky.
Without you, my Chroniya, who keeps my time rife,
My existence would then be owned by the afterlife.

Luna closed her eyes, attempting to put Tycho's information and the poem together. Did anything relate to the other? Was there really a plausible way to destroy the Time Belt? Was the answer right there on this page she gripped so tightly between her fingers? Thoughts swirled too quickly in her brain to properly comprehend.

"Luna!"

Luna popped her eyes open and saw Riff, Elbina, Constance, and Clorin dashing toward her. All of them had chocolate cake smeared on their faces, even Constance.

"Enjoy yourselves?" Luna asked curtly.

"Elbina bought an entire chocolate cake for us," said Riff. "It was awesome. Here, we saved you a piece." Riff placed a thin slice of cake on the page Luna was reading. Luna picked it up, noticed a bite had already been taken out of it, but ate the rest of it, and brushed the crumbs off the page.

"So, did you find anything?" asked Elbina, wiping her face on the sleeve of her jumper.

"I think so," Luna replied between bites of cake. "I think I understand a bit better now what it will entail to escape the Time Belt, and how Focalok fits in."

Constance squirmed impatiently and growled, "Well? Spit it out!"

"In the poem 'The Next Levels,' Focalok is referred to as 'the place to change the date.' That poem Ann Lou kept says, 'For you cannot be both lost and found.' If you put those two together, I think it means we have to go back in time to our old dimension and make sure we get born. Before we can escape the Time Belt, we have to ensure we have existences to get back to. But I think there's more to the story. I think there's a way to destroy—"

"Well, let's get going, then!" barked Constance. "What are we waiting for?"

Luna began to answer as diplomatically as she could. "I think first, we need to—"

"Listen, you moronic Earthling," Constance snapped. "I've done my part. At this point, you're just holding me back. I'm not wasting any more time in this timeless place. Let's get a move on, or I'll make sure none of you gets out of here."

Luna gulped. Even though she had no reason to fear a Cipton, especially in front of two other humans and a half-Epitonian, she didn't want to anger Constance any further. And Constance had a point. She deserved her chance at an escape.

So Luna gave in. "Okay. Let's go to Galalok. First, Riff and Elbina and I will find the potions we need." Before Constance could erupt again, Luna added hastily: "And we'll help you find yours, too."

Luna and Elbina sat in the apeirotope and watched as Vivalok receded, shrank, and finally disappeared behind a puff of grey clouds. Luna's thoughts returned to her mother and Ann Lou, hollow and pale, floating forlornly on dreary Mortalok. She hadn't wanted to leave them there; just thinking about it made her feel sick. But the possibility that they might figure out how to escape the Time Belt gave her hope. Ann Lou and Henrietta would not have to rest for eternity in that dreary place if Luna could help it.

Once the two Jalopies had landed on Galalok, the group gathered in the dim moonlight to plan their search for Knitsy's soul fragments.

"What was Mum's clue again?" asked Elbina.

"A-three-five, Zed-Zed-three, J-one-five-two," said Luna.

"Right," said Elbina. "Er, do the towers have names?"

"Not that I remember," answered Riff.

"That's not a bad guess, though, Elbs," said Luna as she pulled out the atlas and opened it to the Galalok page. She traced her finger around the perfect grid of thousands of dots. "Actually," Luna continued, "I think you have the right idea." She laid the atlas on the ground so everyone could crowd around to see. "Mum's clue sounds like grid coordinates. See how the map is divided into rows and columns? The first row could be A, and the first column could be 1, and so on."

"That would make sense!" said Riff. "So how do we orient ourselves? Where are we in this grid?"

Luna pointed to the gargantuan tower in the distance, the one that loomed over every other tower on Galalok. "That's our first marker. It's here on the grid." She traced her right index finger to the largest dot on the map, which was at the south end of Galalok. "I believe that's also to the pathway to Focalok."

"Are there any other indicators on the map to help us know where we are?" Elbina asked, lacking any confidence in their plan.

"Constance, which tower number is your last potion located?" Luna asked.

Constance squirmed and then muttered, "B-six."

Luna surveyed the map. "That should be this one," she pointed to a dot in the second row and six columns from the left. "That's the tower just over there that we were in before," she said, pointing to a tower in the distance and looking at Riff. "That means if we want to orient ourselves at A-one, it should just be over here."

Luna led the group to the start of the grid, just six towers to their right.

"Okay, then," said Riff, hopping from one foot to the other. "Where first?"

"A-three-five!" howled Clorin.

"Good memory, little man!" Riff clapped him gently on the back.

"What about me?" called Constance.

Luna looked back and saw the desperation in Constance's quivering body. She felt angry toward the Cipton. It wasn't as if she had done anything to help them. But Luna remembered her mother always saying to the siblings to help others and to not expect much, if any, help back.

"Right, sorry. Got caught up in the moment," Luna started. "Riff, why don't you help Constance get her last potion? Then you and Constance can do tower Zed-zed-three right after."

Constance vibrated with excitement.

"I have to do that one again?" Riff whined. "The whipping stairs and the sharp, pointy, murderous . . . things on the ceiling?"

Luna knew it was asking a lot of her brother to do that tower again. She understood his fear. But she knew he could do it. "Take two steps at a time," she said reassuringly. "Remember to use the shield. And, Constance," she added, addressing the now impatiently pacing Cipton, "keep him safe. Please."

146

THE CIPTON'S LAST POTION

Riff saluted Luna and led Constance in the direction of the tower they had previously gone in. Constance bounded after him with excitement for finally getting a second chance at receiving her last potion.

He stopped in front of the opening to tower B6, sucked in a large gulp of air, and laced his fingers together atop his head. Constance stopped alongside him.

"Go ahead," Riff urged. "I'm just catching my breath."

Constance squirmed with discomfort but slowly slithered through the opening. Riff followed her in. The opening behind them sealed shut with a rumble.

"All right, Constance, listen up. I know my way around this tower. The first challenge to overcome will be these deadly stairs to climb, so it's best if I lead the—"

A torch lit ahead of them, and Riff saw no trace of the rumbling, deadly stairs from last time. A new challenge presented itself. Ahead of them stood a large pipe with an opening in its side.

"The towers *change* every time you go in them?" Riff said, perplexed.

"How about I go first, almighty Earthling?" snarled Constance.

Riff shrugged and gestured for Constance to go first. She cautiously manoeuvred herself into the pipe. Riff squeezed in behind her, and they began to climb. The diameter of the passage varied as they wriggled up, left, or right, following the strange pipe's course. Seams and pinholes let in tiny amounts of light, but Riff couldn't see much of anything beyond Constance.

Soon they reached a four-way intersection.

Riff sighed. "Which way do you reckon?"

"Don't be so impatient," Constance murmured. She poked her head into the passage on the right, which was quite narrow, and squeezed a portion of her jelly body through it to sense the best way forward.

Riff's eyes bulged at her dexterity, but he realised that he's seen stranger things. Then she checked the other two directions.

"Left," she concluded. "Right and straight lead to dead ends."

"Brilliant. Let's go," Riff said, astonished at her sudden helpfulness.

They continued through the pipe maze in this way, with Constance scouting out the options at each intersection. Finally, they reached the end of the pipe. Riff flopped himself out and stood up, then patted Constance's jiggly body.

"Well done. I'd still be in there four months from now if you hadn't been here," he said.

"You're . . . welcome," Constance muttered.

Riff smiled. "Warming up to me now, are you?"

Constance just growled.

The pipe had deposited them in a tall and wide room with an

opening far up the wall of the room. To Riff's horror, this room was entirely filled with water. They had to swim up to the landing. It had to be hundreds of metres upward.

A thin, clear veil encircled the room, keeping the air separated from the water. Riff cautiously put a finger to the veil's surface. It felt rubbery, and with little force his finger was able to penetrate the veil and enter the area with the water. No water spilled into the air area in which they stood.

"What's going on in this room?" Constance asked.

"We need to swim up to the landing all the way up there," Riff said, squinting at the next opening. "I'm not sure I can hold my breath that long."

"Well, I can," Constance said curtly. She plunged her gelatinous self through the veil and started wiggling her way up through the water.

Riff bit his lip. He needed to keep up with her. He took a deep breath in, pushed his body through the veil, and found himself fully immersed in the water. He had never been swimming in his life due to Earth's unfortunate atmospheric conditions, so the feeling of holding his breath was unnatural to him.

Constance was far ahead of him now, about halfway up the room. He began to dog paddle his way up toward her. A few strokes later, his lungs started to battle with him—he needed air. His heart was pounding, and he began to panic. Riff accidentally gulped in a large breath and filled his lungs with the water, causing him to cease swimming and grab his throat.

Riff thrashed in the water, sinking toward the ground level. His vision started to blur, and Constance was well out of sight now. He screamed for help as his mind started showing him shapes and colours. He felt like he was dying.

This was it. He had died trying. And they hadn't even reached the tower for Knitsy yet. He had died trying to save a blobby prisoner that he didn't even know. Riff imagined his body with a rope sticking out of his stomach in Mortalok. That was where he was headed. He might as well just stop struggling . . .

Just then, Riff took a giant gulp of air and heaved heaps of water everywhere. As he came to, he realised that he was in a small bubble floating through the water.

"Huh?" he said, placing his hands on the bubble and feeling a jelly-like wall around him. He was inside Constance. He was in her stomach, and she inflated herself into a bubble.

Constance and Riff reached the landing with the opening within minutes of floating upward. Constance rolled onto the landing and easily pushed through the veil, bringing them back into a region with air. She spat Riff out roughly, and he tumbled in front of the opening.

"You—you saved me," Riff said, clutching his ribs. "Thank you."

"It's fine, I guess," wiggled Constance in an uncomfortable squirm. "My father would've helped if he were here."

"Is your father the prisoner stuck in your potion bottles?"

Constance nodded with a sad sigh.

"I'm sure he'll be glad to see you again . . . if we ever figure out how to get him back, of course," said Riff.

"I just need that last potion first. Let's get it quickly," Constance said, squirming past Riff toward the opening.

This opening had the shape of an L. Riff bent at the waist and managed to fit through. Constance slipped through easily, taking no notice of the opening's shape.

Riff was glad to see a similar room with a potion as he had seen the last time he had been through this tower. The same small room contained a hovering, gold-flecked potion in the centre. This potion, too, was crying. The pair walked up to it. There was a label on the potion with a series of raised bumps, like Braille. Probably Cipton language.

The potion floated just above Constance's head. With a small spring, she leapt into the air and snatched the bottle in her mouth. She then placed the potion on the ground and gently slithered over the label with the raised bumps.

"Same as the other two," she said.

Constance uncorked the top of the potion with her mouth and dripped a part of her blobby body's substance into the bottle. The golden liquid stirred and turned white. The tower rumbled and quavered. Riff gasped but caught a glance at Constance—she looked happier than he'd ever seen her.

The centre of the floor revealed a hole, and Riff and Constance tumbled through the innards of tower B6.

CHAPTER 12

THE QUEST FOR KNITSY'S SOUL

"**E**lbina, you and Clorin can go to tower J-one-five-two," Luna directed.

"Without you?" Elbina croaked. "I'm not sure I can do it without you."

Luna grabbed Elbina's shoulders. "Elbs, I know how brave you are. I've seen it! You've always had it in you. Do it for Ann Lou!"

Elbina swallowed hard. "Okay."

But Clorin started tugging at Luna's trousers. "I want to go with *you*!" he whined.

Luna was just about to push Clorin toward Elbina when she chirped, "It's okay. I can go on my own."

While Clorin wrapped himself firmly around Luna's leg, Luna looked up into Elbina's eyes. "You sure?"

"Positive." Elbina's eyes gleamed a spark of confidence as she smiled.

Luna hugged Elbina tightly. "Be careful, Elbs. I need you safe."

Elbina took Luna's comment with felicity. "Thanks, Sis. You be careful, too." She started walking, then looked back and signed "I love you" to her sister.

Luna smiled and held up her hand with the same sign back.

Luna bent down and patted Clorin on the back. "Ready?" she asked him kindly. He hopped off her leg, nodded with a smile, and took her hand in his claw. Together, they started down the row to the thirty-fifth tower. Along the way, they could hear the faint cries of the soul fragments that were trapped in the dimly lit, topmost rooms of the towers.

They reached tower A35 and looked up. Goosebumps formed on Luna's arms as she recognised Knitsy's voice coming from the top of the tower. Luna hurried Clorin through the small dark entrance at the tower's base. Clorin fit through it easily, but Luna had to crouch. Even so, she bumped her head. Wincing, she squatted lower and waddled in.

Torches lit up before them, revealing an even smaller opening in the wall in front of them. The opening behind them rumbled shut, causing Clorin to leap into Luna's arms. They were locked in the tower until they were finished. Clorin looked into Luna's eyes for reassurance, and she managed a smile as she let him down. He gulped as he stared at the next opening. He puffed his chest out and huffed a small, husky breath, then wriggled through the opening. Luna had a tougher time, but Clorin helpfully tugged on her arm, and eventually she broke free of the hole. She stood up in the dark chamber and dusted her hands on her trousers.

Torches lit up, revealing a round, high-ceilinged room similar to the one in the tower she and Riff had been in. However, there was no spiral staircase this time. Instead, a pan, like one on a set of balances, sat on the floor in the centre of the room. The pan was big enough to hold two people and was harnessed to a rope that ran up into the opening, through a series of four pulleys, and down again. The free end of the rope dangled high over their heads. In line with it, three boulders of different sizes hovered in mid-air.

"Do we need to go there?" Clorin pointed up to the opening.

Luna nodded. "Yes, we have to get up there somehow. I just need to figure out how. Let's see what's in the basket," Luna chirped, trying to sound carefree for Clorin's sake.

Clorin skipped over to the pan, jumped on it. Luna followed him on the pan and noticed a holographic panel in the centre. Clorin reached out his claw toward it.

"Don't touch it!" she yelped.

Clorin looked at her, wide-eyed.

"I'm sorry," Luna said. "I just want to be sure we don't make a mistake." She had no idea how to explain this scenario to a toddler when she couldn't even understand it herself.

Clorin lowered his arm to his side and kept quiet.

The wordless panel depicted the three boulders in order of size. Apparently they were supposed to choose one. Luna peered up again at the pulleys. She remembered learning about them in school. Pulleys were typically used to lift heavy loads with less force required to do the actual lifting. Luna also noticed that above the opening but below the pulleys was a scanner emitting a red beam across the diameter of the room. Parallel to the beam was a large axe—ready to be swung, she assumed, if they failed the challenge.

Luna considered their objective. In order to raise the pan, a mass had to be attached to the hook at the free end of the rope. Presumably that was what the boulders were for. But there were three boulders. Which was the correct boulder to choose? It would make sense, she thought, to choose the heaviest one—to get them up there quickly.

But then she looked at little Clorin and reconsidered. If she chose too heavy of a boulder, they'd be lifted past the opening and into the scanner beam, triggering the axe to slice them to their deaths. The pan had room for two, but Clorin was pretty small. Surely the largest boulder was meant for a load heavier than one adult and one child. So Luna decided it had to be either the medium boulder or the small one. But which one? If she chose the small one, there was a chance they might not even be lifted all the way up to the opening.

Luna closed her eyes in thought. When pulleys are stacked on top of each other, the load is spread evenly among them. There were four pulleys here, so, essentially, a boulder one-quarter of Luna and Clorin's combined mass would pull them up. The hook was much closer to the ceiling than the floor, so the maths worked out in her head. The boulder would need a much longer trip downward than they would need upward. The smallest boulder looked the right size according to her calculations.

Luna gulped. Of all the times in her life she had wanted to be correct, she was really hoping this would be one of them. "Clorin," she croaked. "Would you like to tap the picture of the littlest boulder?" She pointed. "Right there."

Clorin jumped happily and jabbed his claw into the correct picture. They watched as the smallest of the three levitating boulders floated over and attached itself to the hook at the end of the rope. They heard a short buzz, and the small boulder became subject to gravity and started moving toward the floor. The pan started to rise—slowly, compared to the boulder, but steadily, much to Luna's relief. Clorin peered over the rim of the pan.

"So high!" he shrieked.

Luna's heart hammered as they inched closer to the opening and the scanner beam that would trigger the axe. The boulder reached the floor, and the pan was perfectly level with the opening.

"Oh, thank goodness," Luna sighed, wiping sweat from her forehead.

Clorin began to clamber off the pan.

"Careful!" said Luna as she steadied him on the landing. Then she, too, scrambled off.

They walked side by side through the next opening. The torches lit up, and they saw a catapult on one side of the room. Luna had the glum thought that she and Clorin would be the projectiles. On the opposite wall were a target and, above it, another opening.

"Looks like we get to take another ride," said Luna.

Clorin ran over to the catapult and hoisted himself into the main bowl, and Luna climbed in after him. Inside the bowl was a cup-like seat. Luna sat in the seat, and Clorin jumped in her lap. Immediately the torches around the room dimmed and the ones around the target grew brighter. Then a slingshot, its pouch loaded with a ball of fire, materialised in front of them.

"Oh, no," thought Luna. Although the Time Belt had restored her eyesight, she didn't know if she had enough hand-eye coordination for this task.

"Can I try?" Clorin asked.

"Erm . . ." Luna hesitated. She guessed that their accuracy at hitting the target with the slingshot would determine the accuracy of the catapult. If the catapult's aim was off, they would hit the wall hard. But Luna didn't trust herself to make this shot—and she figured if anyone had a coordinated bone in their body, it would be Clorin, son of two Pyroll champions.

"Sure, Clorin. Go for it."

Clorin held the slingshot in his left hand. With his right claw, he pulled back the band and the ball of fire, bringing them up close to his nose. He closed one eye, took aim, and then released the slingshot with a small huff. The ball of fire arced away. Luna pressed her head back into the seat and slammed her eyes shut.

A small *ping* against the target triggered the release of the catapult. Luna whisked open her eyes and held Clorin's small arm as they flew through the air toward the target. On their downward arc, they made the landing in front of the opening.

"Good shot!" said Luna, hugging Clorin. "How did you do that?"

Clorin beamed with pride and said, "I pretended I was throwing the Pyroll to Riff!"

Luna had landed awkwardly, scraping her leg on the landing. Small beads of blood dripped down her leg, but she was more concerned with checking Clorin for bumps and bruises. His arm was leaking a tiny bit of eelich. Luna knelt and applied pressure to the wound until the flow of the smoky substance stopped. Clorin didn't seem to mind. He just pointed excitedly with his other arm toward the next opening.

In front of them was a triangular opening. They tiptoed through it and found themselves in a dimly lit room that was identical to the one at the top of the previous tower. The sounds of Knitsy's cries filled their ears. A small bottle floated in the middle of the room. Luna ran up to the bottle and stared at it closely, her pupils dilating in the dim light. The bottle was filled with a golden substance, and Knitsy's wails were coming from within. Beads of sweat formed on Luna's forehead. Hearing Knitsy's cries added to the grief of her mother's and Ann Lou's deaths. But Knitsy was alive. Just in pieces. She could see her again. Luna's heart started to pound.

She snatched the potion bottle from the air. This time there was no shock. She peered at the small label. Instead of raised dots, this one had words she could read: *Prove you are part of me, to which I ask one simple plea. Give to me what keeps you alive so that I may properly fertilise.*

Luna quickly uncorked the bottle and held it against her leg so that fresh drops of blood could enter the opening of the bottle. The cool glass of the potion bottle against her skin felt comforting. It felt like a small embrace from Knitsy. Luna watched as the golden liquid swirled and transformed into an opaque white liquid.

"Nan, we're coming. I promise," she whispered.

The entire tower shook and rumbled. The centre of the floor opened up, and Luna and Clorin slid down through the belly of tower A35, landing on the ground outside.

* * *

Elbina walked along row J, whispering to herself as she counted the towers. "One forty-nine . . . one fifty . . . one fifty-one . . . one fifty-two." Tower J152 was shorter than the ones around it. Elbina hoped that meant the potion would be easy to reach. Knitsy's cries, faint but distinct, were emanating from the dimly lit room at the top of the tower. She ran through the dark opening without a second thought.

Instantly the floor dropped out from under her, and she was free-falling through blackness. She screamed and reached out with her hands, but there was nothing to grab onto. Finally, she landed, uninjured. Something had cushioned her fall. When her eyes adjusted to the dim light, she saw that she was sitting on a pile of bones that essentially made up the entire floor space of the room. She shrieked and scrambled off the pile. As she stood up and brushed white bone dust from her clothes, she saw a basket on the floor in front of her. It looked like the sort of basket one sees on a hot-air balloon. Above the basket were some beams that looked like supports for a balloon. A deflated red cloth was draped over one of the beams.

Elbina looked up into the dark passage through which she had fallen. High above was a tiny dot of light, only a little larger than a pinhole. Elbina wondered if it was the light at the top of the tower, where the potion was. If so, she thought, it must be very high up.

Cautiously, Elbina walked over to the balloon basket. It was just large enough to hold her, but it didn't seem very sturdy. It was made of a papery material. She climbed very carefully over the side and into the basket. In its centre were two crankshafts that were perpendicular to one another. She seized the crank of the horizontal shaft and pulled with all her might, trying to rotate it clockwise, but it would not move. Next, she tried to rotate the vertical crank. It gave way easily, and after only one revolution, a flame appeared under the deflated cloth and beams. Elbina watched as the cloth began to inflate and expand into the shape of a balloon. Beads of sweat formed on her face and ran down her cheeks. When she let go of the crank to catch her breath, the flame went out, and the cloth deflated to its original form.

"Ughhh!" she grunted. "Why is nothing easy?" She pulled her long hair away from her eyes and tucked it behind her neck.

She turned the vertical crank again and again, reinflating the balloon. After several revolutions, she felt herself being lifted off the ground.

"Ah!" she exclaimed, amazed at her progress.

She continued to crank the shaft as fast as she could. The balloon floated higher, lifting her upward slowly. Then a bump startled her. The basket was scraping against the wall of the passage. The fragile material of the basket was shredding rapidly as it dragged along the rough surface.

Elbina desperately grabbed the other crank and found that it was much easier to turn now that the basket was off the ground. The balloon-and-basket contraption zigzagged toward the opposite wall but also began to descend now that she was neglecting the other crank.

"No!" she shouted. She gripped one crank in each hand. By turning them both, she was able to steer the basket in a fairly straight line.

Elbina was so focused on coordinating the two mechanisms that she didn't realise she was fast approaching the opening in the wall through which she needed to pass. The balloon carried her past the opening. She gasped and quickly let go of both cranks, hoping she'd float back down to the landing. Suddenly an intense warmth washed over her. She looked up to notice that the fabric of the balloon had caught on fire. That pinhole of light she'd seen earlier wasn't the top of the tower—it was a fiery blockage.

The fire quickly spread to the flimsy basket. Elbina felt her shoes burning from beneath her. Her hope drained. She had assured her sister—her best friend—that she would be okay on her own. She'd been as confident as Luna or Ann Lou or their mother, but now it seemed there was no way she would make it out alive. She concluded she was neither as smart nor as strong as any of them. Now they'd all be stuck in the Time Belt forever—because of her.

Then Elbina caught herself. If this was the end, she didn't want to go with self-deprecation radiating through her body. She'd go like a hero, just as her sister and mother had.

Elbina jumped up, pushing off the basket floor with every ounce of strength she had left. Mid-flight, she could feel the fire burning through her jumper. To her utter shock, she dropped squarely onto the landing. She ripped off her jumper and rolled around. Her face ached and burned. And her arms. And her legs. She clung to the edge of the landing and looked down at the balloon contraption as it fell into the depths of the tower. Fire consumed the cloth, and the basket remains floated around her as feathery ashes.

She had done it. She survived. Perhaps she wasn't as feeble and useless as she believed. Elbina trembled as she got up. She touched her face with her fingertips, then winced and fell on her back as the burning sensation surged through her body in a fiery wash. As much as she wanted to writhe in pain, she knew Knitsy needed her. She had to keep moving.

Elbina sucked back her urge to cry and limped through the next opening. She found a completely different scenario in front of her eyes. Another opening was right across the room from her, but a gaping divide separated her from safety. There was a vertical pole next to her and another one across the divide. Attached to the poles were two ropes that extended across the divide, one about five feet above the other.

Elbina took several deep breaths, then reached a shaky hand out and lightly touched one of the ropes. Ignoring the pain that ripped through her hand, she tugged on the rope to check its sturdiness. It seemed secure.

Elbina gripped the top rope with both fists, then stepped onto the bottom rope. Her body was now suspended above the divide. One wrong move, and her time was up.

As Elbina crept slowly along the ropes, she managed to smile for a few peaceful moments as she thought of Hayden. What would he think of her latest achievement? He'd be so proud of her! He'd swing her around in a circle and embrace her tightly. She thought of his shining green eyes, warm dark skin, wavy black hair, and his wonderfully exuberant smile. She wished more than anything she could hold his hand again, kiss him deeply, and make him his favourite foods while he told her stories of Epiton. Then she could brag about the work she was doing with the ERA, and he'd be even more proud. And Luna! How proud she would be!

Elbina was so immersed in her thoughts that she hadn't noticed that the two ropes had slowly rotated as she crept along. She was now oriented upside down. Upon realising her new position, she looked back at the pole where she had started from. It was coiled around itself, as if it were made of a rubbery material. The other pole had also begun to do the same. The distance between the two ropes was fluctuating rapidly, straining Elbina's limbs to their extremes. The poles were twisting, swaying, and wiggling in circles—and Elbina was only halfway across the divide. Struggling to hold on, Elbina hooked her feet around one of the ropes and swiftly pulled herself hand over hand. She was twisting and turning so often that she couldn't even see clearly in front of her. Then the pole she was heading toward recoiled suddenly, flinging Elbina with such force that she lost her footing and the grip of one hand.

"Ahhh!" she bawled. She hung onto the rope even though the skin on her fingertips was breaking open. The pain was unbearable.

The self-deprecating thoughts re-entered her brain as fear of death seized her. Elbina stared into the abyss. She wondered if it would be better to let go. Would anyone care if she was gone? Luna and Riff could get through this no problem without her help. They didn't really need her. She looked up at her bleeding fingertips and was ready to release her grip when the other rope caught her from underneath, pushing her back into position. Stunned, she pulled herself the rest of the way across without thinking further, then hopped to safe ground.

Elbina watched as the poles returned to their original vertical forms. She kept watching, frozen, until the ropes across the divide stopped swaying. How had she managed to escape death? Could it have been the spirit form of her mother? Or Ann Lou, making sure she kept going? She was needed. She was worthy.

"Thanks, Mum. Thanks, Ann Lou," she said tearfully, tasting blood from her lips.

She picked herself up again and limped through the final opening. Before her was a floating potion bottle emitting cries that she recognised as Knitsy's. Elbina struggled to walk to the centre of the room. Very gently, she wrapped her ripped hands around the glass bottle holding the golden potion. She felt a sense of warmth envelop her as she held it close to her chest. She felt Knitsy in her presence. Perhaps Knitsy was the one who had saved her. She felt protected. Loved. Wanted.

Elbina noticed the scrawl on the label. *Prove you are part of me, to which I ask one simple plea. Give to me what keeps you alive so that I may properly fertilise.*

She thought in silence for a few moments. She tried reasoning as Luna would. *Give to me what keeps you alive.*

"Of course," she said breathlessly. There was blood all over her body, but the freshest was that on her fingertips. She squeezed a few fingers together to collect a small stream of blood in the top of the bottle. The liquid turned from golden to white with a quick swirling motion.

"I'm here, Nan. I've got you." Through tears of pain and relief, Elbina smiled.

The tower rumbled, and Elbina fell through the floor and slid safely to the ground outside tower J152.

* * *

Riff and Constance tumbled out of tower B6 with Constance's last potion securely tucked into her gelatinous stomach. Constance rolled to a graceful stop, only to be flattened when Riff landed on her.

"Sorry, mate," he said, though he was secretly happy to have landed on such a plushy cushion.

"Get off me, you massive Earthling! You're squishing me flat!"

Riff got up and peeled Constance off the stony ground so she could reconfigure herself into her usual blobby form. She shook herself back to normal and immediately bounced away without another word.

"Oi!" said Riff, galloping after her. "You're not off the hook yet!" He snatched her in his burly hands and held her in front of his face.

"How many times do I have to tell you not to pick me up!" Constance blubbered, trying her best to squirm out of his grip.

Riff scolded her. "The deal was we help you and you help us."

She relaxed to a goopy consistency and started dripping out between his fingers. Riff felt bad for her. "As soon as I get my potion, you won't have to work with me ever again. All right?"

Constance sighed. "Fine."

The two walked for ages past thousands of towers and eventually found their way to tower ZZ3. Once they made their way through the opening and into the first room, Riff was glad to see the opening just down a flight of about ten stairs and ahead just about twenty metres. To his left was a thick black tube on a stand. There was a box filled with some objects beneath it.

"The opening is just over there," Riff said. "Be careful, the stairs tend to move in these towers."

He and Constance cautiously made their way down the stairs and up to the opening, although this opening was blocked off by a giant metal door. Riff pushed against the door and Constance flattened herself against it, hoping it would budge. But it stayed sturdily shut.

"What do we do?" Riff asked. Constance shrugged her jelly shoulders.

Riff ran back up to the black tube and inspected it. It was lying horizontally on the stand. It had an on / off switch, currently set to off. Riff flipped the switch.

Instantly, a giant laser beam shone out of the tube. Riff heaved himself out of the way of the bright light. The beam's diameter was about the size of Riff's palm. It was collimating across the room and ending just above the metal door.

"Hmm," thought Riff. "Maybe we can melt the door."

He tried adjusting the laser and the stand but neither budged.

"Bollocks."

"What's in the box?" Constance asked.

Riff ruffled through the box of objects next to the laser. A few objects were mirrors, others were glass lenses about as big as Riff's head.

"I think we have to guide the beam to the door with these objects. Reminds me of when I was a kid back at school," Riff told Constance. "My friends, Matt and Joe, and I used to melt things when the teacher wasn't looking during science class. One time we managed to melt one of the legs on Matt's desk." Riff let out a hearty laugh and a smile spread. "We got in so much trouble."

"What's the point?" Constance asked, sternly.

"Oh, erm, right. We can probably use these mirrors to guide the beam to hit the door. Let me show you."

Riff walked down a few steps and, dodging the beam's intense light as stealthily as he could, held one of the mirrors at an angle downward from the beam.

"See, the beam bounces off the mirror and now it's hitting the ground. I wish I could just hold this mirror in place somehow—oh! It stays on its own."

The mirror stayed in mid-air in the orientation Riff held it. He then placed a second mirror at a forty-five-degree angle to the stairs, which also held itself in place.

"So now the beam is also bouncing off of this mirror. And the beam is directed perfectly at the centre of the door," Riff said.

He rushed over to the door to watch the beam. Constance slithered over and the two waited for something to happen. The door stayed perfectly intact.

"Nice going, genius," Constance snarled. "Now we have a laser beam that could blind you *and* a sealed shut metal door!"

Riff thought for a moment. There had to be something else in the box. He rushed over to look at its contents. There were two giant clear glass lenses, one whose two sides were convex, and the other whose two sides were concave.

Riff hurried back over to the bottom of the stairs just in front of the door. He held up the concave lens in front of the beam. The beam spread out wider on the door.

"Nope, not that one," said Riff. "We want the beam to focus on one spot on the door. That might make it melt. Let's try this lens."

Riff held up the convex lens in front of the beam and, consistent with his hypothesis, the beam focused to a single point on the metal door. Within seconds, the door started to melt.

"It's working!" Riff exclaimed. "I can't believe it! Wait till Luna hears about this!"

Riff punched the air in victory while they waited for the remainder of the door to melt into a puddle. Once there was a hole big enough for the two of them, the laser beam shut off and the floating optical components fell from mid-air.

Riff smiled at Constance. "Bring on the next challenge."

The two entered the next room, which was completely dark. They were immediately shackled and pinned to the wall. Riff couldn't move either of his arms, and he hung from his tethered hands. Then torches lit around a large circular room.

Riff gulped. "I think I see why that door before had been sealed shut . . ."

Before them was a giant creature—more like a monster. The monster was brown all over and had saliva dripping from its mouth, which contained a set of razor-sharp teeth—no, three rows of them. Spikes poked out of every inch of its head, four legs, and two tails. Its body was oozing what looked like lava from pores that patterned the entirety of its torso.

It was humming a low growl, and its yellow eyes and black slits of pupils were fixated on Riff and Constance. Riff could just make out an opening right behind the monster. They had to somehow free themselves of these chains, avoid the monster's clutches, and get through the opening.

"Constance, it's been a pleasure," Riff said, half crying. "I think we're monster meat."

The monster still stared them down, licking its lips and revealing more razor-sharp teeth in its hideous mouth.

"Every monster has a weakness. Is there something in the room that you see that might be able to help?" Constance asked.

Riff moved his eyes to look around the room rather than his head—he didn't dare make any sudden movements in case the monster lunged. And then he saw it. An ice block. It was about the same size as a big boulder and was off to the side of the room.

"There's an ice block over to the left. I have no clue what it's used for. But it's something," Riff said in a whisper, trying to reduce the movement of his lips.

"Perfect," said Constance. "You try your best to stay alive."

"What are you—" Riff started.

But Constance had already slipped out of her shackles and flopped on the ground.

This movement angered the monster, and it let out a grim shriek that shook the tower. It curled up its back, and its torso started to bubble beneath the surface. It let out another shriek as it uncurled its back and spurts of fire began shooting out of its pores.

Flames ripped toward Riff, and he screamed as several of them hit his hands squarely in the palms. The pain coursed through his hands, and he writhed in place, hoping to unshackle himself, but the chains were too strong.

Riff searched the room for Constance, and he found her slithering toward the ice block. She looked as if she'd been struck with the fire-balls, but her gelatinous exterior kept her safe from harm.

"Constance, help!" Riff yelled.

The monster focused its attention on Riff now. It pawed at the ground and pounced.

"Arghhh!"

But then Riff's left hand had been freed from the chains. The monster had tripped over something and one of its tails slashed the chain off. Now Riff dangled from his right hand. He could see that Constance had managed to flatten herself and trip the monster. She returned to her blobby form and headed back to the ice block. She started to push on it.

The monster had regained its stance and again glared at Riff. It leaped toward him, but Riff managed to swing himself out of the way in time. The monster smashed its head into the stone wall of the tower. It shook bits of rock from its face and growled at Riff. It bared its deadly sets of teeth and lunged again. The teeth caught Riff's right hand, setting him free but causing a massive cut across his forearm. Riff fell to the hard ground and rolled away as a tail came straight for his head. Blood trickled down his arm and painted the ground he rolled on, as well as his clothes. He gritted his teeth, climbed to his feet, and took off in Constance's direction.

The monster shrieked again as it curled and uncurled its back. Its pores shot out another round of fireballs toward Riff and Constance. They hid behind the ice block but heard sizzling sounds as the fire started to melt it.

"Push!" shouted Riff.

Riff and Constance slid the ice block toward the monster as it lunged for a bite at their heads. Narrowly missing the attack, Riff and Constance continued pushing the ice block until it met the monster's skin.

"It's not doing anything!" Riff said, covering his eyes in fear.

"Just be patient!" retorted Constance.

The monster curled its back again, its pores ready to bubble and spew. It shrieked even louder than before, causing Riff to cover his ears.

But then, as the monster uncurled its back, it shrieked in a higher pitch, sounding more like it was wounded. The ice block was preventing it from producing fire and decreasing its health all at once.

"Now, while it's distracted!" Riff exclaimed.

Riff scooped Constance in his arms and ran for the small opening just ahead of him. It was metres away, feet, inches . . .

Riff dove just as the monster lunged at his legs. He tucked and rolled through the opening, which was much too small for the monster to get through. The monster let out one last shriek of defeat and walked away. Riff and Constance took a few moments to catch their breath. They were both happy to find another potion floating in front of them. But as Knitsy's cries filled the small room, Riff felt helpless. He had always been particularly close to Knitsy, and hearing her in distress was painful. Riff walked up to the potion bottle and read its label aloud.

"'*Prove you are part of me, to which I ask one simple plea. Give to me what keeps you alive, so that I may properly fertilise.*' What does that mean?" he asked Constance.

Constance knew she owed Riff some sort of thank you. She told him, "Remember that I had to put part of myself in my potion? Maybe you can put in some of that stuff that I can smell coming off you."

"Right," remarked Riff. He uncorked the potion and was enveloped by the sounds of his grandmother. He positioned his bloody palm above the opening of the vial and dripped a few drops of blood into the gleaming golden liquid. As the blood mixed into the solution, the potion turned white.

"I've got you, Nan. We're nearly there," Riff whispered to the blood-stained bottle.

The floor beneath them opened up with a rumble, and Riff and Constance tumbled down and out of tower ZZ3.

CHAPTER 13

A Soul's Reunion

Luna and Clorin ran through the grid of towers in Galalok with their focus on reaching the large tower on the south side of the town as fast as they could. The south tower appeared enormous from row A, so Luna imagined how large it would actually be once they reached the end of the seemingly endless rows of towers.

As they reached row AC, Luna noticed someone limping a short distance away from them. It was too dark to distinguish who it was in the spooky moonlight. Clorin gripped Luna's shirt and froze. Luna knelt down to him and tried not to look or sound hurried.

"It's okay, Clorin. I'm here to keep you safe. We have a long way to go, so let's keep moving, okay?"

Clorin nodded. Suddenly the stranger tripped on a cobblestone and fell to the ground. The stranger didn't even try to get back up. That, or they were unable to.

"D-do we help?" whispered Clorin, pointing a shaky claw toward the stranger.

Luna hesitated. She wanted to go quickly in case her siblings were waiting for them or, worse, needed help. But Clorin was right. The stranger was clearly in distress.

They slowly approached the prone figure. It appeared to be a human. The person's arms, legs, and face were bloodied up and burnt. Luna's heart sank when she recalled how few humans were actually in the Time Belt. The only ones she had come across were her family. The moonlight contoured the figure's bony build and protruding cheekbones with an eerie glow. Luna darted to the stranger's side and knelt.

"Elbina? Elbina! Are you all right?" Luna rolled her sister over and brushed the hair away from her face.

Elbina's eyes fluttered. She made some gurgling noises, but no words came from her burnt lips.

Luna shook her sister gently. "You need to stay with me, Elbs. Say something!"

Elbina weakly reached into her trouser pocket and shakily pulled out the white potion.

Luna took it with a sigh of relief and put it with her potion in her flannel pocket. Her face welled up with tears. "Elbs, you've done so well. I'm so proud of you! And so is Nan. And Mum. And Ann Lou. You—you've helped us all so much."

Elbina's head rolled to the right side. Her breathing was laboured.

"No!" shouted Luna. "You are not going anywhere! Let's get you some help!"

Luna lifted Elbina from the ground as gracefully as she could. Even as a twenty-one-year-old, Elbina was still extremely light to carry, even for Luna. Luna didn't exactly have a direction in mind once she had situated Elbina on her back. Should they go back to Vivalok? There must be a doctor there, or at least some creatures with an understanding of basic human physiology. Or maybe there was someone in the giant tower who could help, but that tower was still hundreds of rows away. Luna stepped forward, then backward, unsure where to go. She had to help her sister. The fact that she had not kept an eye on Ann Lou on Vivalok before her disappearance pained Luna to her core, and she needed to make up for it. She decided to continue in the direction of the giant tower. Focalok was within reach, and that was their last stop, she figured. Elbina just needed to stay alive long enough for them to escape, however that was meant to happen.

With Elbina on her back, Luna started to run down the cobblestone path, holding her sister's limp arms close to her chest. Clorin ran at her heels. He would pass her every so often but then fall back to let her lead. By the time they reached row CD, Luna was gasping for air. She stopped and put Elbina down, leaning her against her legs as comfortably as she could. Elbina's head hung as if she were asleep.

"I can help!" said Clorin.

Luna explained gently, "You're too small, Clorin. You can't carry her."

"I can carry anything," Clorin said. He then pulled Elbina over his small shoulder, taking care not to hurt her with his claws. Her torso hung over his small shoulder, and her legs hung down his back. Clorin didn't even seem to be bothered by the added weight. He just huffed, puffed his chest out, and zoomed off toward the giant tower.

Luna watched in awe as Clorin disappeared into the darkness. She had nearly forgotten that he was part Epitonian. Due to his frequent episodes of anxiety, he did not display the hubris and fearlessness of the typical Epitonian, but he certainly possessed Epitonian strength. Even at his young age, Clorin was far stronger and faster than a human adult.

Luna ran in the direction Clorin had gone, toward the giant tower that loomed over the rest of Galalok. She was slowed somewhat by lingering stiffness in the leg she had injured in the tower with Riff. As she ran, she wondered if Riff had made it through the tower for Constance's relative and the one for Knitsy all right, and she hoped that Constance hadn't abandoned him. Luna also thought about Elbina and how amazing she was. Luna felt horrible for assigning her a particularly dangerous tower—and yet, despite being all by herself, despite her injuries, Elbina had managed to get Knitsy's potion. Luna's thoughts turned dark, wondering what her life would be like without Elbina in it.

"No," she muttered to herself. "Not while I'm still fighting."

At row ZZ, one row before the south tower, Luna stopped to catch her breath. The shape of the south tower was unlike that of any of the other towers she'd come across so far. It was rectilinear, like the skyscrapers Luna had seen in her school textbooks. It was so tall that its topmost point was indiscernible from the darkness of the sky around it.

"Zed Zed," Luna recalled out loud. It occurred to her then that she had sent Riff and Constance to tower ZZ3. She ran past the first two towers in the row, then stopped and listened. Not only did she hear Knitsy's cries, but she also heard piercing screams that belonged to her brother. She felt a stabbing pain in her stomach.

"Riff!" she shouted. She looked up and down the tower, but the only entrance was the one at the base, and it was sealed. She tried again. "Constance! Help him!" But there was no way they could hear her. All she could do was wait. After she had paced around the circumference of the tower about five times, the entrance opened, and Riff and Constance tumbled out.

"Riff!" Luna shouted again, running to his aid. She noticed his bloodstained shirt, and then her eyes turned to his palms, which were burnt. She knelt down and placed her hands on his shoulders. "Are you all right? What happened?"

Riff, still sitting on the ground, nodded calmly. "Constance got us through the first tower, no problem." He smiled at Constance, who, much to Luna's surprise, gave him a weak smile in return. "This tower, though." Riff looked down at his trainers in embarrassment. "I thought I was going to be monster kibble."

"You're okay, though," said Luna. "I'm relieved." Then she hesitated, not wanting to sound dismissive of the ordeal he had just been through. "Did you . . . manage to get the potion?"

Riff reached into his pocket and pulled out something with his thumb and index finger. Shakily, he lifted his hand up in front of Luna's face and showed her a small bottle.

"Brilliant, Riff! Just brilliant!" said Luna excitedly. "We have them all!" Riff smiled in return.

Then Luna heard a slithering noise beside them. She whirled her head around in anger and snapped at Constance, "And where are you going?"

Constance sighed and turned around. "The deeper-voiced Earthling said—"

Riff broke in. "Let her go, Luna. She's been really helpful. We have to let her do what she needs to do."

"Fine. Go, then!" Luna shouted at her. Constance drooped slightly but continued away from them.

"I told you she helped me," said Riff. "You don't have to be nasty to her."

"I just—seeing you like this, all bloodied up . . . I just feel like she . . . well, I feel like she could have done more." Luna collapsed on the ground next to Riff. This was the first time she had stopped to gather her thoughts since leaving Elbina with Clorin. She buried her face in her hands.

Riff gingerly placed his uninjured arm on Luna's knee, avoiding contact with his palm. "Luna, it's going to be okay. We've got all of the potions. We can get Nan back. We're all okay."

"But we're not," Luna choked. "Elbina's not fine. She's nearly dead. And Ann Lou. I didn't save her. Now I know why Mum was so protective of me. She did a much better job watching us than I have."

"You can't put that much pressure on yourself. It's not your job to watch us. We're not little kids anymore. We all wanted to help get each other out of here. And . . . if that meant only a couple of us would leave in the end, I don't think any of us would have done anything differently. That's what family is for."

Luna went over Riff's words in her mind. He was right. Their family was brave—braver than any other family she knew. The McHubbards were a special family. Oddities and all, they were hers. And she was theirs.

"So," said Riff, "not to put the pressure back on or anything, but where is Elbina? Why did you say she was nearly dead?"

Luna hopped to her feet. "Clorin took her to the south tower. They must be inside waiting for us. We need to find help for her!"

Luna helped Riff up and led him to the entrance of the south tower.

"Whoa," said Riff, admiring its size.

"Let's go!" said Luna.

The two ran up a set of stone stairs toward the opening, which was disproportionately small compared to the size of the tower. Luna knelt in front of the dark opening, which was about the size of a dog door, and crawled through on her hands and knees. Riff followed her through, using his elbows instead of his hands.

Once inside, they stood up carefully in the complete darkness. Luna half expected a line of torches to light up in front of her eyes, but after a few moments, a twinkle of light flickered. It was just a speck at first, but then it multiplied into many specks throughout the room. The lights floated slowly around them, bringing Luna a peaceful feeling amidst the stressful situation.

"Looner?"

Through the specks of light, Luna saw Clorin in the corner of the room. She rushed over to him and embraced his small body. "Where's Elbina?"

Clorin pointed with his claw. Elbina was slumped on the floor nearby. A few specks of light floated past her face, and Luna saw that patches of her hair were missing and her face was nearing unrecognisable, except for her bony features.

"Elbs!" Riff cried, running to her. He tried to hold her face with the sides of his hands.

"Be careful!" Luna scolded. "You could hurt her!"

Riff tenderly brushed her cheek. "What do we do?"

"I—I don't know," said Luna.

Then Clorin tapped Riff's shoulder. "Riff?" he asked, pointing to the other side of the room. "What's that?"

More specks of light materialised, filling the room with a soft glow, and their gazes fell upon a circular dais with a soft light glimmering from within it. They walked over to inspect it and crept up the set of stairs. The light was coming from a shimmering pool of white liquid at the top step. Luna noticed three empty potion bottles on a stair nearby.

"Give me your potion, Riff," Luna directed, holding her hand out toward him.

Riff obeyed and shuffled through his pockets again for the white potion he had obtained. Luna took it and uncorked it, and Knitsy's cries filled the room. Luna tipped the bottle, pouring its contents into the pool.

"Are you sure you know what you're doing?" Riff asked.

"Looner always knows what to do," said Clorin.

Ripples formed in the shimmering pool, followed by waves that sloshed and then settled back down. Luna then took the other two bottles from her pocket. She uncorked them, wincing at the sound of Knitsy's cries, and then dumped them both into the pool. Choppy waves formed in the pool and grew to a height of a few metres, then died down again. Riff, Luna, and Clorin watched, mesmerised, as all the specks of light flowed together and formed one large bubble of light above the pool. The bubble radiated warmth and floated down into the pool and burst, releasing sparks of light that rained down into the pool. Again, the liquid rose, but this time it formed a luminous white shape. Sparkles formed inside it, first white but soon developing into all the colours of the rainbow. The sparkles swirled around and painted in the details so familiar to Luna and Riff: the slim figure, the short hair, the cane.

"Nan?" cried Riff. Neither he nor Luna knew what to do. Could they touch her? Could she even see them?

A torch behind them illuminated the room, and their questions were answered. Knitsy held out an arm in front of her and gasped in awe at her physical form. She looked up then and saw Riff and Luna standing there. A smile spread across her face, and she stepped wobblishly down the dais with her cane and onto the floor. Luna and Riff embraced her. Luna breathed in the scents of black tea and smoke that were still in Knitsy's clothes after all these years.

"You guys found me," Knitsy croaked. "I didn't know if I would ever get out of there."

Riff and Luna stood back and looked at their frail grandmother. Her clothes were the same as they always were. She wore an ankle-length dark green skirt and a white turtleneck with gold earrings and a string of pearls around her neck. Her wedding ring was on her finger as it always had been, and her cane was the same one that she regularly smacked Riff in the leg with. Her white hair was done just as nicely as always, almost as if she hadn't been trapped in three potion bottles for however long she had been here. She looked no older than the last time they had seen her when she disappeared in the Time Belt's vortex. The only difference about Knitsy physically was that she appeared to be breathing just fine. No coughing fits ensued.

"You must've been so scared, Nan," Riff said, helping her take a seat on the outer rim of the stage. "They kept you all bottled up in there for all this time?"

"It was scary. Even though I was in there, I could see you. You're able to keep an eye on your family while you're in the Time Belt, but nothing else. You probably heard my potions weeping a bit loudly," she confessed, blushing.

"So you know everything?" Luna asked.

Knitsy nodded. "Ann Lou. Your poor mother. Elbina. And him," she said, gesturing with her chin toward Clorin. "I figured that devilish-looking husband of Ann Lou's would make for some strange offspring."

"Nan, he's really sweet. He's your great-grandson," said Luna, putting her arms around Clorin.

Knitsy chortled and smiled at him. "Come give your great-granny a hug, young lad."

With some gentle urging from Luna, Clorin stepped forward nervously and took Knitsy's hand in his claw. Then he smiled and hugged her.

"See?" said Knitsy. "I can be sweet sometimes."

"Nan," said Riff, "what do we do about Elbina? She looks really ill."

"Nothing we can do now, I'm afraid. If she's alive, that's enough for now. We just have to get out of here, and then she'll be back to normal."

"So you know how to get out of here?" asked Luna.

"Not a clue," Knitsy responded.

Luna sighed. "Well, Ann Lou gave us a bit of a lead. We just need to get to Focalok."

Knitsy pointed to an octagonal-shaped opening along the wall in front of them. "Right through there."

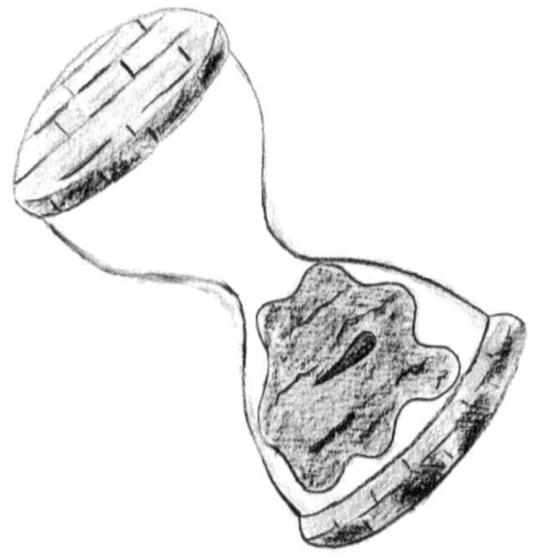

CHAPTER 14

FOCALOK

There it was. The passageway to Focalok. They were nearly there.
"Let's go! We need to hurry to give Elbina a fighting chance!"
Luna gestured to everyone to get up.

Knitsy looked down at her shoes in humiliation. Luna cocked her head. "Are you all right to go, Nan? We have to hurry!"

Knitsy shook her head. "I'm really sorry for all the pain I've put you through. I shouldn't have said what I said back in the Time Belt on the way to Harvinth. I was so selfish. I—I've caused too much hurt to this family." Luna watched a tear slide down her cheek, something she had never seen before.

"Nan," Riff said in a warm tone. "I've just given this talk to Luna. You were anything but selfish. Wanting your daughter to stay alive instead of you? Any of us would have switched places with her if we had the chance. You were really brave."

Knitsy's head slowly rose, and she gaped at Riff with tearful eyes. "I've missed you, my boy."

He kissed her on her head. "Let's go. I'll help you." He held out an arm for her to take. She took it and walked unsteadily toward the opening with Riff, who also trembled as he walked.

Luna ran over to Elbina and picked up her head in her hands. "Clorin, do you feel comfortable carrying her again?"

"Can I have chocolate cake after?" Clorin asked.

"You can have as much cake as you want once we get out of here. I promise."

"Woo hoo!" Clorin hooted. He carefully put Elbina over his shoulder again. Riff and Knitsy went through the opening first, and Clorin followed.

Luna went through last. Finding herself in complete darkness, she followed the sound of the others' footsteps. Soon a small pinhole of light appeared. She squinted at it, wondering what it could possibly be. Then the pinhole started to grow exponentially, blanketing Luna with bright white light and a warm, blustering wind. She had experienced this warm light several times in her life now. She knew exactly where she was—or, at least, exactly what she was about to experience.

Rhapsodic orchestral sounds filled Luna's ears as the warm light completely surrounded her. The floor beneath her feet disappeared, and she stopped running. She tumbled forward through the white space as images of her life popped up all around her. She watched herself on her first birthday, sticking her nose into a cake. She saw herself as a toddler, unwrapping a book on Christmas. She saw herself receiving all As on her report card and losing her two front teeth. Millions of other memories surrounded her, too, many of them taking the form of sounds, smells, tastes, or tactile sensations, since she hadn't had her eyesight for most of her adult life. Her fingertips felt her favourite lines from a book in Braille. She heard her family's cries as they struggled through Cipto during the Planetary Diagnostic test. She tasted stews Elbina had made for dinner, and she smelled Riff's cologne stinking up the hallway at their home in Portsmouth. A feeling of euphoria flooded her body and mind as she re-lived these memories. As her senses were flooded with more memories, she felt her body being lifted higher and higher.

In most of Luna's earlier memories, many of them were visual since she still had sight in her childhood years. There was a man in a number of these memories that she did not recognise. Often he was standing next to her mother and smiling as Luna was doing the things toddlers do. Sometimes he was hugging her and kissing her cheeks. Could this be her father? During Luna's childhood, whenever Knitsy made remarks about him, Henrietta would quickly hush her up. Luna had always wanted to know about her dad, but the most she'd ever gotten out of Knitsy was that he left when Luna was five years old, never to be seen or heard from again. She got the sense then that she was supposed to hate him, but seeing him now in these memories, Luna thought he had kind eyes and a warm smile. Nothing in these memories suggested she should hate or fear him. He had a muscular build and was much taller than their mother. His untidy red hair resembled Riff's. In one memory, the man hugged Luna, and she could feel his warmth on her arms. As more memories streamed through her, she tried to pick out the ones of her dad and lock them in her brain. Then, during a memory of drinking a cup of her mother's tea, Luna closed her eyes. Suddenly she no longer felt her body tumbling through space. The memories stopped, seeming to fade away in the depths of the Time Belt, taking with them the warm blanket of happiness and leaving her with only sadness.

Luna opened her eyes. She and her family were now standing on a slate platform under a bright white sky. Clorin set Elbina down gently, and Riff and Knitsy stood guard near her as Luna placed her flannel under her head like a pillow. Luna turned to look around. The platform was circular and gave them a 360-degree panoramic view of Focalok. The light on Focalok was so bright that the land, if there was any, was as white as the sky. At the centre of the platform was a spiral ramp with the hourglass Jalopy at the top of it. Next to the Jalopy was an exact size replica of the Bank's sphere on Vivalok, but without its golden pipes and myriad clocks. The sphere at its top was completely full of black liquid Chroniya.

Luna saw also that they were not alone here in Focalok. The hooded figure from the Bank was standing near the Jalopy, and next to him was Constance. The hooded figure's husky voice broke the silence.

"Two families at once—what an unexpected bunce!"

Suddenly Luna saw a second Cipton alongside Constance. This Cipton was a bit larger than Constance but lacked her murky colour. This Cipton's body was so clear that Luna hadn't seen it at first.

"Where are we?" asked Riff.

"If you've managed to travel all this way, surely I shouldn't need to say," said the figure.

Luna stepped forward and spoke firmly. "We'd like to have our go at getting out of here. We know we have to travel to the past."

The figure shook its head. "Miss McHubbard, I appreciate your thirst, but you did not arrive here first. This family," he went on, gesturing toward the two Ciptons, "has shown me patience, so I ask for your simultaneous obeisance."

"But our sister is nearly dead!" Luna cried, pointing at Elbina's limp form. "We have to go first!"

Constance's gelatinous body bubbled with anger. "Do you think we're not hurt as well? Do you only think of yourself, you selfish Earthling? So what if she goes to Mortalok? Big deal! My father has been stuck in those potion bottles for many years!"

Constance's father touched her shoulder gently. "There, there, dear daughter. We must remember to be kind."

Luna felt at a loss. Each time the Bank filled up with Chroniya, only one escape attempt could be made—Tycho had been very clear about that. Constance and her father had beaten them to Focalok. There was nothing Luna could do to change that or expedite the process. She had to accept the situation and hope that Elbina could hold on until they got their turn. Luna glared at Constance, who mimicked her stance and stiffened her gelatinous structure. But Luna felt a wave of sadness for the Ciptons. They couldn't help themselves. They were doing the same thing she was: trying to escape their phantom existence in the Time Belt and get back to their lives on their home planet. Luna sighed, relaxed her posture, and exchanged her angry look for one of understanding. Constance relaxed slightly.

Luna spoke up, swallowing her pride. "Constance, I'm sorry for giving you such a hard time. I got lost in my own mission here. We're . . . really lucky to have found you."

Constance bowed her head and said, "Earthling, I . . . appreciate your understanding." Then she turned slightly and looked at the other Cipton, who nodded. Constance turned back around and looked at Riff next. "You are the one who deserves thanks. I wouldn't have my father back without you. You showed me kindness when few others did. I know I have been difficult at times. But I had to find him. We have to try and make things right for our dear planet Cipto."

"Very good, Connie," said the other Cipton warmly.

Luna burst out with a thought. "Hang on. Connie? As in Cipto's shining star?"

"Yes," she nodded. "That's me. And this is my father, Rodney."

Rodney reached out a blubbery hand to Luna. "How do you do, kind Earthling?" he asked.

Luna shook Rodney's hand with astonishment. "I thought you were just a fable."

"While we're lost in the Time Belt, we're all just fables," Rodney replied. "I wouldn't be surprised if your planet has fables of its own about you all. I'm sure Connie and I are all the rage on Cipto at the Storytelling Ceremonies."

Luna couldn't resist asking Rodney a question. "Pardon my bluntness, but aren't Ciptons supposed to be nice all the time? Your daughter had her moments, sorry to say."

"Luna, don't be rude to the blobs!" hissed Knitsy.

"No, ancient Earthling, it's a valid question," said Constance. Addressing Luna, she continued: "If you managed to pay any attention to our story, you know that I became quite ill. I lost my translucence, my personality . . . everything good about me in the eyes of Cipton society. That's why I'm this puddley colour rather than clear like my father. And it's why I've been short with you. But I simply cannot apologise. It is who I am now."

Luna nodded and held out her hand. "That's fair. Can we put our differences behind us?"

Constance squirmed in discomfort. "I don't particularly like you." Then she slithered over to Riff and held out a blobby hand. "But I like you."

Riff fist-bumped her and said, "The pleasure is all mine, Constance."

Rodney said, "We should be going, Connie. No time to waste."

The hooded figure raised a skeletal hand toward the Bank replica and recited, "At the expense of others, I ask you to drain. For there is a glimmer of hope that Rodney and Connie may no longer exist on this plane."

The level of the dark liquid in the Bank replica started moving downward, draining somewhere they couldn't see.

The hooded figure then waved his hand, and the stone at the top of the hourglass Jalopy opened. To the Ciptons, he said: "Your Jalopy is ready to go, but there is one last rule you must know. Only the inmate may travel back; Rodney must go alone to Cipto's pitch black. Should he complete the mission, dear Connie will be freed and disappear as fission. Should he fail, both of you shall end up in eternal jail. You will get no more chances, so make the most of your circumstances."

Rodney turned to Constance and held her jelly hands in his. The Ciptons' mouths curved upward into smiles.

Then Constance seemed to waver, her smile slightly dimming. "Do you know what to do, Father?"

Rodney replied cheerfully: "One of the multiverse's greatest story-tellers said it best: 'For you cannot be both lost and found, Only one suits the father of ticks and tocks.'"

Luna noticed his reference to E. Bowser III's poem, and she nudged Riff.

Then Rodney's smile faded also. "I apologise, dear daughter of mine. For getting us into this mess. I hope I can fix it."

"Don't worry, Father. I'm just so glad I got to see you again," Constance replied, her voice quavering.

Constance reached into her side and pulled out her orb. Carefully, she transferred it to Rodney's blobby hand. He put the orb in his mouth and swallowed it, then slithered up the ramp into the Jalopy and settled into a comfortable spot in the cinched part of the hourglass. The hooded figure waved his hand again, closing the Jalopy and sealing Rodney inside.

Connie and the McHubbards watched from the platform as the hourglass Jalopy accelerated upward and quickly disappeared into the white light of Focalok. Then the panoramic view of Focalok faded rapidly from white light to completely dark. Clorin panicked and started squealing with fright. Luna felt a sharp jab at her side and heard Knitsy start cursing under her breath.

"Ouch, Nan! Be careful with your cane. You'll hit Elbina!" Luna said. She held one arm around Clorin's shoulders, and another was holding Elbina's hand.

"I can't bloody see anything!" Knitsy growled, still poking around with her cane.

"What is going on?" Riff exclaimed.

The hooded figure's voice filled their ears. "This mission won't be one to experience with your eyes. It's a different sense you'll use to analyse."

Then they heard Rodney's voice in surround sound all throughout Focalok. He was talking to himself.

"Okay, Rod. You can do this. You must do this."

The McHubbards quickly realised their panoramic view had shifted to Rodney's perspective. They were listening to his mission unfold.

"Good luck, Father," Constance said under her breath.

CHAPTER 15

RODNEY'S MISSION

Rodney flew alone in his Jalopy out of the warm bright light of the Time Belt's grips and into the darkness of outer space. He was anxious to get to Cipto and wanted nothing more than to jump back into the routines of his old life there: the Storytelling Ceremonies, listening to the local Pyroll team practice, and bouncing along the roads as happy as can be. But first he had to complete one last task. There was no time for messing around, and certainly no room for error.

"Okay, Rod. You can do this. You must do this," he muttered to himself.

He knew what he had to do, to some extent, but executing the plan was the beastly task at hand. Rodney told the Jalopy to travel back to the time period right before Connie was born. In order to succeed, he'd have to make sure Connie became his daughter again. If she were to exist as his daughter on Cipto again this time around, that would mean she would technically be in existence both on Cipto and in the Time Belt. According to E. Bowser III's poem, one cannot exist in both realms, so Connie's rebirth as his daughter would break her out of the Time Belt. But it would be tricky. Very tricky.

Another difficult part would be finding the cure for Connie's illness. Her illness, after all, was why they had attempted to reverse time and ended up getting stuck in the Time Belt.

As the Jalopy zoomed past a supernova, Rodney started formulating his plan. He'd go back to the doctor first to find out which planet the cure is on and what he would need to do to get it. Then he would retrieve the cure and have it with him, all before Connie was born, so that he could give it to her as soon as her illness developed.

Rodney's thoughts were interrupted by the shuddering of the Jalopy as it entered the atmosphere of the dark planet of Cipto. More excited than scared, Rodney tightened up his body as the Jalopy descended. It landed on its side, then rolled to a stop. Rodney relaxed and let gravity pull him out of the neck of the hourglass. Then he slithered along the glass to the stone that sealed him in. He pushed against the stone gently, and it tipped onto the stony ground of Cipto with a thud. Rodney exited the Jalopy, shivering with joy as his body moved from the cool stone to the rocky ground of Cipto, the planet he so dearly missed.

He could hear a muffled commotion coming from perhaps fifty metres ahead of him. It was the familiar sound of a Storytelling Ceremony in progress at the arena. He headed toward the sound. As he drew nearer to the arena, he could hear Ciptons trading stories about their dreams of visiting other planets, their perspectives on what they thought stars looked like, and their take on skim versus whole Moolweep. He so badly wished he could take part in this ceremony. How the other Ciptons would praise him for the story of his travelling to the Time Belt and back! And his soul being stuck inside small bottles! And his daughter, Connie, so bravely collecting them all so that he could have a second chance to save her! They might think he was crazy, since technically Connie wasn't born yet and he'd be telling them stories of the future. But they would still listen and enjoy. It was the Cipton way to accept all stories with curiosity and wonderment. But he had to keep his head focused. He had to find the doctor. The doctor always attended these ceremonies. Occasionally the audiences would get rowdy, but Ciptons were generally very peaceful, so the doctor was usually free to listen in on some storytelling circles.

Rodney slithered into the arena, resisting his urge to join a circle and spew out everything he had encountered in the Time Belt, or would encounter. He bounced in excitement as he wove his way among the circles, each of which was aquiver with excitement. As Rodney passed by one circle, one Cipton recognised the sound of his slither.

"Rod!" said a haunting, silky voice. "Where have you been?"

Rodney stopped abruptly. His partner! How had he forgotten to keep an ear out for her? He had been so focused on finding the doctor and saving Connie that he had forgotten about the old friends and family he would run into.

"Avaira!" Rodney called back, slithering to her side. "Oh, I'm so happy to see you again! How have you been?"

"I just left you about twenty minutes ago at the hut, so I'd say that I'm doing very well," Avaira replied with joviality.

"Of course," said Rodney, trying his best to behave as the others expected. "Avaira, dear—can we form our own, more private circle? I have to tell you a story. It's important you hear it."

"Of course, Rod. Let's huddle a bit closer to the entrance. Toric is telling the story of the time he fell into the Pyroll arena; I can barely hear myself over his fortissimo."

As they slithered off together, Rodney said, "Do you know where Doctor Cornelia is?"

Avaira touched Rodney's shoulder with concern. "Are you hurt?"

"No, but . . . our family will be."

Avaira squirmed in discomfort but trusted her husband. "Doctor Corneeeliaaa!" she bellowed across the arena in her powerful Cipton voice.

A few minutes later, Dr. Cornelia was huddled with them. "I see you've been working on your vocal projection, Avaira. Well done. Are you drinking at least eight cups of whole Moolweep per day to keep your throat healthy and strong?"

Avaira nodded. "Doctor, my partner requested your presence. He said he has a story he wants to tell us."

Dr. Cornelia jumped into the air with excitement, her body making a suction noise as she leapt and another when she landed. "Do tell!"

Avaira and Dr. Cornelia huddled close to Rodney as he told them the whole story of the future—including Connie, her illness, travelling to the Time Belt, and his temporary escape granted by a strange figure as his one and only chance to put things back to the way they were previously. The Ciptons listened intently, interrupting only to "ooh" and "aah" occasionally. Once Rodney reached the part of his story about his return to Cipto and his plan to save Connie, the doctor cleared her throat.

"If this story is true as you say, which would be incredibly sensational, you are in luck. Since you'll be treating the disease early, Connie will need only two doses of the medicine. It's called cryocillin. Actually, given the severity of the illness you described, make that three doses. Best of all, the medicine is right here on Cipto."

Rodney gulped. "Where? Please don't say—"

"The northern polar ice cap."

"That," sighed Rodney, drooping into the stony ground.

"What's wrong?" Avaira said hurriedly, bobbing up and down.

"It's so far away," lamented Rodney.

"Oh, that's not the problem," said Dr. Cornelia. "You can take a Jalopy up there. The problem is the Choovers."

"Choovers?" inquired Avaira and Rodney simultaneously.

"You haven't heard Toric's story about how he survived the Choover attack? It's such a good one!" gushed Dr. Cornelia, dancing up and down. "Choovers live in the ice. They're fairly brainless and don't intend any harm. But that doesn't make them any less hungry."

Now Rodney was quivering violently. "S-so, where exactly is the cryocillin? How do I find it?"

"They're small pods that are embedded in the ice underground. You can't miss them. They smell like mould." Dr. Cornelia wrinkled her face. "Nasty odour, if you ask me. You should just be able to pluck them from the ice wall. Be careful, though—strong odours usually lure the Choovers. That's how they find their prey."

"Of course it is," noted Rodney. "Then what?"

"Take the cryocillin home and store them in the freezer. When Connie's fever begins, just squeeze one of the cryocillin pods, and its juice will come out. Connie will drink it right down; children love the taste. Do the same thing the next day, and once more the day after that. That's all you need to do—she'll be good to go."

"Excellent, doctor. Thank you for your help," said Avaira, bobbing graciously.

"My pleasure. This will be an excellent story to tell once you return from your mission, Rodney. Good luck to you!" The doctor bounded away to the nearest storytelling circle to make up for her lost time.

Rodney and Avaira had a private moment. Avaira whispered, "Can I go with you?"

"So you believe me?" Rodney said, his slumped form becoming more structured.

"If we really are going to have a daughter someday," said Avaira warmly, "I'll do anything I can to help you save her."

"You realise that if I fail, I'll disappear forever and Connie will never exist for you?"

"That's why I'm going to help you. We're a good team." Avaira's blobby hand touched Rodney's, and they smiled broadly.

"Let's get to my Jalopy. It's over there," said Rodney, poking his head toward where the hourglass Jalopy lay.

They slithered to the hourglass Jalopy, went inside, and squashed themselves together, forming one large Cipton blob. They realised then that they could not close the stone lid from the inside. So Avaira went back to the arena and returned with several friends who were happy to help and, thankfully, didn't ask too many questions. Avaira went back into the Jalopy, and their friends closed the stone lid for them and hastened back to the arena for more storytelling.

The Jalopy cabin lit up green, and the voice of the Jalopy recited, "Hello, Avaira of Birthing Class 4055 and Rodney of Birthing Class 4057. The Jalopy is ready to depart. Please state your destination."

"The northern polar ice cap of Cipto, please, kind Jalopy," stated Rodney sweetly.

"Enjoy your trip."

"Thank you," Rodney and Avaira replied simultaneously.

The Jalopy accelerated upward into the darkness of Cipto and proceeded north of Rodney and Avaira's hometown. Neither of them had ever been to the northern polar ice cap. They both were anxious about the dangerous trek, yet they remained quiet, each of them determined to keep calm for the sake of the other.

A hard jolt told Rodney and Avaira that the Jalopy had landed. Together they pushed the stone lid open. Immediately, a blast of icy wind stung their faces.

"Avaira, it's freezing here!"

"It's an ice cap, Rod," Avaira teased good-naturedly. "It's to be expected."

"Do you think we'll freeze to death?"

"Not if we keep moving. Come on, this way! I think I smell mould."

They crept down onto the ice, which was so cold it was painful to slither on. With Avaira leading the way, they followed their keen sense of smell toward the source of the mouldy odour.

"Stay close," warned Avaira as she carefully slid forward.

"I can't help where the wind is blowing me," said Rodney. "Augh . . . it's so cold! I can feel myself solidifying!"

"Shake it off, Rod. The smell is coming from this hole here. We need to go in. It's only going to get colder!"

Rodney swished his body back and forth a few times, shaking off the frost that was forming on him. "Okay, let's go. Try to keep quiet in case of . . . you know . . . Choovers." He said the last word of his sentence very quietly.

Avaira didn't respond; she had already entered the narrow tunnel. Rodney followed and squirmed his way after her. A few feet down, the tunnel widened, and he dropped down onto the floor of an ice cavern, joining Avaira who had just landed there herself.

Avaira was right: it was even colder under the ice than it had been on the surface. Rodney could hear her sniffing the walls of the cavern in search of the cryocillin. He sensed that they were getting close. The smell of mould filled his body. He didn't want to get any closer to it but knew he had to for Connie.

"Aha," breathed Avaira. Rodney heard a sucking sound, followed by a pop. "Got one!" mumbled Avaira through a mouthful of ice. She spat the ice out and kept the cryocillin safe under her tongue.

The awful smell of the mould was strong on Avaira's breath. Rodney could not help twisting away from her. With the stench in her mouth, Avaira could no longer track mould smells in the air, so Rodney took the lead. He sniffed around the cavern and found another tunnel from which the odour was emanating. This time, Rodney went in first.

The icy tunnel walls robbed their bodies of heat from all sides, causing their slithering muscles to go numb. Unable to slither purposefully, Rodney could only lurch forward and try to gather momentum as the tunnel sloped downward. Soon he was spinning out of control and yelling, "Whoa-oa-oa-oa!" Finally, he collided with the end of a T-intersection and bounced backward into Avaira.

"Rod, pull yourself together," she whispered, sounding less jovial than before. "We need two more cryocillin. You have to keep quiet!"

Following Rodney's nose, they chose the left branch of the T and continued down the tunnel more carefully. As they rounded a bend, they heard a persistent sniffing noise up ahead. They stopped in their tracks.

"Wh-what was that?" Rodney whispered.

"I'm hoping it was your stomach and not a Choover," breathed Avaira.

Silence.

"Should we keep going?" Rodney questioned.

"Of course!" Avaira replied in an impatient whisper. They continued along the tunnel as the pungency of mould grew stronger. Rodney swished the frost off his body again. The smell was very strong now.

"Found another," said Rodney. He attached his mouth to a spot on the ice and sucked hard. Out popped a cryocillin, along with a mouthful of ice. Rodney wasn't expecting all the ice, and he had to cough loudly to keep from choking.

"I've never heard you make that sound before," said Avaira.

"What sound?" coughed Rodney.

"That growl. Maybe you should see Doctor Cornelia once we get back home."

"I didn't growl."

Something bumped into Rodney's face, and he yelped in surprise, spitting the remainder of the ice in the face of whatever had touched him. The creature roared a pained, echoing bellow in shock at being struck.

"Choover!" shrieked Avaira. "Move away!"

Rodney and Avaira slid backward as fast as they could go, which, thanks to the ice, was much faster than they could have slithered. They felt the Choover lashing out at them wildly with its sucker-tipped appendages.

"Keep going!" yelled Avaira, who veered through the tunnels with ease by slaloming each turn. Rodney was bouncing every which way, trying to keep his wiggling body out of reach of the nearest sucking leg of the Choover. He ended up rolling as he lost control, which helped him gain speed.

"Rod, are you still there?" called Avaira.

"Yeeeeesssss!" Rodney cried as he rolled.

"We should spit out the cryocillin!" yelled Avaira. "Choovers are drawn to strong smells."

"But we need them!" said Rodney as he caught up to Avaira.

"We can spit them out of that hole where we entered the ice cap. Choovers don't seem to go up to the surface. I think they're too big to get out."

"Okay," said Rodney dizzily as they got closer to the entrance. "I'll try anything at this point!" He was starting to feel nauseated.

Once they had reached the mouth of the cavern, Avaira said, "The opening to the surface is directly above us. On my ready. Three, two, one, spit!"

Avaira and Rodney successfully spit their cryocillin up through the tunnel and out the entrance hole. The Choover was now in the cavern, but with no more mould smell, halted its threatening movements. It reached one of its spidery legs up the narrow passage in hopes of sucking up something to eat, but its reach fell just short of the surface.

Avaira and Rodney pressed themselves against the cavern wall, trying to stay quiet. Eventually the Choover grew tired of reaching, pulled its leg back down, and retreated into the depths of the ice tunnel.

"Well, that was fun," said Avaira, bouncing with glee.

"One more to go!" Rodney said, matching her happy energy.

The two went back down into the ice cap, following the path they had been on. They sniffed the air for mould, but they could smell nothing. They moved even farther into the depths of the tunnels, sliding down small ramps and jumping down a step every so often. Still, no mould smell.

"Do you think Connie would be all right with just two cryocillin?" Avaira asked as she sniffed the wall next to her.

"I'm not taking any chances. We have to get three," Rodney stated firmly.

"Sounds good, Rod."

They continued down the tunnel. Suddenly they smelled something. They both sprang up and down with excitement, suctioning the ground.

"Do you smell that?" Avaira exclaimed. "That's either one *giant* cryocillin or a whole bunch of them!"

They dribbled themselves down the tunnel and arrived at an opening that led them into another cavern. An overwhelming smell of mould surrounded them. Rodney could feel dozens of cryocillin under his body. He quickly rolled to the side and sucked one up.

"Got one!" he said. "Now, let's get back to the Jalopy!"

Suddenly the entire cavern shook with the noise of multiple very loud growls.

"What?" Rodney yelped, flattening himself.

Growls erupted all around as a pack of Choovers encircled them. Rodney felt a powerful suction on his back. A Choover had latched onto his body and was trying to vacuum up his soft body like gelatine through a straw.

"Avaira! I'm caught!" he cried, flapping his body in every direction.

"Flatten yourself, Rod!" she called.

Rodney obeyed and flattened himself to the width and height of a pancake. The suction from the Choover's leg was broken, and Rodney fell to the cavern floor. Immediately he and Avaira started for the surface. As they tumbled, rolled, and bounced along the tunnels, they could feel the walls shaking as the pack of hungry Choovers pursued them.

"Form one!" called Avaira.

Rodney understood. He bounced into her, and they formed one Cipton ball. They sped along with a quicker velocity now but slightly less controlled.

"To the right!" Rodney called.

"No, to the left!" Avaira countered.

Their gelatinous unit smashed into the end of another T-intersection, causing them to bounce back toward the approaching predators. They collided with a Choover's surprisingly hairy head, then bounced off it and landed at the T.

"Left!" Avaira repeated.

"Okay, dear," said Rodney.

They tore to the left, bouncing up steps and propelling themselves up icy ramps. Avaira continued steering as they neared the cavern below the narrow passage back to the surface.

"We have to separate, Rod! We won't fit!"

Avaira broke from him and jumped for the tiny hole above their heads. She reached it and wiggled herself through.

Rodney, still in the cavern, gasped when he heard the Choovers approaching. He floundered into a jump and barely managed to wedge himself into the narrow passage. He began to shimmy himself upward. The first Choover to reach the cavern thrust a leg upward, catching Rodney off guard just as he thought he was safe. The suction started, and Rodney felt himself being pulled down. Unable to flatten due to the tightness of the hole, he panicked.

"Avaira!" he bawled.

Avaira, safe on the surface, stuck her jelly arm down and stretched it until she reached Rodney's hand. "Arghhh!" she cried, straining herself to pull him to safety.

Rodney could feel the Choover winning. There was nothing he could do but accept his fate. He was going to lose.

But Avaira had a different plan. She released her grip on Rodney and then, as quickly as she could, swept their cryocillin into a pile and shoved them across the ice to get them away from the hole. She could hear the Choovers stampeding in the direction of the cryocillin, pursing their smell through the ice. Moments later, Rodney emerged from the hole, a bit battered but otherwise whole.

"Let's go home," he said, breathing a mouldy-smelling sigh of relief.

* * *

The Jalopy brought Avaira and Rodney back to Cipto, where their hometown was bustling with activity. Everyone was setting up for the first Birthing Ceremony of the Cipton year. Many Ciptons were bouncing with excitement for the babies soon to be birthed. Others, mostly the parents-to-be, were slithering anxiously back and forth.

"I'm actually quite nervous, Rod. What if we're bad parents?" Avaira said, tensing up her body until her normally blobby form looked like a Pomberian plumpnut.

"I know that we are—well, will be great parents. Connie is marvellous. You'll just have to wait and see," said Rodney, smiling.

This put Avaira at ease, and she released her tense form.

"Everyone meet at Jellon Springs, please and thank you!" boomed a Cipton, whose voice carried across the entire town of darkness.

Every Cipton paraded their way to Jellon Springs, the location of every Birthing Ceremony in history, as well as a nice holiday location for Ciptons to enjoy the hot springs. Once the Ciptons arrived in Jellon Springs, which was only a few blocks away from the Pyroll arena, each individual found a seat around the largest of the springs, Bubble Billows. The suction noises as they bounced in their seats united into a loud, echoing buzz. Avaira and Rodney sat together in the first row, along with the other prospective parents.

Then a fanfare sounded, and an announcer's voice boomed:

"Welcome, my fellow Ciptons, to the 5001st Birthing Ceremony in Bubble Billows. It feels great to be back in Cipto's renowned Jellon Springs! You have all travelled near and far to be with us at one of the most exciting events of our community!"

The crowd boomed with cheers. Rodney and Avaira huddled up against one another in excitement.

The announcer continued. "Oh, I see we are ready for the pan to be lowered!"

The crowd cheered even louder. Some Ciptons were even somersaulting in air.

A sizzling noise permeated the air, meaning a giant pan had been placed across the diameter of Bubble Billows.

"And now, the heart of the ceremony and, indeed, of what makes us Ciptons," the announcer said. "Dear friends and family, the Birthing Ceremony reflects the Cipton values of ecological conservation and responsible stewardship of our beloved planet. Those of us who have passed on pledged from a young age to donate their bodies to new life. Our new offspring will carry on their old bodies and form new personalities for the community to enjoy. And naturally, it is also the time when we celebrate those who have gone before. Please rise so that we may show them our gratitude. Our ancestors truly make us what we are."

The crowd quieted instantly. Each Cipton formed their blobby bodies into a taller version of themselves for a few moments, before flattening back down from their lack of bones to keep them upright for long.

"And now," said the announcer, "bring in the goo!"

The crowd immediately roared with glee and resumed their jumping and squealing.

A splattering noise filled the pan on top of the hot spring.

Avaira said into Rodney's ear: "I just hope we get chosen this time."

"I told you, it's going to be just fine, dear!" Rodney reassured her.

"Bets are almost closed, folks!" boomed the announcer. "Lock your bets in with the usher at the end of your aisle!"

Last-minute bettors squirmed through the tightly packed rows to get their predictions in.

"Put twenty on Rodney and Avaira! They've been waiting for ages!" squealed one Cipton to an usher.

"If anyone's going to become a parent tonight, it's my man Pup!"

"Vitreo! I just put five hundred on you, buddy! Show me the money!"

Bets were being thrown every which way, and Rodney was starting to get nervous.

There's nothing to be nervous about, he told himself. He had lived this part of the timeline once already. Surely Connie would fall in love with them just as she had the last time.

The announcer's voice reverberated through the arena again: "Aaall right, folks! The betting is closed. And now begins the next section of our ceremony . . . Building the Babies!"

The attendees practically lost their minds at this point. Some Ciptons bounced clear out of their seats. Even the prospective parents got caught up in the excitement and started smiling and quivering.

"Start tossing in your ingredients!" said the announcer.

A Cipton behind Rodney shouted, "Here's some blubberberries to give the babies a fuller, more blobbish form!" and spat about twenty rotund berries in an arc over Rodney's head and into the now boiling pan.

Avaira squeezed Rodney's hand in anticipation.

"Books! For knowledge of Cipto society!" shouted another Cipton from across the arena, who spewed out a line of books from its stomach.

"Who said you could take my books, Lido?" shouted his angry partner.

Others in the crowd continued tossing in sundry items, from rocks and furniture to mushpuddle pies, a bit of brandy, and a few Pyrolls. The mixture bubbled vigorously. Then the brewing pan began to rise from the hot spring. Rodney could feel the warmth of the brewing pot rising up. The babies were nearly done.

"Now for the last but most important ingredient," said the announcer. "Moolweep from the prospective parents, to give the babies their grit!"

The parents around Rodney and Avaira started rapid-fire spitting Moolweep into the pan.

"Shoot!" said Avaira, sharply. "We didn't have time to get Moolweep from home before coming here!"

"I'm sure it's fine, dear," Rodney said.

The mixture bubbled high, and the heat from the pan washed through the entire arena, prompting a wave of murmurs that started in the front row and travelled concentrically all the way to the most distant seats. Finally, the murmurs quieted down to dull whispers, and every Cipton in the arena leaned toward the pan and listened. Soon the sound of hundreds of tiny, squeaky voices rose up from the pan, sending the crowd into a whooping celebration.

After several tries at quieting the crowd, the announcer said: "You've all done it! Fantastic input from the community, simply fantastic. I have a feeling this batch of babies is going to be our healthiest and happiest yet. Now we start the next and undoubtedly most anticipated part of the ceremony, the Choosing of the Parents!"

Rodney scrunched his face at the bellows from the crowd. He was exponentially more nervous now. The plan had to work.

The announcer continued. "And listen—quiet, please—I'm being told we already have one baby emerging! Welcome, Baby Number One from Birthing Class 5001!"

A small and curious gooey head poked out of the pan and stood frozen upon hearing the strange crowd ahead of it. All the parents in the front row began showing off to the baby, trying their very best to get its attention.

"Over heeere, little ooone!" called Avaira, waving her wiggly arms in the air.

"That's not our baby, dear. Connie is a bit later," Rodney said.

"Oh, Rod, are you sure?"

"Positive. That's Pup's baby. Just listen."

Avaira listened as the cooing baby moved toward Pup, who jumped up and down in his seat, making rapid suction noises before landing with a splat. The baby laughed and slithered into Pup's waiting arms.

"Well, everyone," gushed the announcer. "Our first pairing!"

Pup's bettors in the crowd also tumbled with excitement. Rodney's heart began to pound. He wasn't sure why he was starting to get nervous. What if something went wrong? No, it's not possible. The first pairing went exactly as Rodney remembered. Everything would be fine.

Another baby Cipton emerged from the pan. This one turned and made a happy squawk at its friends who were still in the pan attempting to get out. The crowd boiled with excitement again.

"Come on, Vitreo!" shouted one anxious bettor.

Rodney felt Avaira dancing in her seat. "Not this one either, dear."

"No?" said Avaira. She sighed and slumped back down into her seat.

Vitreo, who was sitting next to Rodney, shook his body clumsily, trying to get the baby's attention. The baby just looked blankly at him.

Rodney whispered to Avaira, "I feel bad for this chap."

The baby turned around and slithered to the other side of the centre circle, then hopped happily into the jelly arms of another Cipton parent.

"Nooo!" shouted the Vitreo bettors in the crowd.

Rodney and Avaira listened and cheered politely as a few more babies chose their parents. Then, a very small baby poked her head up and climbed out of the pan. Rodney recognised her quiet slither as she approached the prospective parents.

Rodney nudged Avaira. "That's her!" he whispered. "It's Connie!" Rodney and Avaira began their choreographed dance, alternately twisting around one another and bouncing stomachs. Rodney's heart was racing now. He was sure Connie would pick them. Everything was in alignment, happening as it had his first time around.

Vitreo was dancing for Connie's attention as well, but—there was no polite way one could put it—his moves were sub-par. Connie swerved in the direction of Rodney and Avaira, and a smile started spreading across her tiny face.

"Come on, Connie," said Rodney under his breath as he and Avaira continued their dance. "That's it . . ."

Connie was close now. She scrunched up her little body in preparation to leap into Avaira's arms. Then she took a deep breath, and her face shrivelled up in disgust. "Blech!" she squeaked, inching her way backward.

The mould! How had Rodney not realised the mould would make them smell bad to her? She didn't want smelly parents!

"No, no!" cried Rodney, horror-stricken. "Come back, sweet girl! It's your father, remember? And Mommy! It's us!" Seeing the confusion in Avaira's face—and desperate to make everything all right, as he had promised—Rodney left his chair and started to bounce toward Connie.

"Hey!" shouted Vitreo. "That's cheating!"

A whistle sounded, and an usher called out: "Foul! Rodney, Class 4057."

Immediately the announcer's voice boomed: "Rodney of Birthing Class 4057, you are in violation of the Birthing Ceremony parental rules. You and Avaira are hereby eliminated."

Rodney heard Connie hop into Vitreo's arms. "No . . ." he cried. "That's not possible. She's mine! That's my daughter!" Rodney's voice grew louder as he sobbed, his tears pooling all around him.

Vitreo said, "I'm surprised at you, Rodney. Can't you be happy for me?"

"No!" screamed Rodney. "Please, Vitreo! If you let me have her, you can take anything of mine you want. My hut. My food. You name it. Oh, Vitreo, please!"

The crowd was booing Rodney now. Even Avaira was shaking her head. The announcer quieted the crowd down, then spoke explicitly to Rodney. "You are not her parent!"

A black, swirling wormhole opened up in the sky directly above them. The diameter of the looming event horizon expanded until it was the size of the entirety of Bubble Billows. Rodney stared up at it in fear and defeat. He had lost. He had failed himself, Avaira, Connie, and all of Cipto. His body wobbled with sadness. All that was left to do was surrender to the grip of the Time Belt—or wherever he was going this time; he wasn't sure. But he probably deserved it, he thought.

No one, not even Vitreo, seemed to notice the powerful sounds of thunder or the strong winds beginning to lift both Rodney and Connie from the land of Cipto. Connie screamed in terror as she floated out of Vitreo's arms and up toward the dark wormhole. Rodney tried his best to grasp her one last time. His jelly hands met her jelly body as they flew upward in the strong winds, and they entered the depths of the vortex together. Cipto would live on without the existence of Rodney and Connie. They would remain a fable for eternity.

CHAPTER 16

THE ULTIMATE SACRIFICE

Luna and Riff listened in horror toward the dark panoramic view of Focalok as Rodney and Connie were sucked into the wormhole, never to exist again. The darkness around them transformed back into the bright white light. The hourglass Jalopy returned to its place in Focalok, empty of any Ciptons. Rodney and Connie's one chance was used up.

Luna wheeled to the right, where the Time Belt version of Constance stood next to her, to see her slowly turning into smoke and dissipating into nothingness. Luna reached forward to grab on to her, but Constance just bowed her head in acceptance. Her mouth wobbled in sadness. She mouthed a "Goodbye" before completely disappearing. Luna closed her fist around the smoke as it vanished. Thoughts raced in her brain about how valiantly Rodney had fought to keep his daughter and the unfortunate ending through all the pain he endured. A lump formed in her throat. She wondered if Knitsy would be able to perform her mission successfully.

Luna looked over at her family. Knitsy and Clorin were curled up on the floor, asleep. Riff had tears streaming down his face.

"Who knew those jelly blobs had such hard lives?" he said.

"At least we helped them as best we could," Luna said, trying to offer some comfort.

Luna heard groans from the opposite side of the room. Elbina was starting to come to her senses. Riff wiped his tears away, and he and Luna went over to check on Elbina. Her eyes were closed, and her face and hands looked puffy and swollen. Her body was trembling as if she were in horrible pain. Her laboured breaths turned into gasps for air. She reached her arms out for someone to help her.

"It's okay, Elbs, I'm right here. It's Luna. You're doing great," Luna said, her voice hoarse.

Riff patted Elbina's head gently as tears returned to his eyes.

Luna looked over her shoulder toward Knitsy. "Nan! Wake up!"

Knitsy rubbed her eyes and looked around. "Did the blobs make it back?"

"No," said Riff quietly.

"Oh, well, that's no good, is it?" said Knitsy, doing her best to be sympathetic.

"Nan, it's your turn," Luna said.

"Huh? Me?"

Luna stood and faced her. "Nan, you have to go back and make sure Mum comes into existence again. That's all you have to do. Don't worry about it if you can't ensure the rest of us get born. As long as Mum is born, that means the rest of us will have a chance."

Elbina was still trembling and whimpering. Riff tended to her, though there was nothing he could do except hold her hand.

Knitsy watched the agonising scene. "She's got some fight in her yet," she said. "Help me up."

Luna helped Knitsy slowly to her feet and handed her her cane.

Knitsy smoothed the wrinkles from her skirt, then faced the hooded figure. "Erm, sir? I'm ready for my mission."

The hooded figure raised his head. "How many times do I have to explain, that you cannot depart when no Chroniya remains? The Bank must be completely filled before your mission can even begin to be fulfilled."

"What's he saying?" said Riff.

Luna sighed deeply and narrowed her eyes at the figure. "He's saying we can't go because all the Chroniya was drained for Rodney and Connie's mission. We have to wait until the people of Vivalok spend enough Chroniya to fill it up again."

Riff groaned. "That'll take ages!" He stood and addressed the figure. "Is there anything we can do to bypass that rule?"

The figure raised a bony finger to his chin. "Ah, a shortcut. It's possible but difficult somewhat. Should you want to give it a whirl to save the dying girl, the ultimate sacrifice can be made, for something must be paid."

"Are you saying . . ." Luna began.

"Ah, I see you are smart. You know the answer, though it breaks your heart."

"What's the strange rhyming bloke saying now?" Knitsy asked.

"He's saying . . ." Luna took a deep breath. "He's saying if we don't wait for the Bank to refill with Chroniya, Nan can still go on her mission, but even if she succeeds, we can't all go back to reality. One of us will have to stay behind. Forever."

Knitsy and Riff's mouths hung open. Elbina coughed and struggled as tears rolled down her cheeks.

Riff turned toward Luna. "I'll sacrifice myself. No questions asked."

"No, Riff!" Luna shot him a look. "I'll do it."

"You? You're the brains here. When have I been of use in any situation?"

"All the time, you git!" Luna barked at him, hands on her hips.

"Why don't I do it?" Knitsy said softly.

The siblings looked at her.

"Nan, that's ridiculous!" Luna directed her anger at her grandmother now, her voice trembling.

Knitsy held up her hand. "Think about it. When your mum died, I gladly would have traded places with her for your sakes. I couldn't, but I was willing to sacrifice myself for you then, and I'm willing now. I could go to the other side in peace," she said. "You guys don't need your old grandmother anymore."

Clorin had awakened during the commotion and was now staring at his aunt, uncle, and great-grandmother with interest. "What about me?" he chirped.

"No, Clorin," Luna said with as much patience as she could muster. "You're not going anywhere, either." He stared at her with his beaming red Ann Lou eyes.

Luna turned back to her grandmother and pleaded. "Nan . . . you can't sacrifice yourself. I need you."

"I need you, too," said Riff, treading over to her. He held one of her arms gently and Luna held the other.

"Old Nan has a tough job to do now. Let me rest. I'll need it. Besides, I can watch you nutty lot whenever I want in the afterlife. I'll pull pranks on you! Anytime you hear a swear in the wind, you'll know it's me."

Luna and Riff whimpered. They didn't want to let go of their grandmother.

"It's settled, then," Knitsy said. "Don't be sad yet; let's see if I succeed first. We might all be going to the same place soon enough if I have the same luck as that poor old jelly chap."

Luna and Riff tugged Knitsy for a final embrace. Neither of them could find words to express their love and gratitude. Clorin followed their example and wrapped his small arms around his great-grandmother's leg. Luna inhaled her grandmother's scent through gasping breaths, knowing she'd hold on to it forever. The sight of her flowing white hair, the sound of her coughing, even the thwack of her cane against their legs . . . Knitsy was still a beautiful memory to hold close.

Elbina's wails brought them back to the moment. They needed to act fast.

Knitsy reached down to give Clorin a pat. "Goodbye, my dear. You be good now, you hear me? Don't swear like your uncle," she said with a wink. Then she slowly stooped down to Clorin's level to give him his own hug.

She walked with difficulty over to where Elbina lay twitching and moaning on the ground. Knitsy crouched, kissed the tips of her own fingers, and then touched them to Elbina's forehead. "You're going to be all right. Nan's got you covered."

Walking over to the hooded figure and facing him with confidence, Knitsy said, "I'm ready."

The figure let out a deep chuckle. "I see you've made your whole family soppy. Now make your way to the Jalopy."

Riff and Luna walked Knitsy up the spiral ramp until they all stood just outside the Jalopy. The hooded figure raised its skeletal hand toward the Bank replica below them, and it suddenly filled to the brim with the dark liquid Chroniya. Keeping his hand in the air, he recited, "At the expense of Knitsy McHubbard, I ask you to drain. For there is a glimmer of hope that the McHubbard family may no longer exist on this plane."

The dark liquid drained once again until the Bank was completely empty. Knitsy gave Luna and Riff each a kiss on their foreheads and then looked up at the Jalopy. Riff helped Knitsy in and lowered the stone lid.

Alone inside, Knitsy said, "Well, here goes nothin'." Her eyes twinkled as she spoke.

"Hello, Knitsy McHubbard. The Jalopy is ready to depart. Please state your destination," said the familiar voice.

"The Cat's Chin. Portsmouth, England. June twenty-ninth, 2169."

"Enjoy your trip."

The panoramic sky of Focalok changed from white to a colour view from Knitsy's perspective. Knitsy signed "I love you" to her grandchildren through the glass, and they signed the same in return. It was the last communication they would share in this plane of existence.

CHAPTER 17

Knitsy's Mission

As Knitsy flew out of Focalok and into the starry universe in the hourglass Jalopy, many thoughts swirled through her head. The last time she was in a Jalopy, she had been travelling on her way to Harvinth with her grandchildren. Upon entering the Time Belt, an ominous voice, probably Father Time, had called her forth and asked her to change one event in her life up to that point. Millions of images had passed before her eyes like a reel of all the events in her life. But the only change that she could fathom was to have switched places with her daughter, Henrietta, back when they all moved to different planets. It was all for the sake of her grandchildren. The mysterious Father Time had deemed her decision selfish and punished her by banishing her into a wormhole that split her soul into three pieces. It was terrifying, and Knitsy understood now that she had to act with her head and not her heart if she was going to succeed in ensuring the existence of her descendants.

Just because she temporarily existed for this mission didn't mean she was in the clear. She had to be smart, cunning, logical—things she usually wasn't. But she had a loose plan. And if it meant she could see her daughter alive again one more time, it was worth the risk.

The Jalopy passed through a vast ring nebula with stunning multicoloured rings, surrounding Knitsy with enchanting colours. Her body felt relaxed for the first time in . . . well, as long as she could remember.

She hoped her success meant a bountiful life for her grandchildren and great-grandchild. Although she wouldn't be with them anymore, she'd rest easy knowing they had full lives ahead of them.

As the Jalopy neared its destination, Knitsy pressed her face against the sturdy, cool glass. Her heart practically lunged out of her turtleneck when she saw her home. She watched the pale yellow dot grow larger as the Jalopy approached. Earth's black and brown patches were beautiful to see again after eight years on the sandy, barren planet of Olfinder.

Knitsy fidgeted as the Jalopy began its descent, bouncing her legs and picking at hangnails. When there was nothing left to pick, she resorted to tapping her fingertips together and rubbing her palms for warmth. The Jalopy homed in on Europe, the U.K., England, and finally, the very southernmost point of England and Knitsy's very own city of Portsmouth. To anyone else, Portsmouth would have looked like every other lifeless patch of the Earth, but to Knitsy it was her home of seventy-five years. Portsmouth looked beautiful in the warm light of sunset. As the Jalopy coasted toward its landing, Knitsy saw neighbourhoods and landmarks that triggered countless memories almost as vivid as the reels she had seen in the Time Belt. There was the Fratton train station, whose tracks hadn't been used in at least a hundred years, and her childhood home on the road parallel. Then there was her and Henrietta's home, and Houndwell School, where all the McHubbards, including

Knitsy, had received their early educations. She gazed lovingly at each landmark. And then there was the pub. Her favourite pub.

The Jalopy came to rest on the rock-hard ground and attached itself to the tunnel that would allow Knitsy to walk into the pub without exposure to the deadly contamination of Earth's environment.

Knitsy remained in the Jalopy, hesitant and beginning to question the plan. How was she supposed to relive part of her mid-twenties as an eighty-two-year-old woman? She wondered if her wrinkled hands could pass for a younger age—perhaps sixty-five instead? She peered down at her hands and gasped upon seeing that all her wrinkles had completely vanished. Not only that, she was now dressed in skinny grey jeans, white trainers, and a large, woolly green jumper instead of the floor-length skirt and turtleneck. She continued inhaling deep, incredulous gasps. She grabbed the skin of her belly, surprised at how tight it was. Her fingers flew up and pulled her hair from its high ponytail so that it fell in front of her eyes. It was dark brown, nearly black—just as Henrietta's was before she greyed. She breathed deep breaths, in awe of how much air her lungs could take in. She laughed gleefully, enjoying the feeling of the blood rushing throughout her twenty-four-year-old body. She felt flexible, light, and full of energy. She might yet be able to execute her plan successfully.

Knitsy pushed open the stone lid and crawled out of the Jalopy into the windowless, dreary tunnel, which led to a large, secure door. She knocked tentatively at the door to The Cat's Chin, holding her breath in anticipation for what was on the other side.

A tall, stocky security guard opened the door and looked her up and down.

"ID?" he asked in a deep tone through a bushy brown moustache.

"Erm," Knitsy stammered. She felt her left wrist, nervous that if he scanned her microchip, it wouldn't show the correct age.

"Yeh can drink water tonight or leave," the guard said, narrowing his eyes at her.

Suddenly a jolly voice rang out from behind him. "Knitsy Hampshire!"

Knitsy looked to the source of the voice and felt a smile warming her body. It was her best friend, Meg Islington. Meg was shorter than Knitsy, with bouncy blonde curls and skin the colour of smooth milk chocolate. Her face was impeccably made up, as always, and she was wearing a short black dress that showed off her curves. Standing next to Meg was Bowie Tennerow, their friend from The Blue Barnacle, the restaurant where they all worked. Bowie was much taller than anyone else in the pub this evening, as he was most evenings. He was wearing yellow contact lenses, a faux-fur jacket over his bare chest, ripped blue shorts, and combat boots. He had freckles all over his body and blue hair that was shaved on the sides.

Knitsy chirped with happiness and ran past the guard and into Meg's and Bowie's arms. The guard sauntered in after Knitsy with a scowl on his face. Bowie waved at him and said, "Relax. She's twenty-four today. There are some underage kids walking in if that'll make you happy."

The guard huffed and marched back to his post.

"Happy birthday, Knits!" said Meg, playfully punching her in the shoulder. "What took you so long? I need to start telling you to come two hours early just so you get here on time!" Meg's blonde curls bounced as she spoke through her shimmery red lips. Knitsy almost thought Meg's eyelashes would touch her face every time she blinked.

"Meg gave me a full face of makeup while we were waiting for you," said Bowie, admiring himself in Meg's pocket mirror. "Usually, she only gets through the eyes, but now I have the full face on . . . I'm not mad about the foundation, though."

"Sorry, I . . . lost track of time," Knitsy replied.

"Did Paul give you the long shift today? I messaged you like twenty-five times," Meg whined.

"Yeah, it was busy today. The Marsh family was there," said Knitsy, remembering a particularly difficult party she had served once.

"Ugh, bless you. Let's get you a drink, then," Meg said, raising a hand to the bartender.

"Already ahead of you," smiled Bowie, passing Knitsy a cocktail. He smiled at her, displaying his gapped front teeth. "Sip it up, Birthday Girl."

The three stood at the bar for a while, gossiping about the unruly customers and staff at the restaurant. Knitsy was amazed at how easily the memories flowed. They were all there inside her mind, little pieces of information she could access as readily as if she truly were twenty-four again.

"I no joke was about to quit yesterday," said Meg. "You'll never guess what one customer said to—"

A pack of boys across the pub were laughing uncontrollably around a long wooden table.

Meg whipped her head around to look at them. "Well, they're being quite obnoxious, aren't they?"

Knitsy followed her gaze. Normally she'd have scowled along with Meg, but one of the boys caught her attention. He was laughing along with the others, but not hysterically. He was sitting slightly hunched. He almost looked as if he didn't want to be there at all, as if he were faking his way through the evening. He wore large round glasses and had dark brown hair that was parted down the middle and curled to either side. His face was sprinkled with freckles, and his cheeks were rosy. He was wearing a black woollen jumper similar in make to Knitsy's and a patterned bow tie.

"Knits?" Meg said, waving a hand in front of her eyes.

Knitsy blinked. "Hm? Oh—sorry."

"Does one of those obnoxious men . . . interest you?" Bowie asked, leaning into her.

One did. Her husband. But he didn't know that yet. Neither did her friends. Nor, technically, was she supposed to know either. But Knitsy couldn't help staring at him. Besides Henrietta and her grandchildren, he was the person she loved most in this world. Even more than she loved Meg and Bowie. Her heart leapt into her throat, and goosebumps formed beneath her jumper. She swallowed. A sad feeling washed through her body, and she closed her eyes.

"You all right?" asked Meg.

Knitsy nodded. She didn't know what to say, so she looked at her feet.

"Do you want us to wingman for you?" Bowie said, clapping his hands together. "Matchmaking is my favourite!"

Meg joined in. "Oh! Please, Knits? Bowie and I need you to triple-date with us. Bowie's boyfriend is starting to drive me nuts. I need a buffer."

"Same here, honestly," said Bowie.

Knitsy tried to find words. "Erm . . . Well, I, uh . . . Maybe he'll come over by himself."

Bowie craned his neck to survey the group. "The nerdy one? Makes sense; he's wearing an oversized jumper as well."

"Do you want to change real quick, Knits? We can swap clothes if you want him to really notice you," Meg offered.

"Oh, please! She's a head taller than you," Bowie scoffed. "All her bits would be showing. It wouldn't be Knitsy if she wasn't wearing a jumper on a night out. She needs to be her authentic self."

Meg laughed. "Yeah, all right. Let's go, Knits. Gonna get you your man!" Meg took Knitsy's arm and started to pull her across the room.

Knitsy gulped. She hadn't spoken to her husband in decades. What if he didn't fancy her this time around? What if she made some small error that botched the grand plan? She couldn't bear the thought. "No no no! Please, I'm all right," she said, attempting to pry Meg's sharp fingernails off her wrist.

But Bowie was pushing her shoulders forward.

"You two are mad!"

When they reached the boys' table, Meg smiled confidently. "Hello, lads!" They all stared at Meg, slack jawed.

One of the boys popped up instantly from his seat. His body was sturdily built, with bulging muscles under a tight T-shirt. He had short, buzzed brown hair and a tight jawline. He looked Meg up and down, then gestured to his chair and said in a low voice, "My, my, fine lady. You sit here."

Knitsy's stomach lurched at the sound of his voice.

"No, thanks," said Meg. "I'm here strictly to introduce my best friend to your friend in the corner." Meg pointed at the hunched, bespectacled boy, and his piercing blue eyes bugged out. Knitsy dropped her eyes to her feet, imagining how silly she surely looked in front of him.

"Macky? Our little Macky lad? Who knew all the girls would be after him!" said the boy with the buzz cut, starting a cascade of whoops and hollers from the boys around the table.

Macky's face turned the same shade as Knitsy's.

Meg just said, "Can we borrow Macky?"

"Up you go, lad!" one of them said, and the boys on either side of Macky shoved and poked him until he stood up and went over by Knitsy.

Then the boy with the buzz cut turned his attention to Bowie. "And who do we have here?" He scratched his chin. "I've seen you before."

"Pardon?" Bowie blinked at him.

"I've seen 'im, too," said one of the other boys at the table. "'e was on the news with the prime minista."

"That's it," said the first boy. The others murmured in agreement. "How do you know the prime minister?"

"He's my boyfriend's grandfather," Bowie said nonchalantly. "His family invites me to events and such."

The boys glanced at one another, chuckling and snorting. The boy with the buzz cut spoke again. "Well, well! Do you think you could possibly introduce us to the prime minister? We'd *love* to meet him!"

Bowie laughed. "Um, no."

The standing boy ambled up to Bowie and stood directly in front of him. "Well, if you want to borrow our Macky lad, you need to introduce us."

"Erm, guys, just leave him be," said Macky softly.

The boy winked at Bowie. "We'll listen to sweet ol' Macky lad this once. But our business isn't over." Then he went back to his seat.

Meg rolled her eyes and walked Knitsy away. Bowie and Macky followed behind them. Once they reached a quiet place at the bar, Meg pretended to gag herself. "Your friends are horrible," she said to Macky.

"I'm sorry about them. That was my brother, Burl. I don't particularly get on with him and his mates, but my brother is some of the only family I've got."

Meg said, "Well, you should be *our* friend!"

Bowie stood up then and said, "Let's leave these two alone, Meg. I could use another pint."

Meg stood up. "So could I." She picked up her purse, then said to Macky, "Oh—it's her birthday! Treat her nicely!" She and Bowie headed to the bar, leaving Knitsy and Macky alone at the table.

The boy smiled shyly at Knitsy. "Erm, well . . . Happy birthday!"

Knitsy blushed. "Thanks."

"So, what's your name?" Macky shoved his hands into his pockets. He had a Scottish accent.

Knitsy looked at him, their eyes meeting for the first time. "Knitsy. Knitsy Hampshire." She felt a warmth surge into her body.

His eyes twinkled. "That's a really cool name. Mine's Mack Gorgan. He smiled and pushed a free strand of hair behind his ear. "I only go by Mack. Not Macky, just to clear that up. My brother just calls me that to annoy me."

Knitsy knew all this, of course. But she had to play along. She smiled. "You from around here?" she asked, twiddling her fingers nervously.

"Mum, my brother, and I moved here last month from up north. Near Glasgow," he replied.

Knitsy's heart sank. She knew his family history. But she continued smiling.

"I've seen you at The Blue Barnacle before," he noted. "My girlfriend and I have eaten there a couple times."

Girlfriend. Right. Knitsy had forgotten about the girlfriend.

"Girlfriend, eh?" Knitsy said playfully. "What're you doing here talking to me, then? She'll surely come for my arse if I'm not careful."

Mack laughed. "Well, I *was* forcibly lifted from my seat."

Knitsy so badly wanted to flirt her way to his heart, but she knew she needed to play it safe and do exactly as she had done the first time around to avoid any mishaps. "Well, you and your girlfriend should come to the restaurant next Sunday. We always put on a nice roast."

Mack smiled. "I'll—I mean, we'll be there."

Burl shouted from across the room. "Macky lad, we're on to the next pub! Don't hold us up!"

Mack sighed and shut his eyes for a moment, then opened them and smiled at Knitsy once more. "It was really great to meet you."

"Bye," she said. Her stomach was full of butterflies. She felt light-headed and rested an arm on the bar to steady herself.

He waved to her and walked back to his table, his back hunched the way Knitsy knew so well. She breathed a sigh of relief and went to the bar to join Meg and Bowie. They pulled her into a tight circle.

"Tell us everything," Bowie said, hopping from one foot to the other.

"He has a girlfriend."

"So?"

"So, it would be an arsehole move for me to step in where I'm not welcome," replied Knitsy. "Right?"

"Yeah," said Meg, putting her arm around Knitsy's waist and pinning a stare on Bowie, "Knitsy's not a homewrecker, like *some* people we know. She has morals."

"Screw morals! This girl needs to become a wild child," Bowie said, shaking his hips. He took a small round object from his pocket and offered it to Knitsy. It was gold in colour and about the size of a pearl. She took it from him and looked closely at it. It was a device that clipped to the nasal septum and dispensed a bit of flavoured smoke every few minutes. It was also quite fashionable at the time. Knitsy eyed it with a gutted feeling. She knew this moment would eventually lead to the lung disease that left her subject to coughing fits and dependent on breathing patches. But her friends didn't know this. She had to pretend she had never used the device before. She hesitated, then awkwardly clipped it to her nose.

Bowie beamed. "Knitsy Hampshire, Mission Wild Child, step one: try a SeptaSmoke."

Knitsy coughed as the device emitted a zesty orange smell into her nose, which filtered to her lungs. After a few more puffs of smoke, Knitsy became used to the device.

Wow, she thought. *I've missed this.*

Meg checked the time on her microchip.

"Is that the time? Blimey, I need to be up early tomorrow. I'd better get home."

"But the party was just getting started," whined Bowie.

"Why don't you say that tomorrow when we're working at seven a.m.?" said Meg.

Bowie just uttered, "Oh, right."

"Want a lift home?" Meg asked Knitsy. "I'm safe to drive."

"Erm, no thanks. I've got my . . . car out front," said Knitsy.

The friends walked out of the pub and made their way down the tunnel. Small transport pods were taking people from the pub to their cars in order to avoid contact with the outside world. Knitsy waved goodbye to her friends and as soon as they were gone, she took a transport pod to the hourglass.

After the Jalopy recited its usual greeting and question about where to go, Knitsy replied with, "Twenty-nine East Suffolk Close."

"Enjoy your trip."

The ride to Knitsy's old flat took no more than one minute. She immediately recognised the run-down studio from the outside. The dark green front door, the brick exterior, and the chipped pitched roof were all the same. The Jalopy parked at the entrance to the tunnel to the flat and Knitsy made her way safely through it. She arrived at the front door and turned the handle.

It was locked.

"Bollocks," she muttered. "Of course I don't have the keys."

She dug in her trouser pockets and there the keys were. Where she always put them.

"Brilliant," she said, unlocking the door.

The flat was the same. Things strewn about. Bed unmade. Dirty dishes in the sink. She lived alone and worked a lot, so flat upkeep was a rarity for her.

She entered the bathroom and caught her reflection in the mirror. How strange it was to be looking at herself nearly sixty years younger. She saw many similarities between her and Henrietta—the hair, the rosy cheeks, the eyes. She smiled and walked into her kitchen. The fatigue was starting to get to her, so she ate a few biscuits and collapsed on her bed.

* * *

The following Sunday, Knitsy was wiping down a table at The Blue Barnacle when she heard someone clear their throat behind her. She turned her head and saw a couple standing there. It was Mack and his girlfriend. Mack waved shyly. The girlfriend was thin and very pretty, with long, wavy blonde hair and fair skin, but her face was scrunched up in distaste.

Knitsy hid her dirty cleaning rag behind her back and blushed. "Hi," she said.

"Are you going to seat us?" asked the girlfriend. "We've been waiting for five minutes."

Knitsy glanced over at Meg, who was meant to be hosting, but she was in deep conversation with Bowie. "Sorry," said Knitsy. "You can sit here; it's all clean now. I'll get cutlery."

"Thank you," Mack said as he slid past her into the booth.

Knitsy walked over to where Bowie and Meg were talking and grabbed cutlery from the bucket beside them. Quietly, she said, "Mack's here."

Bowie subtly glanced at the couple. "And that's the girlfriend?"

"Probably," said Knitsy, although she knew very well that it was.

"She's got nothing on you," said Meg.

Suddenly the girlfriend called loudly to Knitsy from across the restaurant. "Excuse me! How much longer do we have to wait?"

Bowie's eyes bugged out. Then he thought a moment. "Step two for Mission Wild Child: get the girlfriend to look bad in front of him."

"How the bloody hell am I supposed to do that?" Knitsy whispered.

"She's got a temper. All you have to do is trigger it."

"Ooh, I know—give her the wrong meal!" Meg suggested.

"No, it has to be worse than that." Bowie thought some more. "How about you put something in her food?"

"That's so mean!" said Knitsy.

"Okay, then *I'll* put something in her food," snapped Bowie.

"Hel-LO?" the girlfriend shouted, prompting stares from other diners.

Knitsy swiftly made her way back to their table and pushed her long hair behind her ears. She looked at Mack.

"I think I'll go for the roast you recommended." To the girlfriend, he said sweetly, "You want the same, Penny?"

"You know her?" Penny growled.

Mack looked nervous. "Remember? I told you I met her at The Cat's Chin last week."

Penny didn't look enthused.

Knitsy piped up, "He told me all about you!" Then she thought: *Why am I trying to keep the peace between them?*

"I'm not hungry," Penny said, slouching back into the booth with her arms crossed.

Mack said to Knitsy, "We'll just share."

Knitsy nodded and hurried back to the kitchen, where Bowie was waiting for the order. "One roast," Knitsy told him. "Don't make it too bad—they're sharing it!"

While Bowie plated the roast, Knitsy ran an order out to another table. She raced back and grabbed the plate of roast, hoping it wasn't full of poison.

Knitsy fluttered up to Mack and Penny's table and set the plate down. Penny eyed her. Then Knitsy left them alone and went to tend other customers as she waited for the drama to unfold.

After several minutes, Knitsy heard a loud *"Ewww!"*

She held her breath and walked back to Mack and Penny's table.

Penny was pointing at their plate, her mouth agape. Then she shrieked: "This . . . is *disgusting!*" Knitsy looked where she was pointing. There, nestled amid the half-eaten potatoes, was a slobbery SeptaSmoke. Penny's face turned red as she screamed at Knitsy: "So you let whatever jewellery you're wearing just drop into the food, do you?"

"Darling," said Mack quietly, "it wasn't her fault. She didn't make the food."

"She's the reason you brought me here! What makes you think you can talk to other girls behind my back?"

Before Mack could reply, Penny shoved the plate of food hard across the table at him. It went over the edge and into his lap. For good measure, Penny dashed a water glass onto the floor. Then she grabbed her purse and marched straight out the door.

"I'm so sorry," Mack said to Knitsy. He stood up, and pieces of meat and potato fell off his clothes and onto the floor. He knelt and started to pick up pieces of the broken glass.

"Don't move!" Knitsy said. She ran to the kitchen to get towels and a broom and dustpan. There was Bowie, wearing a giant grin. Knitsy said, "A SeptaSmoke? Really?"

"I like to combine my missions," he smirked.

Knitsy ran back to the table, where Meg was giving Mack a napkin.

He had cut his hand on a piece of glass. Knitsy handed the broom and dustpan to Meg, then said, "Mack, let's get you cleaned up, all right?"

She took him into the kitchen and cleaned his cut hand, then wrapped it with a clean towel. She proceeded to wipe the food off his clothes as best she could. He stared at her the entire time. Knitsy tried not to meet his gaze but found herself drawn into his mesmerising blue eyes. She paused, and they connected for a moment. Knitsy's breath was lost. She wanted to kiss him, but she hesitated. At this age—at the age her body was—she had never kissed anyone. She was different from her friends. Shy to date. Scared to share an intimate moment. Afraid she didn't look pretty enough. But this was her husband. Even though they weren't married for very long, they had been soulmates. Here, now, Knitsy sensed something in him. A deeper recognition? Or just momentary adoration? She couldn't take the risk. Not yet.

She breathed and backed away from him. "Let me clean your glasses," she said airily, her cheeks turning red.

Once Mack was all cleaned up, he stuck out his left arm to pay via the microchip in his wrist. "How much?"

"Oh, you're not paying for food that was dumped in your lap," Knitsy said.

"I'm more than happy to pay. The roast really was nice. And I'm sure I caused you some emotional damage today."

"It's all right," said Knitsy. "Please, don't worry."

"Well, let me make it up to you somehow," he said. "Would you care to meet me at the pub for dinner? Sometime this week?"

Knitsy's eyes bugged out. "Erm, are you mad? Penny would have my arse!"

"We haven't been doing well, as you can probably tell. I've been thinking about cutting it off lately. I'm not sure why I haven't. Maybe because hanging out with her gets me away from my brother."

"Well, I'll only see you when it's over between you two. I'm not going to cause any more trouble."

Mack smiled. "So . . . Friday? Six o'clock?"

Knitsy laughed. "All right, then. Why not?"

"I'll change into something nicer by then, I promise," he said, looking down at his stained shirt. "I think Penny and I will be having a chat tonight."

"I'm sorry," Knitsy said solemnly.

"Don't be. I like people who are nice and make me laugh. People like you."

Knitsy was at a loss for words.

"Thank you, Knitsy Hampshire. I'll see you Friday."

Mack started to walk away. Knitsy stood there watching him. Then he stopped, turned, and looked at her one more time. She couldn't be sure, but it seemed almost as if he wanted to lurch forward and kiss her but stopped himself. He raised a hand and waved. "See you Friday."

Knitsy waved back. As soon as the tunnel door closed, she ran to Meg and jumped into her arms.

* * *

That Friday, Knitsy arrived at The Cat's Chin early, wearing her favourite dress, a knee-length tartan V-neck. She read the menu over and over while she waited for Mack to arrive. She glanced at a table in the back corner, where Bowie and Meg were sitting. They shot her a thumbs up, as they were going to secretly watch the date unfold.

Was it a date, though? Or was he really just apologising for the scene at the restaurant? That was Knitsy's worry the first time around. The worry this time was entirely different. If she was successful, her daughter would be born, and all their progeny currently trapped in the Time Belt would be saved. If she failed, she, her grandchildren, and Henrietta would cease to exist. She took a SeptaSmoke from her purse, clipped it on, and sucked the smoky scent—Earl Grey Tea, her favourite—firmly into her lungs. She noticed Meg glaring at Bowie as if to say, "Look what you've done to her." Knitsy closed her eyes and breathed the smoke out, letting the calm wash over her. Then she unclipped the SeptaSmoke from her nose and tossed it back into her purse.

She glanced at the entrance and saw the security guard scanning Mack's chip and motioning him inside. Knitsy lowered her eyes to her menu, pretending she hadn't seen him. She heard his cautious footsteps approaching.

"Erm, hello Knitsy," Mack smiled, pushing his hair behind his ears. "You look lovely."

She felt queasy but mustered up a meek "Thanks."

Mack leaned down, and Knitsy froze. His soft lips met her cheek. Then he looked embarrassed, as if that was too big of a step, and he quickly sat down.

He held out a rectangular package. "This is for you."

"What for?"

"Well, I never gave you a proper birthday gift."

Knitsy gaped at him. A present? She gingerly tore the brown paper wrapping to find a framed drawing of herself. It was a stunning portrait, all in pen. The details were immaculate.

"This makes me look beautiful," she said.

"No," Mack said. "You make the drawing beautiful. I just draw what I see."

Knitsy studied it closely. "You're . . . so talented. How did you learn to draw like that?"

Mack smiled. "I've always been quite shy. I would draw whenever I felt alone. Drawing brings out my personality. It's my happy place."

Knitsy thought of her grandchildren—their grandchildren—and the special talents they had: Luna's writing, Elbina's cooking, Riff and his music, Ann Lou's athleticism. *They certainly didn't get them from me,* Knitsy thought.

"I love it," Knitsy said, hoping her face wasn't too dark a shade of red. "Thank you so much."

"It was my pleasure."

"So," she continued. "How's Penny?"

Mack brushed his hands together as if dusting them off. "It's over. I don't want to talk about her, though. I want to know everything about you."

Relief. But now Knitsy had to reveal things about herself. She bit her tongue. What could she safely say? Only things in her first twenty-four years of life. But sorting memories on the fly and screening out everything from the latter sixty or so years was going to be difficult.

"Erm, I've lived in Portsmouth my whole life. I work at the restaurant, as you know. You've met my two best friends. My favourite food is sweets."

Mack chuckled. "What kind of sweets?"

"I really like cakes. Any sort of cake."

Mack smiled so hard that his cheeks formed two large spheres on either side of his mouth. He cocked his head slightly. It was the kind of smile that melts a person—where someone can't even look into the other's eyes for fear of disintegrating on the spot. Knitsy looked at the table, hoping the fluttering in her stomach would subside. She felt a soft hand grasping hers.

Suddenly, the activity at the tunnel door grew rowdy, and Mack drew his hand away from Knitsy's as he swivelled to see what the fuss was about. Knitsy heard Mack sigh. It was his brother Burl and his posse.

The boys hollered for drinks as they approached the bar. They were clearly already inebriated. Mack's brother had his arm around a girl. The girl happened to turn toward Mack and Knitsy, and when she saw them, she elbowed Burl and grinned. It was Penny.

Burl pointed at Mack. "Oi, lads, look who it is!" He and Penny staggered up to Mack and Knitsy's table, followed by the others. "Macky boy!"

Knitsy's stomach turned as the boys surrounded their table, sloshing drinks in their faces.

"And he's already got himself a new girlfriend!" Burl shouted. "What a cad, eh? Well, I'll tell you what, little bro. I'll treat your old girl nice." Burl leaned in and gave Penny a sloppy kiss as the other boys hooted and shook the table.

Mack said to Knitsy, "Just ignore them."

On the outside, Knitsy was the shy, inexperienced girl who hid herself in oversized jumpers and didn't rock the boat. Inside, she knew so much more about the world than she had then. Since she was in her young body, Knitsy still felt the same fear. But she also had a new perspective on these boys that she hadn't had last time. They were acting like children. In Knitsy's mind, they deserved ridicule.

So she picked up her waterglass and threw the water into Burl's face and said, "Go home, Burl. You're drunk. You're not impressing anyone. You look like an arse."

Burl's face fell as it dripped with water. For a brief moment, he looked unsure what had just happened. Knitsy froze, squeezing the glass tightly in her grip and wondering if she had made a terrible mistake.

Then someone across the bar laughed.

Burl couldn't think of any sort of comeback and mimicked Knitsy by splashing his drink squarely into her face, with much greater force than she had done to him.

Mack lunged at Burl, but another boy pushed Mack to the floor.

"Mack!" Knitsy screamed.

Knitsy heard chairs squeak across the room and watched as Bowie's fist flew into the face of Mack's assailant. She gasped as a fight ensued. Mack scrambled to his feet, and Meg pulled him and Knitsy back to the corner.

"The prime minister's little buddy is trying to take us on. How cute!" Burl cried, shoving Penny to the side and pushing Bowie sharply in his chest.

The rest of the boys took hold of Bowie's arms, and Burl began to throw punches. Bowie writhed in pain, unable to defend himself against six muscular men.

"No!" shouted Meg and Knitsy. Mack leapt onto the back of one of Bowie's captors. The boy let go of Bowie, who then used his free arm to clobber his remaining captor in the nose. Meg even joined in and tossed Penny to the ground. The boy underneath Mack staggered around a bit but then flipped Mack over his head. Then he shoved Mack to the floor, pinned him down, and began choking him.

Knitsy watched in horror as her husband's face turned a cool blue shade. If only she had composed herself back at the table! But she was not willing to give up. She needed him alive. She heaved herself at Mack's attacker, who let go of Mack and instead turned to her, pinning her down. Mack gasped for air, then hopped up, grabbed an empty glass from the table, and cracked it against the boy's head. He collapsed, but then the other three boys took hold of Mack. They held him high, then threw him to the floor and pummelled him with their fists. Blood streamed from his face.

Finally, the security guard came around. He quickly overpowered the boys holding Mack.

"Lads!" Burl shouted.

They all stopped and stared at their leader.

"My brother can't end up dead. Mum will ask too many questions. Let's go."

They assembled and headed for the exit. But, on the way, Burl grabbed the back of Bowie's shirt and yanked him backward.

"Remember our deal," he whispered into Bowie's ear.

Burl let go of Bowie and left, along with his gang and Penny. Knitsy's stomach churned. Meg ran to Bowie. Knitsy held Mack's face in her hands and cried. His eyes were closed, and his breaths were small and hoarse. Knitsy looked over to Meg. "Is he all right?"

Meg nodded.

Knitsy stared back at Mack and held him close. She could smell the iron in his blood. With one slip-up, one smart remark, she had nearly lost it all: not just Mack, but Henrietta and the grandchildren and that funny little great-grandson too. Red stains spread across her dress; it was surely ruined, but she didn't care. Mack was alive.

* * *

Knitsy and Mack met up a week later at his house. Luckily, Burl and his friends had run off to torment someone else. Mack's mother had kindly made her a cup of tea and offered her a plate of sweet cakes while they waited for Mack to come downstairs.

When he did, Knitsy saw his bruised black eyes, swollen lips, and broken nose. The moment he saw her, he smiled wide. She winced, thinking how much it had to hurt. But his smile never faded.

"Come to my room. I have to show you something."

Knitsy turned to his mother. "Thank you for the sweet, Ms. Gorgan."

"Oh, dear, call me Etta," she said with a wink.

Knitsy followed Mack up the stairs to his room. She stood in the doorway in awe. His room was entirely filled with art. All four walls and even the ceiling were drawn upon with different shapes, colours, and scenes. Paper, pens, and brushes covered an art table and part of a desk, and paint stained the floor. It was a scene of beautiful disarray.

Mack took her hand and brought her forward, shutting the door behind them. His body brushed past hers as he walked to his desk. He gestured for her to sit down at the chair facing it.

She sat down, and he turned the chair toward the desk and pushed her into a comfortable spot. Then he knelt beside her. His warm skin grazed hers, and she felt an electric shock reverberate through her body. The smell of paint wafted into her nose and into her mouth and throat. She wished she could swallow the smell and keep it inside her forever.

In front of her were sheets of heavy paper and a tube of paint. Two brushes lay next to a shallow dish. She looked at him, confused and flushed.

"I want you to paint your happiest vision of life, and I'll paint mine," he instructed. He squeezed some paint from the tube into the dish. It was black, and its consistency was like that of pudding. Then Mack took one of the brushes and dipped it into the creamy paint.

Knitsy looked at her sheet of paper, puzzled. Her happiest version of life was . . . him, Henrietta, their grandchildren—all together. But that would never happen.

"Don't overthink it," he said, starting on his art. He turned the paper this way and that as he worked. Occasionally he leaned down close to the paper, his glasses nearly touching the fresh paint. Knitsy watched him, mesmerised by his deep concentration.

She noticed his drawing didn't have any colour after his brush would slide on the paper.

"Erm, no colour? What kind of ruddy paint is this?" she asked.

He looked at her with a small laugh, his cheeks also flushed. "You don't need colours to make art. Just draw from here." He placed his hand over his heart.

Knitsy peered at her paper, shrugged, and dipped her brush in the colourless goop. She drew what was on her mind, unafraid of his reaction for the reason that he couldn't see it since she was a terrible artist.

Once they were both finished, Mack stood up and turned off the lights. He hopped back over to Knitsy and knelt again. Her heart hammered when his face was within inches of hers.

"Look!" he exclaimed.

Knitsy gasped as she saw their paintings bloom gradually into full, vibrant colours. Mack's painting showed him and her twirling in a field of grass. Flowers bloomed behind them. There was a waterfall. Knitsy's cheeks were a rosy red. Her eyes were a grassy green. Light shone around her as if she were an angel.

"Whoa," she breathed, her heart pounding.

"Like it?" he asked, slightly sheepish.

"I love it. That's bloody brilliant."

"What did you paint?" he asked quietly.

They both looked at her painting. It wasn't as perfect as Mack's, but it clearly showed the McHubbard grandchildren, Henrietta, Knitsy, and Mack around the rickety table in the McHubbard home. They were all laughing about something. Henrietta's bouncy grey hair, Luna's black glasses, Elbina's Gasser, Riff's red hair sticking out from under his cap, and Ann Lou's prosthetic arm were all there. Knitsy teared up at the sight of their loving faces. They were perfect, even in her imperfect painting.

Mack stared incredulously at it. "Is that me?" He pointed to Knitsy's painted version of him.

Knitsy nodded, hanging her head in embarrassment.

Mack smiled brightly. "A family. The most beautiful family I've ever seen."

"How are all these colours so . . . bright?"

"It comes from your heart," Mack whispered into her ear.

He slowly pulled her chair back from the desk and felt for her hands in the sweet glow of the paintings. He helped her to her feet and gently moved his hands around her waist. Their faces moved closer as he gently pulled her in. They paused as their noses touched, their breaths synchronised. Knitsy's heart was nearly pounding through her chest, and she could feel his doing the same.

His hands went slowly up her back, along her shoulders, and onto her rosy cheeks. His touch was soft, gentle, and familiar. His lips parted, and she could feel his warm breath filling her mouth. Their lips met, and Knitsy melted into him, falling slightly in his arms. Mack gripped her face tightly as he kissed her. Knitsy wanted this moment to last forever. All she needed was more time.

* * *

A few weeks later, Mack and Knitsy were sitting in his kitchen when Knitsy's stomach started to gurgle. She rushed to the bathroom and held her head over the toilet. The colour drained from her skin, and she started losing energy quickly. Knitsy promptly hurled into the toilet and lay there with her arms clutching the seat.

Mack came rushing in after her. "Let's get you to bed!" he exclaimed.

Mack and Etta helped her up the stairs and into Mack's small bed. He brought her some water and put a flannel on her forehead. He looked concerned. Knitsy remembered feeling confused the first time around, but this time she knew. The plan was working.

"Mack?" said Knitsy weakly.

He sat on the edge of the bed.

She breathed deeply and stared into his eyes. "I'm pregnant."

He sat back, but his shock quickly faded to a big grin. He stared lovingly into her eyes. "A beautiful family."

He kissed Knitsy and lay down next to her, their hands clasped across her stomach. Henrietta was in there somewhere. The thought made Knitsy cry both happy and sad tears. She was with her daughter again. To save the future McHubbard generations, all she had to do now was make sure Henrietta was born.

* * *

Over the next few months, Mack and Knitsy were together every day. They met up with Meg and Bowie at The Cat's Chin every Friday evening and danced the night away in their little happy group. Mack would show up at The Blue Barnacle during every one of Knitsy's shifts and bring her sweets. Bowie eventually whined enough that Mack started bringing in sweets for him and Meg as well, which Knitsy loved.

Over the winter, Meg noticed how gaunt Bowie was getting. He no longer wore his usual ostentatious clothing or makeup, and he grew his hair out to its natural dirty blond colour. Meg thought he was hiding something. Knitsy knew he was, but after her mistake at the pub, she knew she had to be scrupulously careful to behave as she had before. So she consistently told Meg to drop the subject, implying that she was just imagining things. Meg listened to her friend and gave Bowie his space.

Knitsy became quite close to Etta as well, often chatting to her while she cooked in the kitchen. She hardly saw Burl, which she was thankful for. Mack never spoke about him otherwise. Knitsy eventually moved in with the Gorgans. She still worked at the restaurant and picked up extra shifts so that she could give Etta a little extra money every month for the added burden, which Etta always declined since she was eager for the arrival of her first grandchild and adored Knitsy nearly as much as she adored Mack.

Knitsy arrived at work one day in December of that year to find Meg pacing around tables frantically. Knitsy walked up to her. Meg looked frightened.

"You all right?" Knitsy asked, as she started putting on her apron.

Meg exhaled hard. "Bowie's not here."

Knitsy raised an eyebrow. "He's never on time."

"I know. But he and his boyfriend went to The Cat's Chin last night. We were messaging, but then he stopped replying," Meg said in a flurry. "I'm afraid Burl Gorgan's crew ran into them or something."

"I wouldn't worry about it, Meg. I haven't seen Burl in ages."

Meg nodded. She and Knitsy prepped for their shift, talking about how the baby was coming along and how Meg's relationship was going.

"I dunno," Meg said. "Boys are stressful. Xyler has just been really distant lately. And when we are together, he's rough. Like full of anger. I'm afraid of him sometimes. The only good one is Mack."

"Well, no one's perfect," Knitsy said. "And Meg, Xyler shouldn't be acting that way around you. You don't deserve that. Do I need to have a word with him? Kick him in the arse a bit?"

Just then the restaurant's tunnel door opened, and Mack appeared, trembling. His face was blanched and tear-stained. His hands were covered in blood. Knitsy darted over to him. "What's happened?" She could feel her fingers going numb.

Mack's mouth opened, but no words came out. His eyes darted around the restaurant. Meg hurried over to them.

"What's wrong, Mack?" Meg said slowly, helping him to a seat. "Just say what you can."

Mack shakily sat down and looked into Knitsy's eyes. His mouth quivered as he tried to speak again. "We n-need t-to h h-hide."

"From who?" Knitsy said, taking one of his trembling hands.

"Burl. He-he's on a rampage. He's ju-just . . ." Mack buried his face in his hands and sobbed, gasping and dry-heaving. Meg and Knitsy held him up and stroked his hair.

"What did Burl do?" Knitsy asked calmly.

Mack's mouth trembled. "He's killed our mum."

Knitsy could feel the numbness rising into her arms as the sadness washed over her. This was exactly what she hadn't wanted to relive. With the amazing memories came the horrible ones. They couldn't be separated. She held Mack to her chest as tightly as she could while he sobbed. Knitsy shared a terrified look with Meg.

"You're both coming home with me," Meg said, tearing her apron off. "Let's go. Now."

Knitsy didn't argue. She helped Mack up and kept him close to her as they made their way to Meg's flat.

Meg offered them her bed while she took the couch. They watched the news on her television over the next few days. It wasn't just Etta that was the target of the attack. Many other south England folk were missing. Neither Meg nor Knitsy heard from Bowie, despite sending him countless messages.

Casualties grew over the next couple months as terrorism spread over not only England, but the majority of Europe. When they caught the international news, they found out that every other continent was having the same problem. By mid-April, it was no longer safe to go out by oneself. One news report in particular caught their attention one evening as they sat in the living room playing a game on their microchips.

"This is breaking news from Parliament. We have just been informed that the prime minister is dead."

"What?" Meg said in a horrified tone.

"It is being reported that he died at the hands of the same group that is behind the worldwide terrorist attacks. They have recently named themselves the GeoLapse. Members of the United Nations believe this group is seeking total control of the planet. The British Parliament has voted to redirect funding from environmental rehabilitation to homeland security.

"The United Nations have agreed to provide the remainder of the world's population with a microchip as well as make necessary updates to the current ones in order to better keep track of everyone's whereabouts. This will control the level of attacks and keep us safe. We will provide more information on the prime minister's death once our news team arrives on the scene."

"Bowie," Meg said breathlessly, turning her head back to Knitsy and Mack with tear-filled eyes. "Do you think he's dead?"

"I hope not," said Mack. "Maybe he's hiding." Mack closed his eyes and hung his head in embarrassment. "My brother. My brother did all this. I can't believe he's in the GeoLapse." He looked up at the girls with sorrowful eyes. "I'm so sorry to have gotten you in this mess."

Knitsy placed a hand on Mack's knee. "This isn't your fault."

The next day, the three of them discussed their plans for the day in order to distract themselves from the horrors of the world. Mack went on and on about how excited he was to meet the baby and to be able to take care of her. But he insisted on making things a little more permanent. He wanted to marry Knitsy before the baby was due to arrive.

At this point in the pregnancy, with about two weeks to go, Knitsy was bursting. Meg and Mack tended to her needs, which made her feel guilty, even though neither of them minded at all. Meg, Mack, and Knitsy spent all of their time at Meg's flat. They had been far too scared to go back to the restaurant or out to the pub for fear of an attack. It was safer here anyways, and they enjoyed each other's company.

The three of them decided to have a small wedding ceremony in Meg's living room to keep their spirits up. Meg painted Knitsy's face with the most ostentatious makeup and sewed some white sheets together for a makeshift wedding dress. She even made a veil out of a pillowcase. Mack fashioned rings out of the tines of forks from the kitchen drawer.

Meg wore one of her incredibly short dresses and her highest set of heels. She officiated their elopement by saying a few ridiculous words. "My best friend and her handsome prince are gathered here today to completely rub it in everyone's nose that they are the most perfect couple in the entire universe. Even though I will never find a love like theirs, I could not have asked for a better man to be by my Knitsy's side."

Knitsy and Mack laughed as he pulled his wife-to-be closer to his side.

"Now, Mack Gorgan, do you take this marvellous woman to be your wife, to have and to hold, blah, blah, blah?"

Mack gazed into Knitsy's eyes and pressed his glasses to his nose, inhaling excitedly. "I do." She felt a warmth leave his eyes and swirl into hers. His hands tightened around her back.

"And Knits, my darling dear, do you take this boy to be your husband?" Meg sang.

Knitsy blinked warmth back into Mack's eyes. "I do."

"You sure?" Meg asked jokingly as she glanced at Knitsy sidelong.

Knitsy laughed heartily. "Without a doubt." She winked at Mack.

Meg held her hands to her heart. "Awww, just kiss each other already! Oh, and do the ring thing!"

Mack took the rings out of his pocket. With a shaky hand, he slipped the smaller ring onto Knitsy's finger. Knitsy took the other one and put it on Mack's finger with a bit of a push.

"Well, looks like that's not coming off," he laughed.

Mack took Knitsy's face and kissed her the way he had when they shared their first kiss. It was soft, warm, and electric. Oceans of butterflies flew inside her, around the baby, and filled every crevice of her body as she wrapped herself in him. It was an embrace between their little, growing family.

"All right," said Meg playfully. "I gave you guys the room upstairs for a reason. Off with you!"

That night, as they all slept soundly, Meg was awakened by a loud rap on the door. She held her blanket up to her chin as the knocking continued. She heard voices, laughs almost, from behind the door in the tunnel area. Meg quickly sprinted up the stairs to Mack and Knitsy's room.

To Meg's surprise, Knitsy was sitting up in the bed, breathing deeply and sweating. Mack was holding her hand and counting aloud.

"What's happening?" Meg asked, rushing to Knitsy's side. Knitsy winced, clearly in pain, though she managed not to scream.

"The baby's coming right now," Mack said. "A little early, but eager to join the world."

Meg hesitated. "Well . . . there's someone at the door. They're being rowdy." Her voice grew quieter with each word.

Mack took his eyes off Knitsy and looked at the bedroom door. Terror grew on his face. "We have to keep hidden." He looked back at Knitsy. "Darling? I'm going to have to put you in the bedroom closet." His voice was stern with a tinge of fear.

Knitsy didn't respond, mostly because she was worried she'd vomit on him if she spoke. Meg and Mack carefully sat her in the closet and piled clothes around her. Meg hung some towels and sheets on hangers to shield her body from view.

"We have to check the downstairs, my love," Mack whispered.

Knitsy just whimpered as a painful contraction started. She grimaced and gripped Mack's hand.

The knocks on the door downstairs turned into pounds and clamorous bangs. Mack squeezed Knitsy's hand. "I'll be back, okay? I love you." He kissed her on the forehead and again on her drooling lips.

Knitsy released her grip but started to scream as the contraction became unbearable. Meg reached in the closet and found a balled-up pair of socks, which she promptly stuffed into Knitsy's mouth.

"Keep as still as you can, Knits. You're doing amazing," Meg whispered, kissing her on the top of her head. "I can't wait to meet this baby."

As Knitsy screamed into the socks, Mack silently shut the closet door. Complete darkness surrounded her. All she could sense was the dryness in her mouth and the creaking of wood as Mack and Meg tiptoed down the stairs.

Knitsy whimpered through the pain as she kept listening. She heard Mack and Meg shuffling downstairs, probably trying to find a place to hide. The bangs on the door and the voices in the tunnel grew louder and louder until finally there was a *CRACK!* Loud footsteps barrelled in and spread through the entirety of the downstairs. Angry voices shouted as Knitsy began to hear fragile objects being smashed. Knitsy winced every time something crashed.

The thunderous footsteps continued. Bodies thwacked against walls and furniture.

And then, a piercing scream. Meg's scream. "Xyler! What are you doing?"

Meg's subsequent screams penetrated Knitsy's body, and she released screams of pain alongside her best friend. She couldn't even sit up at this point. The baby was coming. She had to start pushing to end this nightmare.

Whoops filled the downstairs area as Meg's screams echoed, faded, and ended with a thud. The hearty laughter made Knitsy's blood boil. She felt as if she were exploding but couldn't tell if it was from the pain or from living her worst nightmare all over again. It had to be a mixture of the two.

"I just saw that door move!" boomed a deep voice, which Knitsy immediately recognised as Burl's. Loud footsteps led to a spot directly below Knitsy. She could hear the muffled voices fairly clearly. Mack must have been hiding in the pantry. Tears began to stream down Knitsy's cheeks.

"Well, if it isn't Macky lad!" thundered Burl, followed by shouts from his posse.

Knitsy could hear Mack below her, whimpering. A contraction nearly forced a scream out of her, but she held it in, clenching her teeth on the socks, feeling choked by the soft, dry material. Sweat drenched her nightgown. She continued to push, heaving her head backward and resting her back on a pile of clothes.

"So you've got a new bird now, eh?" Burl laughed. "What happened to the dark-haired one? Can I take her too?"

Knitsy gagged at his comment. She heard a girl laugh, probably Penny. Knitsy continued to push, holding her sides and squeezing her eyes shut.

"Y-yeah, we broke up," Mack stammered.

Knitsy heard Mack shout in pain.

"Easy, lads," Burl said calmly. "Give him a chance to speak."

"Why are you doing this?" Mack cried. "You're a monster, just like Dad! Thought we could move down here in peace, but no! You had to put Mum in more danger!"

"Little bro, there is next to nothing left of this damned planet!" Burl said angrily. "The GeoLapse are the only ones promising good things to come. Didn't take much for Dad to convince me."

"Don't call me your brother!" Mack screamed.

"I'll give you one more chance, Macky. Join us. We eat well. We drink well. We can even go outside with these suits. This life is better. What do you say?"

Everyone downstairs was silent, waiting for Mack's answer. Knitsy's whole body was shaking. She wanted so badly to switch places with Mack, but she knew she had to stay hidden. Just a little bit longer. She cried into the socks, the tears still streaming.

"Never!" yelled Mack, his voice growing louder. "You're a coward! No matter what you do to me, my life here is better. It's not about food and beer. It's about family. And friends. And love in your heart!"

Knitsy only wanted to plug her ears.

"Friends? Like your friend here?" Burl asked.

Knitsy heard Mack say weakly: "Bowie?"

"I'm sorry, Mack. My life was on the line. I—"

"The GeoLapse don't show remorse!" Burl bellowed at Bowie. "We lay siege! We are in control!" He directed his tone toward Mack again. "Second thoughts, brother?"

Mack wheezed. "Never."

"Then that's settled. Stand back, boys."

Knitsy heard Mack utter a gurgling sound, followed by a thud. The GeoLapse celebrated their kills, praising themselves with chants as they streamed to the door and exited into the tunnel. Their evil chorus faded away, and Knitsy spit the socks out and screamed into her last push. A baby's cry caused her to shriek and sit up. There was baby Henrietta on a pile of bloody clothes. Knitsy picked up her baby and sobbed. Sobbed at the deaths of her best friend as well as the love of her life. The pain couldn't be blunted, but holding her daughter activated her motherly instincts, allowing her to rock her baby amid both of their cries.

In the darkness of the closet, Knitsy noticed a small glimmer on her left hand. Her wedding ring was glowing. She held it up close to her nose. In the ring's dim light, she saw Henrietta's smile. Mack.

A swirl of white light surrounded Knitsy and Henrietta. It was a wormhole of warmth, beautiful and shining. Knitsy knew that this was it. She had succeeded. Henrietta had been successfully born. "For you cannot be both lost and found," as the poem had said. Henrietta now existed on Earth again, and future generations of McHubbards could continue their lives in the land of linear time.

The wormhole bubbled around mother and daughter as they embraced tightly. Knitsy breathed a deep sigh of relief. Wherever they were going next, they would be together. And the best part was that Mack would be there too. Knitsy's eyes sparkled as she spoke to her ring.

"I'm coming, Mack. And I'm bringing a beautiful family."

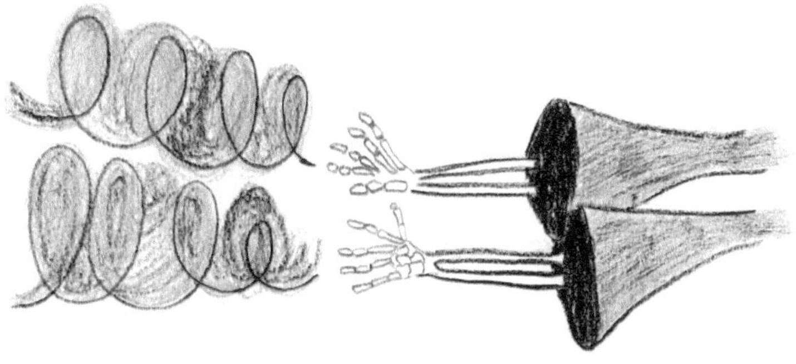

Secrets Within the Bank

Back on Focalok, watching the completion of Knitsy's mission in the panoramic view, Luna and Riff bawled with a mixture of relief, joy, and loss. Knitsy's mission, which took place over nearly ten months in Earth time, unfolded in only a few moments to the watching McHubbard grandchildren from within the Time Belt.

Together, Luna and Riff held Elbina's head up. Her breaths were shallow, and her skin was cold. She didn't have much time left. Clorin danced around them playing some game of his own invention, unaware that his great-grandmother had just relived the greatest horrors of her lifetime.

The hourglass Jalopy reappeared in its place at the top of the ramp. Luna looked up at it. No Knitsy. She was gone. Dead, in the real sense—not just lost in the Time Belt.

Luna looked at the hooded figure. "What now? D-do we go back?"

The figure nodded. "Your grandmother's mission is complete. A strenuous one it was that she managed to beat. You may go back to your realities and once again form your families."

Riff got up slowly, his face full of tears. He gathered Elbina's limp body gently in his arms and started toward the ramp to the Jalopy. Clorin raised his arms up to Riff, but he shook his head. Clorin then raced over to Luna and made the same gesture to her, but she didn't acknowledge him. She only continued staring at the hooded figure. Clorin started to whimper, but Luna held out her hand to silence him. He lowered his arms to his side.

Luna addressed the hooded figure, her voice rising as she spoke. "So you're just going to let Rodney, Constance, and my Nan die? That easily? After all they've been through?"

Riff and Clorin watched Luna sidelong, frozen where they stood.

"Well, Luna McHubbard, those are the Time Belt's rules. Non-existent are Rodney's and Constance's molecules. Your dear Knitsy's strife has landed her in the afterlife."

Luna was not satisfied. "But what good is that? Why are you doing this?"

"What is it with this frustration? Why do you make such an accusation?" the figure said huskily, curling its skeletal hands into fists.

Riff and Clorin slowly backed up the ramp toward the Jalopy, keeping their eyes glued to Luna.

"Because I know who you are," Luna said in a tone of finality. "You're Father Time. Ernesteen Bowser the Third. You created this place, taking full advantage of your grandmother, Ernesteen Bowser Senior's achievement of creating a time machine. You used her invention as a way to destroy creatures' lives."

Ernesteen nodded, clapping her bony hands together. "You and your sister, the amputee, have been reading my book, I see. Well done! You have reached the farthest of anyone."

"Luna!" whispered Riff. "Just come on!"

Luna held her hand up to him.

She repeated to Ernesteen: "Why are you doing this?"

"You couldn't possibly understand planet Thera's bloodshed. My entire family eventually was dead. My grandmother, my mother, and I had to take cover. Terrorism flooded our walls, leading eventually to our planet's downfall. After they took my family from me, that was all they were going to get for free. I vowed to never let anyone cross me with another crime, and if fools wronged me, I'd keep them here for a lifetime."

"I understand the hurt that you've endured," Luna said, surprised at how familiar Ernesteen's story sounded. "Planet Earth went through something very similar. But you can't punish the entire universe. It's not everyone's fault."

"You're wrong!" boomed Ernesteen. "Many are selfish. They deserve for their time to be glitched. I can keep them under my watchful eye, as they continue to act foolish and buy, buy, buy!"

"Why does the Time Belt exist in the Coloratura universe and not any other ones like the Reprisa universe?" Luna asked.

"Silly, sadly limited Earthling! Do you not grasp that I can do anything? My domain stretches far past your imagination—a culmination of all universal congregations!"

"Where is all of their time going?" Luna prodded.

"To me, of course. It is a bottomless source. It will keep me alive for as long as they are willing to self-deprive. Creatures far and wide give up their time so readily, and I can instead use it preciously."

Luna gasped. "You mean to say," Luna started, "that whenever people spend time, it goes to you so that you are granted more time? That means . . . you're immortal?"

Ernesteen laughed darkly. Riff, standing at the top of the ramp with Elbina in his arms, just stared as Clorin cowered behind him.

Luna went on, her fury growing. "You called my Nan selfish for wanting to switch places with my dead Mum. She was trying to be selfless. But you go and manipulate our existence. You make it nearly impossible to get out of the Time Belt. Creatures keep trying and trying, almost all of them just end up giving their whole lives to you. Tell me, who's the real monster here?" Luna cocked her head. "I'd say you're the selfish one. Not my family! I—I won't let you do this anymore!"

Luna sprinted toward the ramp that led to the Jalopy. Ernesteen raised her arms. Instantly, black wormholes spiralled from between the bones of her hands, and she aimed them at Luna, following her as she ran. They were the same type of wormhole that had sucked up Rodney and Connie.

The deranged poet shouted. "You cannot run away! You've earned your fate as my newest prey!"

Luna yelled to Riff as she ran up the ramp. "Get in the Jalopy! Now!"

Riff gently but quickly lowered Elbina into the bottom half of the hourglass, then grabbed Clorin and climbed in. Riff set Clorin in the top half, then went into the bottom half with Elbina, leaving the stone top open for Luna to make a quick leap.

Luna panted as she raced up the ramp. She felt a slight tug on her feet. Ernesteen's wormholes were caving in around her ankles. Her footsteps were being yanked backward. She saw the elongated wormholes stretching like string from Ernesteen's hands. Ernesteen was laughing maniacally at her new prey. They would surely keep her alive for many more decades.

Luna hesitated as the wormholes began constricting the blood flow in her legs. She felt like giving in and just letting her siblings get to safety. "Go!" she shouted to Riff. She felt dizzy and felt herself losing consciousness as her existence started fading away.

But then she felt something grab both of her hands. It was a painful grab and strong. Luna looked up, expecting to see the wormholes rising up to envelop her. Instead she saw Clorin pulling her with all his

Epitonian might. Luna could hear Riff banging his fists against the glass of the Jalopy, rooting Clorin on.

Luna's top half was inching toward Clorin, but she felt her lower half giving way. Finally, her legs snapped back like rubber bands escaping the clutches of Ernesteen's wormholes. Luna scooped up Clorin, heaved both of them into the top of the Jalopy, and pulled the stone down with a smash. The interior illuminated in green.

"Hello, Luna McHubbard, Griff—"

"Vivalok! NOW!" Luna shouted, still panting. Her face was crammed against the Jalopy's glass.

"Enjoy your trip," said the familiar voice of the Jalopy.

As the Jalopy lifted off, Luna caught sight of Ernesteen. The wormholes retracted into her skeletal hands. In the omnipotent voice of Father Time, she boomed: "McHubbards, prepare for your doomsday! This I swear—dearly you will pay!" Then she snapped her skeleton fingers and vanished from the platform of Focalok.

The Jalopy accelerated upward. Luna gulped and looked down at Riff in the bottom half of the hourglass. He was patting Elbina's cheeks, trying to get her to come to, but she lay limply in his arms. Then he looked up at Luna with teary eyes. "I think we're too late. We've lost her."

He was right. Elbina's form started to dissolve into thin air. Riff tried to pull her close, but his arms only wrapped around his own torso.

"Wh-where'd she go?" he screamed. "She's gone! Where is she?" Riff started to hyperventilate and bang his fists on the glass. "Luna, where is she?"

Luna held back her tears and said, as calmly as she could: "She's on Mortalok."

Riff's eyes bulged. "Mortalok? So you're telling me another one of our family will be floating on a rope, screaming gibberish out of their neck for all eternity? This is mad! I need to get out of here!"

Luna pressed her hands against the glass between them and held Riff's gaze. "You jumping out of a flying Jalopy is only going to land *you* on Mortalok, too. If my understanding is correct, and if we're successful, she's going to be fine. We are going to Vivalok to destroy the Time Belt."

Riff groaned. "Luna, why didn't you just let us go back home? We could have been back by now. This is absolute bollocks, and it's all your fault! Why can't you turn off your brain for a damned minute!" He folded his arms and looked away from her.

Luna shouted back at him. "Think of all the innocent creatures we can save! This is bigger than us!"

"I don't give a damn!" Riff yelled, his face turning purple as his tears kept streaming down. "I don't want to keep watching my siblings die! I want to go home! Nan just did all that work, reliving hell for us all, just so we could exist again! And speaking of being selfish—who's the selfish one now? I know you're obviously *way* smarter than everyone in the universe, but I'll tell you—the answer is *you!*" Riff was violently trembling and Clorin hugged one of Luna's legs with sad eyes.

Tears stung Luna's eyes. This wasn't the usual banter between her and Riff. This was a real accusation. A real fight. Maybe he was right. Maybe if she had just sent them all back to safety by pointing the Jalopy back to Earth, Elbina would still be alive.

But something in Luna's gut told her that her plan was worth more. She remembered the line from the "My Chroniya" poem: "All inhabitants who have paid would exit my domain." Anyone who spent time in the Time Belt would be released if the Bank was destroyed. It certainly sounded as if Elbina, Ann Lou, and Knitsy could also get out of the Time Belt if Luna and Riff could just destroy the Bank.

"Riff, please," she begged. "We need to destroy the Bank and the Chroniya. That's our way out."

"We *had* a way out. Do you not understand that?" His angry gaze almost burned. "And what are you expecting me to do exactly? Go with you to destroy it? I'd rather go to Mortalok right now. It'll save me the trip back there once you get us all killed off!" Then Riff's eyes landed on Clorin. "And you'd put our nephew's life at risk, too. You're no family to him."

"You take that back!" Luna cried. "I've taken so much care of him!" Salty tears puddled in her mouth and her chin quivered.

"Look who he preferred to play with. You scared him—just like Ann Lou did."

"Don't speak ill of Ann Lou! She saved us!" Luna shouted. She could hear her blood pulsating in her ears. "We all made mistakes in our lives!"

"But Ann Lou did something about it," Riff retorted.

"Sacrificing herself was not a redemption! She thought she was making everyone's lives better off by doing that. Between the four of us, we could've easily gotten another orb!" Luna's screams pierced Riff and Clorin's ears. But she calmed herself then, and continued in a softer voice. "Let's show Ann Lou that we need her by getting all of us out of here. If we'd gone straight back to Earth from Focalok, it would have been just you and me and maybe Elbina. If we succeed at this, it'll be us and Ann Lou, Nan, Elbina, and Clorin once he's born."

"And if we don't succeed, none of us gets to go back," Riff snapped.

But Luna could tell that her last words had resonated with Riff. He ran his hands through his moppy red hair, took a deep breath, and closed his eyes. Then he nodded.

The Jalopy set Luna, Riff, and Clorin down in the centre of Vivalok, directly in front of the Bank. The town was bustling as usual—diverse creatures entering and exiting colourful shops, buzzing excitedly about their new acquisitions. Judging from their expressions, it seemed they hadn't a care in the world—that all was well in the land of Vivalok. Luna wondered if any of them knew about their loved ones moaning in the endless gloom on Mortalok and imprisoned in bottles in the horror-filled towers of Galalok.

Luna and Riff looked up at the monstrous structure of the Bank, in awe at its twisting pipes and many strange clocks. Luna watched as the massive sphere at the top filled, little by little, with dark liquid as transactions were made in the town. Now that Luna knew where it was going—that Ernesteen's power was growing with each drop—the Bank was a fearsome sight. Luna shook her head and focused her attention back on the task at hand.

Luna said, "We have to dismantle the Bank. If we do that, Ernesteen will be destroyed."

"How are we going to dismantle it? It's huge," said Riff.

"We'll need to pull a Henrietta McHubbard and organise some universal troops. Let's alert as many shops as we can and see if we can recruit help. You could start with the gym. The Rhothgans would be perfect. They're quite used to crashing into things."

"What do we say to them? They'll think we're mad."

"Tell them you know a way out. And that their spent time is being used against them. I'd bet you any of these creatures would do anything to get out of here."

"Yeah, all right," Riff said weakly. He rubbed his temples and headed for the arena.

"Clorin?" said Luna, kneeling down to him. "Do you think you could find some Epitonians and bring them back here? They're the ones that look like you. The ones with the horns."

Clorin smiled. "Yes, Looner!" he said, and he dashed off with ultrafast Epitonian speed in search of his kin.

Luna took the opportunity to bolt in the six o'clock direction from the Bank, toward the book shop. She pushed past a group of young Antympanicans gossiping over the latest issue of *Epiton Stars* and found the till area.

Tycho rolled his eyes and slammed his head onto the counter, causing a customer's purchases to bounce off.

"Tycho . . ." panted Luna, "I need your . . . help." The customers in line stared at her with their various forms of eyes. "The Bank . . . the Chroniya . . . you were right . . . It needs to be . . . destroyed."

Tycho lifted his large head and chuckled nervously to the crowd. "Earthlings! What can we do besides laugh at them? Excuse me for a moment." He made his way over to Luna and narrowed his eyes at her. "What's going on?" he whispered.

"E. Bowser the Third is the mysterious figure always standing by the Bank. She's Father Time. She used Ernesteen Bowser Senior's time machine to create the Time Belt. She takes the time everyone spends and uses it to become immortal."

Tycho considered her findings and nodded. "So, destroying the Chroniya means you destroy time. Thus you also destroy the Time Belt. As a bonus, E. Bowser the Third is destroyed also. The quantum mechanics add up! I like it. But how in Casper's name did I not figure it out?" Tycho scratched his chin thoughtfully with his nasal antennae.

"We need as many creatures as possible to start dismantling the Bank. Now!" Luna said.

Tycho looked around the shop. The Antympanicans had lost interest in their magazine and were leaning toward Tycho. The customers in line were staring at him. The entire book shop was eavesdropping on their conversation. Tycho spoke up for them all to hear: "We have a way out, everyone. Head to the Bank. Let's take it down."

The customers just stared—partly confused, but mostly not wanting to lose their spot in line.

Luna added, "You'll be able to get back all the time you've spent. You can go home! And your loved ones will be returned. Well, only the ones who spent time. But still—it's worth a shot, right?"

An especially translucent and bouncy Cipton boomed over all the commotion, "Let's gooo!" and began slithering slowly out of the door.

Everyone else dropped their belongings and followed the brave gelatinous creature. Luna smiled, feeling this was a glimmer of hope in the darkness. Epitonians, Casperians, Olfinderians, Ciptons, Antympanicans, Minagians, hesitant Pomberians, and many more creatures she'd never seen bolted out of the door, ready to attack.

Luna followed them out and recited the same speech at each shop along the way back to the Bank. Soon enough, and with the help of the gossiping Antympanicans around Vivalok, everyone knew the plan, and a horde of creatures was converging on the Bank. Luna started to run with the stampede. She soon spotted Riff running behind a group of Rhothgans who were rolling down the main road with incredible momentum. She also saw Clorin running alongside a group of angry Epitonians.

The Rhothgans were the first to reach the Bank. Led by the largest of them all, Ignea, they bashed into a tangle of pipes and planet clocks, instantly smashing them to small pieces and sending flakes of gold into the crowd running behind them. The flakes fell around the crowd like confetti and stuck to the creatures' faces and bodies as they continued to deconstruct the Bank. The Epitonians scaled the golden pipes, swinging with ease from one handhold to the next, and easily crushed the planet clocks between their strong claws. Olfinderians surrounded the structure at ground level and sang at the resonant frequencies of the golden pipes, causing them to shatter. Kilo-209 creatures happily munched on some of the pipes. The plan was working. The structure was being destroyed before their eyes.

Then Luna perceived a slight dimming of Vivalok's bright light. Amid the joyous clamour, no one else noticed it at first. But as the light faded to grey, the army of creatures stopped their dismantling and stared up at the sky. Soon it was almost as dark and gloomy as the stormy sky on Mortalok. How strange it was to see darkness, especially in a place normally so light and cheery as Vivalok.

With a crack of thunder, Ernesteen rose from the Bank and flew with ease above the crowd. She brought her bony arms out from under her cloak and raised them toward the darkened sky. Storm clouds snagged on her fingers. She made fists and pulled them to her chest, dragging the storm with them. Rain pelted the crowd. A few screamed as the lightning and thunder intensified.

Ernesteen boomed: "Luna McHubbard, you have made this place a little too cluttered!" Dark, spiralling wormholes emerged from the carpals of her palm, spread out over the crowd, and snapped back like bungee cords. One by one, creatures were whisked up into the wormholes. Luna's army was quickly being obliterated.

She heard Riff shout, "Keep going!" and the creatures obeyed, continuing to dismantle the Bank while trying their very hardest to avoid being sucked into Ernesteen's clutches.

Then Luna heard a thunderous sound from behind her. She whirled around to see Brick and Wrench barrelling down the road toward them. A mass of Ciptons had gathered to form a ramp, and the Rhothgans rolled right up it, one by one, and flew over Luna's head, crashing spot on into the Bank's main sphere. Dark liquid Chroniya spewed from its central golden pipe, spraying the crowd with their spent time.

As the Rhothgans rolled off the wreckage of the Bank, Ernesteen focused a palm in their direction and promptly sucked them up into the darkness. Ernesteen cackled from above: "You may have destroyed this source, but the rest of it will never be destroyed by this workforce!" The wormholes from her palms grew in diameter, now sucking up multiple creatures at a time.

Luna's brain ticked with a thought. The "My Chroniya" poem: what had it said again? Luna ran into the nearest shop, a clothes shop, to take cover from the cacophony outside. She pulled the anthology and read the first couple lines.

My Chroniya, oh the treasure you hold,
Deep, deeper in the depths of the gold.

Luna peered up. She was standing in the till area, just beneath the open golden pipe that protruded from the ceiling. That was it. That was how she could get into the depths of the Bank without being seen. Hopping onto the counter, Luna clumsily jumped up and caught the lip of the pipe with her fingers as her legs flailed around beneath her. Summoning all her strength, she hoisted herself up and reached a weak arm to a horizontal part of the pipe where she could stabilise herself.

Luna caught her breath, then began to crawl. The pipe was dark, which didn't really bother Luna at all. It felt natural relying on her sense of touch, allowing her arms and legs to guide her. When her hands bumped into something, she felt the pipe walls around her. The pipe took a ninety-degree turn upward. Luna lay on her back, then propped herself up on her elbows until she was sitting in the vertical section. Shifting gradually, she managed to stand up. Feeling around, she found pipe wall over her head and empty space ahead of her. So she assumed a hands-and-knees position again and continued crawling.

The pipe maze continued in loop-de-loops, long climbs, and short drops. The pipe from the clothes shop connected to all the other shop pipes. She crawled on, manoeuvring carefully across downward openings. She could smell a mixture of all the foods in the food shop wafting from somewhere farther down the pipeline.

Still unable to see where she was going, Luna heard faint cackles and bangs from below her. It sounded exactly like the scene she had ducked away from by the Bank. She knew she was getting close when another full-body Rhothgan attack shook the pipe system.

Luna's arms reached another downward opening. She could feel openings to the left, right, and straight ahead also. The four-way intersection seemed like a good sign that she was right on top of the Bank. The only way was down, she hoped. Light poked in where parts of the central pipe had been damaged by the Vivalok army.

Luna squirmed around until her feet were in front of her, then dangled them down into the pipe. Beads of sweat poured down from her face. Her heart pounded. What if Ernesteen had heard her fiddling around in the pipes? Or knew where she was headed? Luna was terrified to be doing this by herself, but she had to do it for her family, for the ones who had sacrificed themselves for her: her mother, Ann Lou, Knitsy, and Elbina. Riff and Clorin had played their heroic roles as well. She even felt a degree of gratitude for Constance. All their souls were on the line now, and Luna didn't want to disappoint them. She had to try. It was the only way justice could be done.

Luna pushed herself off the edge and fell straight down the pipe. It took all of her inner strength not to scream as her body accelerated toward an unknown landing. Luna tried to measure her descent by what she had seen from outside, starting from where Ernesteen had been floating just above the Bank, to the level where Wrench and Brick had smashed into the Bank, to eye level with Riff, and, finally, below the soft, cloud-like ground of Vivalok.

Luna shuddered when she splashed into a pool. Never before had she been doused in a pool of liquid, but human instinct prompted her to hold her breath. She tried paddling toward the surface, but an intense gravitational force pulled her down. All around her was still black. Her lungs were giving out. An accidental anxious gasp sucked the liquid into her nose and all through her sinuses. As her lungs filled with the liquid, she sank. Her hands clasped around her neck as she felt her entire body being squeezed tighter and tighter, as if being forced into a tiny hole.

Luna landed hard in a grey place. She sputtered and coughed black liquid from her lungs and stomach. Her hair and clothes were saturated with it, and it stained her skin. All around her was a deafening sound like a waterfall.

Time. She was drenched in a mixture of everyone's time—the same time Ernesteen was collecting to remain immortal. But where was this place? Luna wiped the liquid from her eyes and looked around desperately for clues. The distant landscape looked eerily similar to that of Mortalok, but the ground on which Luna sat was just a small circle floating in empty white space. Near her, Mortalok's Bank, previously just an empty sphere, was being filled by a waterfall of dark liquid Chroniya. Luna peered up and saw that the Chroniya was cascading from a tiny hole in the white space. She realised she must have fallen from that hole—there was no other place she could have fallen from. Chroniya from the Bank on Vivalok was cascading into the Bank on Mortalok.

Luna gasped and stood up as two figures materialised in front of her. It was Henrietta and Ann Lou, still lifeless and attached to their ropes. Ann

Lou still held her Pyroll stick, and her shoulder-length blonde hair floated peacefully around her head. Henrietta's wild grey curls bounced and the hole in her neck was still there. Luna began to cry as she relived the horror of the first time she had seen them like this. As her tears flowed down her cheeks, streaking her stained skin like a reversed mascara, a third figure appeared next to Ann Lou. It was Elbina, now lifeless on her own rope. Although Luna had known that Elbina would end up here, a knot still curled her stomach.

"Elbs! No!" Luna sobbed. "I'm so sorry I didn't do better for you. I'm so sorry! Elbina, no!" Luna dropped to her knees just in front of Elbina's floating rope.

Feeling a presence behind her, Luna turned her head slowly to see two more figures appearing. It was Riff and Clorin. All five of them—Ann Lou, Henrietta, Elbina, Riff, and Clorin—formed a circle around her that began to tighten around the already tiny circle of ground on which Luna was floating.

"No!" she bellowed, dropping her head to the ground. Ernesteen must have captured Riff and Clorin as they were following Luna's orders. She had been a terrible protector. Now the remainder of her siblings and future generation of McHubbards would cease to exist, and it was all her fault. Her back heaved as she wept.

Luna wailed on the ground. For the first time in her life, she had absolutely no idea where to go or what to do. She had always had some hypothesis in her brain or an intuition to follow. But there was nowhere to go from here. Not up, down, right, or left.

Then something brushed against Luna's head. She looked up, and a sixth rope was dangling there in front of her. The rope appeared blurry through her watery vision, but she already knew who it was for. It was an invitation to join the others. And she deserved it. But she was too weak to stand. All the guilt and the emotional experiences that she had endured in this horrifying dimension had sapped what was left of her strength. She just wanted to go home. Or perhaps die—maybe that was better.

"Join us, Luna," Ann Lou said eerily. But her mouth wasn't moving. The roar of the Chroniya waterfall still filled Luna's ears, Ann Lou's voice was coming through quite clearly inside Luna's head.

"Your time is up," the voice said. "Look what you did to all of us. Your rope is waiting for you."

Luna got up. Her eyes were puffy from crying.

"Come on, Looner," Clorin said. His high voice rang sharply in Luna's head. "Listen to my mummy."

Luna turned her head toward Clorin. He, too, floated on his rope.

Then came Elbina's voice. "I can't believe the pain you've caused me. Some best friend and sister you are."

Luna glanced back at Elbina. Questions started to swirl in her brain. The voices of Luna's family were begging her to die. But why did they sound so disingenuous?

"I'm very disappointed in you."

Luna's heart pounded as she looked to her mother. She hadn't ever heard her mother speak to her in that tone. Even though Luna was the oldest, her mother had always doted on her more than any of the other siblings, never so much as raising her voice to her. The accusation felt like a stab to the heart. Luna cried and cried.

"What're you waiting for? Get on the bloody rope!" Riff growled inside her head.

Luna slowly turned to her brother. This accusation made sense, since their last encounter was the biggest fight the two of them had ever had. But Riff had never been one to stay mad. And he had gone out to recruit creatures, as she'd asked. Luna knew something wasn't right. But what was she supposed to do?

"Take the rope *now*," ordered her mother.

"Take the rope," echoed Riff.

"Take the rope. Take the rope. Take the rope," chanted Clorin, Ann Lou, and Elbina.

All five of them began chanting, faster and faster, their voices ringing inside her head. The little circle of ground on which Luna knelt began to crumble at the edges. Little by little, the circle was closing in around her as her family drew closer.

Only a few metres of crumbling ground remained between Luna and the depths of the Time Belt, which would land her an eternal spot on the rope that her family was so concerned about her taking.

Luna looked around for something, anything durable. Her eyes met the Pyroll stick in Ann Lou's outstretched arm. Luna yanked it from Ann Lou's hand and, with all the force she could muster, hurled it at the sphere that was still being filled by an endless waterfall of Chroniya. Luna's eyes followed the trajectory of the stick until it met the glass of the sphere. A crack formed at the point of impact. The crumbling ground was now just centimetres away from Luna's toes. She held her breath as the crack grew and spread outward like a cluster of lightning bolts.

Finally, the glass sphere shattered, pouring out its inventory of dark liquid Chroniya like a tidal wave into the white space of the Time Belt. The ground beneath Luna's toes ceased crumbling, and her family and their ropes dropped like stones. Luna looked down and watched them fall with the liquid.

The liquid below her swirled and formed a giant black wormhole. Her eyes bugged out as she balanced herself on the thin rim of ground remaining. Chroniya began flowing into the wormhole from all directions, carrying with it the remaining creatures from her army on Vivalok, creatures attached to ropes from Mortalok, and potions of souls from Galalok. They were quickly followed by brightly coloured buildings, gargantuan dark towers, and the remnants of golden pipes.

Next, the entire contents of the seemingly endless Jalopy junk-yard—the vehicles that had carried all the unfortunate creatures into the Time Belt—swarmed around Luna and headed for a trajectory into the wormhole. Luna caught sight of the hourglass Jalopy as it whipped past her and plunged into the wormhole.

A final splash of Chroniya carried Ernesteen toward the wormhole. Her skeletal limbs were splayed out, trapped by curling streams of Chroniya. "Luna McHubbard, you have silenced my rhyme! All of this you've done by ridding me of time! In the doom of my wake, something of yours I will gleefully take! Enjoy seeking your prize, for it will be ostracised! Seek low, seek high, whatever you try, you'll never be able to reach Earth's nearly identical ally!" Ernesteen's booming, omnipotent last words echoed throughout the white space, even after her form was flushed into the gargantuan wormhole, unable to return.

Luna was now alone on her circle of ground high above the swirling wormhole of Chroniya. What did Ernesteen's last words mean? What was she taking? More importantly for the moment, what was Luna supposed to do now?

A final spurt of Chroniya answered that question for her. It splashed against her back and pushed her off her small patch of ground and into a freefall toward the swirling dark wormhole that had swallowed her family, E. Bowser III, and all of the Time Belt. The wormhole pulled her into its torrential innards, and everything went dark and silent.

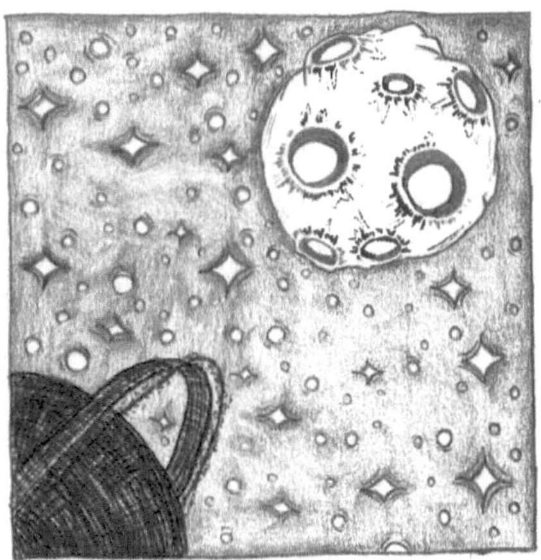

THE THIRD DIMENSION

Luna felt something soft beneath her hands and knees. She flopped to the ground and spread out her arms. The softness was sand. Russian sand. It was cool and soothing against her cheek. She clenched her hands and let the sand sift through her fingers. But then a thought popped into her brain: she was back in Dikson, Russia, at the same point she'd left it.

Unable to see anything, Luna had to readjust to darkness. The vibrant colours of Vivalok and the gloomy greys of Mortalok and Focalok filled her brain; now, she could only imagine the sights around her. She felt a mask beside her on the sand. She grabbed it and rolled over, then slammed the mask on her face and zipped up the top half of her suit.

As she morphed fully back into reality, the environment of Earth slowly rebuilt around her. She heard screams, and other sounds: explosions and thuds and Olfinderians humming their tranquil frequencies as her mother's universal army battled the terrorising force of the GeoLapse. She smiled for a second at the familiar Olfinderian song, but she quickly remembered that she wasn't invisible anymore. She sprang to her feet and felt around for something in her path. She came across a boulder that was about waist-height and ducked down behind it. She sat there, panting and holding her throbbing head. Her forehead felt bruised from the GeoLapse punch to her mask. She could feel blood rushing down the back of her nose and into her throat.

Safe for the moment, she thought about her family. She knew Riff, Elbina, and Ann Lou would be reliving the horrors of their individual missions, but she hoped that they would hold out until they were rescued. She wondered what her mother would think of them all now—not only destroying the GeoLapse but also the Time Belt and saving innocent creatures throughout many universes, including Rodney and Connie. Luna hoped the Ciptons were being rejoiced at their return to Cipto.

Luna's thoughts veered to her grandmother. Certainly Knitsy would be proud, wherever she was. And in thinking about Knitsy and her mission, it was stunning to think that her mum's uncle and grandfather had been GeoLapse. But what stunned Luna more was how immensely brave her Grandad Mack had been. He'd chosen death over life for the sake of love. Luna sat quietly and looked up through the familiar blankness at what she hoped were stars.

"Your beautiful family is back, Grandad."

* * *

Once the universal army had successfully obliterated the Asian GeoLapse headquarters, a Jalopy came to the rescue. Luna and the rest of her battalion were taken to a transfer facility adjacent to the ERA's White House headquarters in Washington, D.C. Riff disembarked from a Jalopy from Prague, Czech Republic, where his battalion had successfully taken down the European GeoLapse headquarters. When he spotted Luna, he ran up to her and hugged her from behind. She recognised his scent instantly, as well as the familiar feel of his large, warm body. She turned toward his embrace and curled her arms around him, exhaling a wave of relief.

"I'm sorry," she said. "I didn't mean to fight with you."

"No, I'm sorry," Riff signed. His response came in through Luna's microchip translation in her head. She had forgotten that he would be deaf again. But he could lip read. "You saved us. I'm the one who should've never doubted you. You've never given me a reason to doubt you before."

Luna tucked her head into his thick neck. She just wanted to stay in this little nook forever.

Then she heard a high-pitched voice say, "Oh my goodness—Apollo, I'll catch up with you in a bit!" followed by fast footsteps. A much smaller being joined their embrace. Ann Lou. Luna grabbed her sister's shoulders and wept into them. Ann Lou's battalion had successfully finished off the African GeoLapse headquarters.

"Ann Lou! What the hell were you thinking?" Luna sobbed, backhanding Ann Lou's prosthetic arm and then pulling her closer again. "You frightened us all to death!"

"I'm sorry," Ann Lou said softly. "I was just so embarrassed for what I did . . . will do . . . to Clorin."

Luna patted her sister gently on the back. "How did you find out?"

"Antympanicans at the Luge Crash gym were gossiping about it when they were rebuilding the walls," Ann Lou said. "The whole of Vivalok knew immediately. I was so ashamed."

"Ann Lou, you should have talked to us," Riff signed, puffing out his big, brotherly chest. "There's nothing we can't help you figure out. Besides, it's not going to happen this time around. Clorin will be much happier. And he's going to love you."

Luna hadn't thought about Clorin's disappearance, and how he was back in Ann Lou's newly pregnant stomach. She reached out and felt for Ann Lou's belly, which was all rock-hard abs, showing no sign of pregnancy yet.

Ann Lou placed her hand gently over Luna's. "I'll make sure of it."

Quiet but fast-paced footsteps approached and stopped in front of them. Luna dropped her hand from Ann Lou's stomach and listened.

"McHubbards, come with me. I have to show you something."

Luna recognised the voice as that of Jung-hoon, a member of the Korean branch of the ERA who had helped bring their mother's plan to fruition. He sounded calm but slightly excited. Luna joined hands with Riff and Ann Lou as they followed Jung-hoon down a hallway and through a secure door to the White House. Luna smiled as she felt the metal of Ann Lou's prosthetic left hand and Riff's sweaty right hand. She couldn't wait to hug Elbina.

Jung-hoon herded them into a quiet room within the ERA headquarters. He presented them with steaming cups of tea and a silvery tray full of biscuits of all flavours. The siblings devoured them within minutes, and Jung-hoon replenished the tray as well as their teas. As the siblings made their way feverishly through the second helping of tea and biscuits, they told Jung-hoon about their experiences in the Time Belt. Jung-hoon soaked in the information, listening intently and with great interest, especially at the moments they mentioned their mother.

"That's incredible what you've all endured. I can't believe you managed to destroy it . . . wow," said Jung-hoon breathlessly, sitting back in his chair. "It all makes sense. The ERA has been studying the Time Belt's purpose for years. We've been so afraid of it—especially when you arrived in Harvinth without Knitsy. We knew something terrible was going to happen. But here you all are. You survived it all and landed back here to tell the tale. I'm so sorry it happened to you, though."

Luna heard scuttling footsteps coming down the hall. Jung-hoon hopped out of his chair. "Oh, here she comes," he said. Luna could tell from his tone that a smile was spreading across his face.

Luna was so ready to hold Elbina in her arms. She stood up and shifted her weight between her feet in anticipation. Her best friend was coming—she could feel it. She was so proud of her sister for everything she had done, for the strength she'd shown by holding on until the very last second. Luna heard Riff and Ann Lou stand up beside her and was surprised when they both exclaimed simultaneously, "Nan!"

It made sense that Knitsy was here as well. She had spent all of her remaining time in order to replenish the Bank so that she could perform her mission. And thus, she was here in the flesh. Luna heard Knitsy coughing as Ann Lou and Riff hugged her tightly.

"Come here, you Time Belt destroyer," said Knitsy.

Luna fell into her grandmother's arms. She wanted so badly to take away the weight of the painful memories her grandmother had re-lived. And in the end, none of it had mattered. If Luna had destroyed the Bank sooner, Knitsy wouldn't have had to live through the horrors again.

"I'm so sorry, Nan," Luna sobbed into her arms. Luna was shaking so violently that she could barely stand.

Knitsy helped Luna to a chair. "Sit, sit, all of you now. Come on, you two," she barked at Ann Lou and Riff. They immediately followed her orders. Luna sat slumped in her chair, still trembling.

"Luna," said Ann Lou, placing a gentle hand on Luna's shoulder, "why do you keep saying you're sorry? You got us all out of there."

"But N-Nan sh-shouldn't have g-g-gone through that all ag-again.

I-I should've f-f-figured it out s-sooner," Luna cried, ploughing her fingers into her face.

"Luna," Knitsy said in a sweet voice, "no one in the history of the entire universe and beyond has been able to get out of there. You figured it out. You! From Earth! And they say we're the thick ones," she laughed, glancing at Riff, who laughed with her.

Luna hunched over, squeezing her temples.

Knitsy continued. "I'm thankful I got to see my Mack again. I'd do that a hundred times over if it gave you a little extra time to figure out how to save everyone. You did amazing. Your mother—" Knitsy choked up but swallowed, coughed a few times, and tried again. "Your mother . . . would be very proud."

Reassurances from her siblings allowed Luna to raise her head from the tense grip of her fingers. "Really?"

"Definitely," said Knitsy, rubbing Luna's back.

Luna couldn't entirely forget her mother's taunts just before the wormhole formed. But the reassurances from her family alleviated some of the pain. She felt slightly better.

"Speaking of Mum," said Ann Lou, "since we all came back from Mortalok, does that mean she's somewhere around here too?"

Luna shook her head, her heart sinking slightly again. "No. It's only for people who paid some of their time in the Time Belt—basically those who weren't dead before they got there. Mum is wherever dead people go."

"Heaven," said Knitsy, nodding and closing her eyes peacefully.

"Or the other place," Riff signed, dodging a sharp slap from Ann Lou.

Ann Lou rested her chin in her hands. "Or she's just one with the Earth now."

Then Jung-hoon said from the doorway, "Wherever she is, I promise you she's somewhere good. Somewhere . . . peaceful."

Luna was surprised to hear him speak. She had almost forgotten he was in the room. "I keep forgetting that you must've known our mum quite well," she said, "Maybe better than we did."

"Oh, now, don't say that, Luna," replied Jung-hoon. "She was exactly the person you knew. She definitely had her stern moments, but she was lovely most of the time. She spoke of you all quite highly. I heard about all your achievements, every one of you."

"How well did you know my daughter?" Knitsy asked him.

"I'd say fairly well. Almost . . . too well," he replied slowly.

"In what way?" Ann Lou asked.

Jung-hoon grimaced and fidgeted with his hands. He exhaled and sat down in a free chair in their circle. "We dated for quite some time. For about ten years, actually. Until she died. Obviously, there's nothing like losing a mother, or a daughter," he said, looking at Knitsy sympathetically, "but when she died, I lost a partner. I was devastated. It's been eight years now, but I still am."

Luna could hear him choking back tears. Although she thought it was a bit strange her mother had kept a partner a secret, she felt for him. He had loved her too.

"Are you our dad?" Riff signed with an evil grin spread across his face. Luna elbowed him in the ribs as subtly as possible. He was back to his old self.

Jung-hoon laughed and smiled warmly, wiping a few tears away. "Definitely not. You all are much too spectacular to belong to me."

"Did you know our dad?" Ann Lou asked.

Knitsy and Jung-hoon looked at one another sidelong. "Erm . . ." he started. "Not on a very personal level, but . . . I was aware of him, yes."

"I saw him," Luna said. Everyone turned and looked at her. "When we were travelling to Focalok and we floated through that passageway. I saw him in my early memories. He was really handsome, with fiery red hair like yours, Riff. He had blue eyes like Ann Lou. But that's all I saw. My visual memories stopped after that age."

Ann Lou and Riff smiled. Riff trailed his fingers through his red hair.

"I wish I could've known him," Ann Lou said solemnly.

"No, you don't!" Knitsy barked. Then she quickly covered her mouth.

"What do you mean, Nan?" asked Luna.

Knitsy dropped her hand from her mouth and looked at Jung-hoon. "Do I tell them?" she whispered.

"I can see your lips, Nan," Riff signed.

Jung-hoon nodded and leaned forward in his chair. "I think they ought to know. They're old enough. They can handle it."

"Was he killed by the GeoLapse or something?" Ann Lou prodded.

Knitsy cleared her throat. "No. He was *in* the GeoLapse."

The siblings' mouths hung open. Ann Lou looked especially pained, gripping her prosthetic left arm tightly in her right hand. She held less than fond memories of her accident back in primary school after the GeoLapse attack.

"It surprised me as well. He was a really good father at first. Very musical," said Knitsy, gesturing to Riff. "Very intelligent," she continued, peering at Luna. "And stronger than anyone I'd ever met," she said to Ann Lou. "But he was secretly power hungry and absurdly jealous. Jealous of your mother and her power within the ERA. He wanted to be on top. Joining the GeoLapse was his way of showing power. Somehow, your Grandad Mack's brother, Burl, found him and recruited him." Knitsy fidgeted with the ring on her left ring finger. "Your mother basically had to come up with a plan to destroy him. It broke her."

"You knew she was in the ERA?" Luna asked.

"Oh, of course. She didn't give me the dirty details I wanted, but mothers know all," she grinned. "I was sworn to never say a word. Had to catch myself a few times, but I was proud I kept her secrets."

"So, Dad's . . . dead?" asked Ann Lou.

Knitsy looked at Jung-hoon. He shrugged and said, "I'd assume so. Your mother's plan worked perfectly. All GeoLapse headquarters have been mostly eradicated. There are probably a few left roaming around somewhere, but we were able to track down the main groups. I understand all this news might be slightly unnerving to you in conflicting ways, if I might say."

The siblings exchanged glances of unease and confusion. Of loss.

"We have GeoLapse blood in us," Ann Lou said, sounding disgusted.

"If it makes you feel better, everyone on Earth is related to someone in the GeoLapse," Jung-hoon said. "They grew so exponentially that their population far surpassed the fifty thousand innocent humans remaining at the time of the planet transfer. Your blood is not tainted. Think of everything you've accomplished. You've not only saved this universe, you've saved creatures from loads of other universes as well."

"But we still share the same surname as our dad," said Riff.

"Well . . ." Knitsy started. "Not exactly. Your mother and I legally changed our and your last names to McHubbard when your father joined the GeoLapse. We had to move, and the name change allowed us to stay undetected by him and Burl Gorgan."

Knitsy's grandchildren's mouths fell agape.

"Our name isn't even McHubbard?" Ann Lou said, bewildered. "Then what is it?"

Knitsy squirmed uncomfortably. "Icketts."

Luna Icketts, Luna thought to herself. *McHubbard sounds much more fitting.*

"I feel like I don't even know who I am anymore," sighed Ann Lou.

"You are all your mother's children," said Jung-hoon. "You are brave and smart individuals. You should be proud of yourselves."

The McHubbards stayed quiet. Luna furrowed her brow. Knitsy kept playing with her ring, concentrating deeply on it as she twisted it around her finger.

Jung-hoon rose from his chair. "I can see that you all might need some family time alone. I'll leave you be. Can I get you anything else for the moment?"

"Elbina," said Luna, inching forward on her seat.

"I'm sure she's up with President Murphy in his dormitory. I'll go check," Jung-hoon replied warmly, starting toward the hall.

"Jung-hoon?" said Luna.

He turned back. "Yes?"

"Will the ERA destroy us since we are technically doubles? Our younger selves are still on Earth somewhere."

"No. You've all been through enough. As long as you stay away from your doubles, we are happy to let you roam the universe. Luna, I think you need to let your brain rest while I find your sister," Jung-hoon added with a smile before disappearing down the hallway.

"He's right," Riff signed. "You should lie down or something."

Luna shook her head and signed, "No, my mind can't settle. I just need to know Elbina is okay."

A few minutes later, two pairs of footsteps raced down the marble hallway. Luna recognised Jung-hoon's footsteps and only realised whose the others were once Ann Lou sprang up from her chair and exclaimed, "Hayden!"

Ann Lou ran to Hayden and hugged him. Riff got up and greeted him with a "Hey, mate" and a clap on the back. Then Hayden came up to Luna. His clothes smelled like Elbina. Luna smiled and reached up to clasp his hand.

She said softly, "Where is she?"

Strangely, Hayden hesitated. Jung-hoon jumped in. "That's what President Murphy was just explaining to me," Jung-hoon said. "He said your sister was there and then she wasn't . . . President Murphy, please take the lead."

Hayden remained standing while the rest of the McHubbards sat. "It was so strange. I heard an explosion just outside my room. Elbina appeared in my dormitory for a split second, but then she just . . . vanished. What's going on?"

A lump formed in Luna's throat as her heart started to race. Her brain was telling her that something was wrong.

Ann Lou said, "Is she still in the Time Belt?" Her voice was rising with fear.

"No," Luna said softly. "The Time Belt was destroyed. It doesn't exist anymore." She sat very still.

"Then did she get stuck in the wormhole vortex thing?" said Riff.

"Maybe she's somewhere else in the White House," Hayden suggested.

Luna said, "Elbina should have appeared in the spot where she initially disappeared. Something, or someone, tampered with her return."

"What do you know, Luna?" asked Knitsy quietly.

"Ernesteen said something to me as she was falling into the vortex. I was a bit preoccupied at that moment . . . argh, I just need to remember what she said." Everyone listened closely as Luna muttered to herself. "Doom . . . wake . . . something I'll take . . . prize . . . ostracised . . . seek low, or was it high? Earth . . . nearly identical ally . . ." Then Luna's face blanched. "Elbina."

"What is it?" cried Ann Lou. "Spit it out!"

Luna grimaced. "Ernesteen punished me for destroying the Time Belt. That's why Elbina isn't here."

"Ernesteen took Elbina with her?" Riff signed angrily. He looked ready to jump up and fight the skeletal, hooded figure, wherever she was.

"No. Ernesteen is dead. She's somewhere in the afterlife. But I think she sent Elbina somewhere else instead of Earth."

Knitsy stammered, "Wh-where? Where could she possibly be? Maybe Harvinth? Or Olfinder?" She started into a coughing fit, and Ann Lou patted her on the back.

Luna sucked in her breath as she wiped tears of frustration from her eyes. "No, she's not on Harvinth or Olfinder. She's been sent to 'Earth's near identical ally.' Tycho from the book shop told me about where Ernesteen was originally from. I suspect that Elbina is on planet Thera."

"Where's that?" Hayden asked. He began pacing around the room. "We have Jalopies that are ready to go. Jung-hoon, the Jalopy Cabins in Danforth Commons—I can use those, right?"

Jung-hoon nodded. "Yes, we can all go! Luna, where is planet Thera?"

Luna gritted her teeth anxiously and turned toward Jung-hoon. She remembered Tycho telling her that the Universal Union's technology wasn't yet safe enough to travel to other universes. But maybe the ERA had made discoveries in her absence. "Tell me, Jung-hoon . . . does the ERA have any way to travel to different universes? A parallel universe?"

Jung-hoon sighed. "All Jalopies are strictly in the purview of the Universal Union. They haven't been tested outside of this universe. It would be much too dangerous with the current unknowns of the universe."

Ann Lou glared at the others with her piercing blue eyes. "So she's gone? We've lost our sister, just like that?" She slammed her prosthetic arm against her chair with a loud *clang* that made everyone jump.

Luna collected her thoughts. "There has to be some way to get out of Coloratura."

"What's that?" asked Jung-hoon.

"Our universe. Coloratura. We have to find the portholes to other universes. Black holes," Luna explained, recalling Tycho's teachings.

"There are omnitillion of them in our observable universe," said Jung-hoon, sounding deflated. "How will we know which black hole leads to Thera's universe? What is that universe called?"

"It's called Reprisa," said Luna. "And as to determining which black hole is the correct one, I don't know," she exhaled in surrender. "But we have to get Elbina back. She's my best friend." Tears streamed down Luna's cheeks as Riff and Ann Lou embraced her.

Knitsy struggled to her feet with the help of her cane and joined in the embrace. "We'll find her," she said. "No McHubbard gets left behind. After all, we're a beautiful family, no matter which dimension or universe we're in."

Acknowledgments

Thank you to the team at DartFrog Books for continuing to work with me. I am in awe of your professionalism, and I have enjoyed producing *The Jalopy Chronicles* series with you so far. I look forward to continuing with you for the rest of the series (if you haven't had enough of my countless questions yet)! As always, thank you to Gordon and Suanne for managing me, Mark for this brilliant cover design, Amy for her diligent editing by providing me with a perfectly crafted story, Andrew for the marvellous final proofread, and Simona for putting it all together with the illustrations.

I've had some additional help this time with the chapter drawings thanks to my incredibly talented family. Claire, once again, I can't even express how thankful I am to not only have the honour of being your cousin, but to also have the privilege of having you draw for the books. They are certainly my favourite parts of the books and I hope you are so incredibly proud of yourself. You are a gem, and the world needs to see your art.

A big shout out also goes out to another amazingly talented cousin of mine, Elyzabeth, whose illustrations for chapters 5 and 19 beautifully captured the story. Thank you so much for allowing me to show off your talent. I am so proud to be your cousin.

Thanks to my biggest motivator, my mom, who still sends me screenshots of every punctuation error she finds. I'm also so thankful of the incredible PR you've done for the books. Your old school ways of walking into libraries and hand-writing press releases have proved the most effective. Also, this momager can draw! Check out chapters 11, 14, and 18 for selections of her art as well. Thank you for being my voice, when mine so desperately wanted to stay in the comfort of the pages. Thank you for pushing my limits and believing in me when I didn't.

A massive thank you goes out to my friends and family who have been pushing the story of the McHubbards out to the world. Your endless support is so warming to me and I am thankful for each post, selfie with the book, and conversation you have about it.

To my readers - thanks for sticking with me! I hope you enjoyed the second instalment of *The Jalopy Chronicles* and look forward to the McHubbards' next adventure past the known universe!

About the Author

Caeli Ennis crafted the story of the McHubbard Family in her small flat in Southampton, England during the COVID-19 pandemic. She is originally from snowy Buffalo, New York, where she enjoys nothing more than spending the summertime at the cottage on Lake Erie with her family and friends. Caeli sought to build characters with physical disabilities to prove to readers that anyone and everyone can help save the universe, as she most personally identifies with Luna's visual obstacles. She works as a Development Engineer and in her free time takes the train to new cities, jams on the cello, and plays with every dog that trots by.